Too Deep for Words

OLD LOVEGOOD GIRLS

NOVELS

Grief Cottage (2017)

Flora (2013)

Unfinished Desires (2009)

Queen of the Underworld (2006)

Evenings at Five (2003)

Evensong (1999)

The Good Husband (1994)

Father Melancholy's Daughter (1991)

A Southern Family (1987)

The Finishing School (1984)

A Mother and Two Daughters (1982)

Violet Clay (1978)

The Odd Woman (1974)

Glass People (1972)

The Perfectionists (1970)

STORY COLLECTIONS

Mr. Bedford and the Muses (1983)

Dream Children (1976)

NONFICTION

Publishing: A Writer's Memoir (2015)

The Making of a Writer: Journals, vols. 1 and 2 (2006, 2011)
edited by Rob Neufeld

Heart: A Personal Journal through Its Myths and Meanings (2001)

OLD LOVEGOOD GIRLS

A

NOVEL

GAIL GODWIN

BLOOMSBURY PUBLISHING

NEW YORK · LONDON · OXFORD · NEW DELHI · SYDNEY

BLOOMSBURY PUBLISHING
Bloomsbury Publishing Inc.
1385 Broadway, New York, NY 10018, USA

BLOOMSBURY, BLOOMSBURY PUBLISHING, and
the Diana logo are trademarks of
Bloomsbury Publishing Plc

First published in the United States 2020

LIBRARY OF CONGRESS CATALOGING-IN-PUBLICATION DATA IS AVAILABLE

ISBN: HB: 978-1-63286-822-0; eBook: 978-1-63286-821-3

2 4 6 8 10 9 7 5 3 1

Typeset by Westchester Publishing Services
Printed and bound in the U.S.A. by Berryville Graphics Inc., Berryville, Virginia

To find out more about our authors and books visit www.bloomsbury.com
and sign up for our newsletters.

Bloomsbury books may be purchased for business or promotional use.
For information on bulk purchases please contact Macmillan Corporate and
Premium Sales Department at specialmarkets@macmillan.com

William Iredell Godwin

1905–1977

Generous Uncle

Sit Tibi Terra Levis
(May the earth lie lightly upon thee)

PART ONE

1

1958

The dean and the dorm mistress stood brooding over the student housing plans laid out on the rosewood conference table. It had been a parching August, happy news only for the tobacco growers transporting their precious harvests from the fields to the curing barns. The tall sash windows of the old building, lowered and raised from top and bottom, failed to entice a flutter of air. The sheer net curtains hung as still as in a painting. The dean had prohibited grass mowing and faculty showers until the day before the girls arrived on campus.

"Maybe we could put her in the Lanier room, with Eskew and Linzey," suggested the dorm mistress. "Back in '48 when we had a full house again, we fitted three beds and dressers into Lanier, and those girls hit it off so well they ended up serving as one another's bridesmaids."

Despite the sapping heat, Winifred Darden, dorm mistress at Lovegood College for thirty-one years, displayed the ramrod posture of a woman born in the last century—which indeed she had been, though midpoint in her tenure at Lovegood College she had moved her birth across the dividing line. ("Don't you dare tell a soul, but I am the same age as this century!" she gaily fibbed to each new crop of girls.)

"I somehow can't see either Eskew or Linzey asking Feron Hood to serve as a bridesmaid," said the dean.

"Well, as you know, I wasn't on campus that day and didn't get to meet her and give her the tour. What was your impression of her?"

Susan Fox paused to assemble her answer. Beginning her second year as dean of Lovegood College (though some continued calling her *the new dean*), she still had not become fluent in the southern art of evasive overlay. "At Saxon Hall, we had a teacher who would throw herself off a cliff before saying something negative about a student. The worst thing she allowed herself was, 'So-and-so is not forthcoming.' That phrase kept beating through my head while interviewing Feron Hood and her uncle."

"Not forthcoming," Miss Darden helpfully repeated. "And by that you mean . . . ?"

"I had to guess, from the little her uncle told me, that she was . . . well, that she had been subjected to a wider range of life's misadventures than our typical Lovegood girl."

"I see," said the dorm mistress, who didn't exactly. "Perhaps we might . . . that little annex next to the infirmary that Mr. Sikes converted into a single room in case of a quarantine . . . ?"

"The last thing a knocked-about girl like Hood needs is to feel quarantined. She needs a positive, steadying influence. I had the idea of pairing her with Jellicoe."

"But Jellicoe's already in with Chasteen! A perfect match. Both fathers are in farming."

"But the purpose of college, after all, isn't to settle down with a carbon copy of yourself. We could switch Chasteen to the Lanier room. As you pointed out, it's spacious enough for three. Eskew and Linzey are second-year girls. They're old news to each other. They'll make a pet of pretty little Chasteen."

"But if Hood has been knocked about and isn't very forthcoming—I mean, Jellicoe struck me as such a positive girl. She knows how to appreciate things. When I was giving her family the tour, I was about to show them our new wing with the modern rooms, but Jellicoe said she liked the high-ceilinged old rooms. Her mother asked if they shouldn't at least see what the new wing had to offer, but Jellicoe said, 'No, I like the way more has happened here in this old part, you can feel it.' That is insightful for an eighteen-year-old, don't you think?"

"They might benefit each other. When I was headmistress at Saxon Hall, each girl was allowed to bring one horse. Just one. The rule had been written in stone since the founding of the school. Then this desirable girl we really wanted insisted her horse couldn't be separated from its companion pony. The horse was a skittish thoroughbred, and the pony kept it calm. I made an executive decision, and we got the girl and the horse. And the pony of course. It worked out well."

Not quite sure which girl was meant to represent the thoroughbred and which the pony, the dorm mistress asked the dean if she could elaborate a little on Feron Hood's misadventures.

"Her uncle telephoned and asked for an interview. It was all very last minute, as you know. He's a lawyer down in Lauren County. The niece had simply showed up at his office. Walked across town from the bus station with her suitcase and asked if he would take her in. He had no idea who she was."

"He didn't know his own niece?"

"He had never met her. She was his late brother's child from a very short marriage. The couple divorced soon after the baby was born. There was no contact until the next husband petitioned to adopt the child. Since his brother had recently died, the uncle handled the matter. Then years went by. The mother had died of a fall, and the girl blamed her stepfather and caused quite a scandal.

But she reversed herself at the inquest and continued to live with him for several months before she ran away. She stopped in Chicago for a short time, sleeping in the park, and then decided to head south to the uncle."

"So she knew she had an uncle."

"The mother must have told her if things got impossible, they might throw themselves on his mercy. From what Hood told her uncle, it was not a happy home."

"I wonder why the uncle picked Lovegood College."

"Oh, his grandmother was one of Lovegood's earliest students."

"Really! What was her maiden name?"

"It was Seawell, or Sewell. I made a note of it. But while they were here for the interview, I forgot to follow up on the grand-mother, I was so intent on studying the girl. She was polite but said no more than she was asked. I got the sense she was being very careful until she was sure she had been accepted."

"I will go through the old records," said Winifred Darden happily. "That means Hood will be eligible for the Daughters and Granddaughters Club. That should provide her with some ballast. We've kept everything, you know, even the first yearbooks, which were stitched together by hand."

"There's a problem with transcripts. She ran away before finishing high school. I told them we would work it out."

"Will she be coming as a full-tuition student?"

"You bet your sweet life. And he's paying extra for tennis lessons."

What would it be like, Susan Fox wondered, to move into a school building at thirty and find yourself still living in it at sixty-two? Darden, the dorm mistress, was not a secretive person and had dropped a discreet crumb-path of self-history for the attentive person to follow. Here was a case of a poor, well-born girl reaching marriageable age just as the young men were leaving for World War I, earning her keep by living with rich people and taking care of their children until Lovegood College decided it needed a live-in dorm mistress. Winifred Darden was recommended by a family friend who was a Lovegood trustee. When the student body shrank by half during the Depression, the dorm mistress made herself indispensable in other ways, and by the time the Depression was over, she was going on forty. ("I still wake up and thank my stars for this solid roof over my head, not to mention my beautiful living quarters.")

Making the most of her scant bounty, whereas ambitious Susan Fox, fortunate in all but the well-born start, prospered in her era until she brought the roof down on herself.

"We will all do our part to make it work out," assured the dorm mistress.

"The world is fast-changing all around us, Winifred. In the next ten years, who knows where things will be? Let's hope and plan that we can accommodate the spirit of change without forfeiting Lovegood's values."

"Oh, Lord, in 1968 I will be seventy-two," moaned Winifred Darden, neglecting in the moment to remember she had shaved four years off her age.

2

Throughout her long life, Feron Hood never could describe to her own satisfaction what she had felt when she first saw Meredith Grace Jellicoe. Entering the room, Feron had seen a girl facing the window, intent on some small black object she held in her hand. Sensing a presence, the girl turned, snapped the object shut, and lit up as though the exact person she wanted had just come through the door.

"Are you Feron?" she asked. "I saw you down in the parking lot. You were getting your luggage out of the car. What a shame you missed my mama and brother by about two minutes."

"I saw a woman with a boy. He was sliding down the bannister as I came up."

"That was Ritchie! He was threatening to do that. I'm Merry, your roommate. Which bed would you prefer, window or corner?"

"You got here first. You should be the first to choose."

"I haven't sat down on either bed. I waited so we could choose together."

"Actually, I'd prefer the bed in the corner."

"Really? You wouldn't rather have the bed next to the window?"

"I'm partial to corners." (From the corner, you could see who was coming through the door before they saw you.)

"Well. If you're sure." The girl stepped forward and showed a small black compass. "This is on loan from my little brother, his prized possession. I guess he thinks I need it more. It's an air force compass from World War II. He knows I get homesick, so he showed me how, since this window faces west, I can figure out exactly how our house in Hamlin will be facing me."

Feron must have said something. Or maybe she didn't. After the roommates became close, Merry confided, "You know, Feron, when I say something and you don't answer, I always worry I've done something to make you mad."

She was slim and petite and exhibited a quality of—*in-one-piece-ness*, if that could be a word. Everything was contained in her. As though God, when making her, took great pains to color all of her inside the lines. Her honey-blonde hair was cut shoulder length, and her features were well-proportioned. She could be called pretty, except her nose was too long. Feron was not inside the lines, was tall enough to have cultivated a stoop, and thought of herself as not unattractive but far from pretty.

The roommates unpacked their belongings, which in the meantime had been carried up by Mr. Sikes, a ropey, ageless man. Now they were making their beds.

"Did you come far today?" asked Merry.

"Only from Pullen."

"Oh, that's right. You live with your uncle in Pullen. Miss Darden told me."

And no doubt told you a lot else as well, thought Feron, who had been briefed about Meredith Grace, the lovely girl from the prosperous Jellicoe Tobacco family, after Miss Darden had pounced on her and her uncle at the entrance and lured them into the reception parlor. Then the ethereal old biddy had produced an ancient hand-sewn yearbook, and Uncle Rowan was visibly moved, lingering over his grandmother's class photo from 1875 until he had to rush off to a lunch engagement at the Walter Raleigh.

"As a matter of fact," Feron said, "I was born in Pullen. My mother met my father there."

"Miss Darden said you had recently lost your mother. I hope you don't mind my bringing it up. I can't even imagine losing a mother. Had she been sick, or—"

"No, she fell and hit her head against the radiator. I came home from school and found her."

Bare facts, heavily edited. That's what you did. Starting over on a clean page with every new person you meet.

"Oh, Feron. I am so sorry. I love your name. Is it from family, or . . ."

"It was from some actress in a movie. My mother liked the sound of it. She wasn't sure of the spelling. It turns out there's a village in Ireland named Farran, but we didn't know that. It was a man who sat next to me on a bus just recently who told me about the Irish village. What about your name? Does anybody call you the whole thing?"

"It varies. Daddy's manager calls me 'Miss Meredith.' My brother Ritchie calls me 'Merry Grape' because it makes him laugh. When Daddy is being stern, he does the whole Meredith Grace thing. But I'm used to Merry. I hope you'll call me that."

Squaring the corner of her bottom sheet, Feron felt her stepfather, Swain, materialize just behind her right shoulder. "That sheet has to be tight enough to bounce a quarter off of." When she was little, it had sounded gently instructive, like he was sharing special army lore with her. When she was older, he began lying in wait, hoping to catch her making a mistake. His voice came from lower in his throat when his corrections took a derogatory dive. "Slovenly corners. What did I say about the quarter? You don't *listen*." Slovenly, slatternly, blowsy, hitty-missy. Sluttish, when he wanted to lay on the disgust. He had liked her better before she showed signs of turning into a woman. At which point he started tormenting her in a new way.

3

To acquaint incoming students with its traditions and bind them into the community, Lovegood College put on an orientation pageant in the school chapel. New girls were seated in the front pews, the lights went out, the music teacher launched into Lovegood's processional hymn, "How Firm a Foundation," on the big pipe organ, and up the aisle marched pairs of second-year girls with lighted candles, belting out the stirring verses. They parted into single file at the front of the chapel and returned down the side aisles to take their seats, except for the ones hurrying backstage who were going to be in the pageant.

> . . . *I will not, I will not desert to its foes;*
> *That soul, though all hell shall endeavor to shake,*
> *I'll never, no, never, no, never forsake.*

Feron, acquainted with few hymns in her lifetime, was knocked sideways by the final verse. She turned away quickly to hide her loss of control from Merry in the next seat, but Merry was already snatching up her hand and protecting it in both of hers. A watchful, affectionate roommate would naturally assume that she was thinking of her lost mother, but actually Feron was grieving and yearning for something she couldn't put a name to.

Next came the drama of the school's genesis. Miss Elizabeth McCorkle, the history teacher, who wrote and directed the pageant, also played the part of the founder. Horace Lovegood, successful businessman and ruling elder of the Presbyterian Church, clad in top hat, double cravat, frock coat, and striped trousers, hustled about town, raising money to build a female two-year college on twenty acres he had donated.

The stage then emptied of donors, leaving only Horace Lovegood sharing his dreams with a top-hatted friend: he envisioned a female institute that would meet the requirements of young ladies like his brilliant young sister, had she not succumbed to typhus.

"I want a learning place for young women where they can partake of the same substantial branches of knowledge that their brothers consider a birthright. Of course we'll teach the elegant and ornamental arts as well."

As he spoke the lines, a scrim curtain rose to reveal a painted backdrop of the Lovegood building, much as it looked today, complete with the four-story Doric columns and gracious landscaping. An offstage pitch pipe sounded a note, and a trio of unseen a cappella voices chanted Horace Lovegood's ambitious plan of study for his young women, each verse concluding with the refrain:

> *In hallowed halls removed from strife*
> *Where they may seek the mental life:*
> *Reflect and learn,*
> *Reflect and learn*

The lights dimmed. The organ struck up a sinister dirge with offstage gunshot noises and cries of agony. "However, fate had other plans," intoned Miss McCorkle as Horace Lovegood. "Just as my school was nearing completion, the War Between the States broke out and the building became a Confederate hospital." Instead of seeking an education, local daughters covered their curls with nurses' caps and rushed onstage in bloodied aprons bearing unpleasant-looking pans. And rushed off again.

Lights up once more, and a masked, leotarded figure danced out from the wings, removed Horace Lovegood's top hat and shrouded his shoulders with a fringed silvery shawl, then danced off again. Standing tranquilly in front of the backdrop of the school, the bare-headed founder (Miss McCorkle had expertly slicked down her hair) explained to the audience he was now "speaking from his final resting place."

"Following the War came Reconstruction, and our noble building was once again appropriated, this time by the federal government to house the local Freedmen's Bureau. More dark days were to follow during which much careless damage was done to the premises. However, Lovegood College at last opened its doors to young ladies in 1872. I missed that opening by seven years, though I hung on till the age of ninety. However, there it is . . . there *they* are . . ."

The founder's ghost departed, and girls in billowing Victorian dresses replaced him. They silently strolled back and forth in front of the painted Doric columns, then dropped gracefully to the ground to freeze into a *tableau vivant*.

A tall figure rose from the audience and mounted the steps to the stage, her narrow ankles wobbling slightly in her high-heeled pumps. It was the mournfully beautiful Miss Maud Petrie,

Lovegood's English and Composition teacher. Fingering the throat of her high-necked blouse and looking on the verge of some great emotion, she said that the poem she was about to read had been written by Mary Louisa Summerlin, "who was Lovegood College's class poet of 1918." Miss Petrie drew a paper from the deep pocket of her flowing skirt, put on her reading glasses, which hung on a chain around her neck, and embarked on "The Melodies of Lovegood College":

> *I dreamed I climbed the curving stair*
> *To visit our old room*
>
> *The moonlight shone on my old bed*
> *Dispelling present gloom.*

Delivered in Miss Petrie's mournful, cello-like voice, the elegiac poem floated through the chapel's darkened air, leaving behind scattered images and phrases.

> *Lingering on the lawn till early dusk . . .*
> *Midst friendship's gentle bonds . . .*
>
> *The stars blink out, one by one,*
> *Around the rising moon . . .*
>
> *Far removed from stir and strife . . .*
> *Precious hours of lonely musings . . .*
>
> *The moonlight falls upon my bed . . .*
>
> *When I am at my journey's end,*
> *I'll climb the curving stairs . . .*

In the darkened chapel Feron was trying not to think about the life before her present life. Each made the other seem like a fantasy. The sentiments composed by the starry-eyed class poet had to contend against degrading phrases that might last Feron's entire life.

—Your mother is a congenital liar.

—My mother is a genital liar.

—Ha, ha! And that, too. That, too!

—You don't *think*. So I have to think for you.

—You act like you're so grown up, but you wouldn't last an hour outside my house.

—It's my right.

—You are legally my property.

Feron was also thinking about the girl who sat beside her on the chapel bench. Was a person like Merry born with her openheartedness, or was it seeded and grown, year after year, by people who had raised her to choose the generous and the true, themselves building on some rich soil of forebears?

But what if you had been raised by disappointed people who were always telling you they had expected a better life than this, who had withdrawn into themselves and took shortcuts with truth when it served their needs?

If one escaped those influences, was it possible to put on a good disposition, like a costume, and practice and practice until no one, except yourself, knew what you had been like before?

4

Take that wing chair, Feron. It was the girls' favorite chair in my office at Saxon Hall, when I was headmistress there. Are you settling in at Lovegood?"

"Yes, ma'am, I think so."

"You and Meredith Grace seem to get on well. Or Merry, as she likes to be called."

"Yes, we get along very well."

"In my experience, roommates go one of four ways. They don't get along at all. Or they find each other compatible enough, but each makes her own friends. Other roommates adopt a friend between them and form a threesome. Then there are some who form an immediate bond and prefer the company of each other. You and Merry seem to have done that."

"Merry is easy to be with. There's nothing underhanded about her. We're comfortable together."

"I'm glad to hear it. Now, Feron, I finally received the transcript from your high school. Top grades for three years, then nosedive, then a flatline of incompletes . . ."

"Yes, ma'am. It was not a good time. The incompletes, they were because I left school."

"Your principal kindly sent a letter with the transcript. He wanted to be sure I was aware of the stresses you'd been under. The letter revealed nothing I hadn't heard already from your uncle in our phone conversation, but it's always useful to have another point of view. Meanwhile, I've had a word with your teachers here at Lovegood. It's all satisfactory, even from Mrs. Sprunt."

"I've always had trouble with math."

"Mrs. Sprunt says it's because you missed some crucial steps in geometry, but she says you'll catch up."

"I hope so."

"So far, Lovegood seems to be working out for you. Perhaps this is the place for me to add that you can count on a discretionary ear in this office if ever you feel the need to say more about that stressful period of your life."

Here Susan Fox chose not to go ahead with her Saxon Hall method, where she had coasted on her imperiousness and acted confidently on her instincts. At Saxon Hall, she would have risked it. ("Tell me, Feron, what was it like to sleep outside in that Chicago park? How did you keep warm? What were your thoughts?") Either the girl would be disarmed and plunge into confidences, or she would draw back, but what was there to lose? The confident head-mistress at Saxon Hall, before her comedown, would have waited and tried again.

However, this was Lovegood, where a humbled Susan Fox, starting afresh, was schooling herself in the safer southern art of evasive overlay. "You know, Feron, there's not much that can surprise me after years of listening to girls' stories from the chair you are sitting in now. Will you remember that?"

"I will, Dean Fox. Thank you."

*   *   *

"Florence. Please come in."

"Yes'm, I'll just catch my breath." Florence Rayburn, Lovegood's senior cook, had not climbed the majestic curving staircase to the dean's office since their meeting a year ago.

"Take a seat, Florence." Dean Fox waved her toward the wing chair.

"You carried that chair all the way from Boston."

"You remembered! Yes, girls seem to feel at home in that chair. Not *too* at home, however. The high back keeps a person nice and straight."

The dean congratulated herself as the cook settled into the upright confines of the wing chair. Last year when invited to sit down, Florence had frozen, her countenance betraying a reluctance close to recoil.

We're stepping over a line here, the dean remembered thinking. So be it, she thought this year, let's find more lines to step over.

"Florence, I've had some ideas, if you'll indulge me. You recall our discussion about potatoes last year?"

"I sure do. All that peeling every single day, but the girls, they love their mashed potatoes."

"Have you heard of this new prepackaging?"

"You mean like those TV dinners?"

"This is more recent. Someone peels the potatoes, cuts them up, seals them in a package, and freezes them. You simply open the package and drop the contents into boiling water. I'm proposing we purchase, say, a week's worth—we'd have to work out the numbers—and mash them up and see how they taste. See how they taste to the girls. Are you willing to experiment?"

"Yes'm, but . . ."

"We'll see how they go over with the girls. Now here's my next brainstorm, if you'll bear with me. I want the girls taking the business courses to have some real-life experience with running an enterprise rather than only working out imaginary problems in the classroom. I'd like you to show them how you go about ordering foodstuffs, calculating quantities and prices, allowing for built-in problems like breakage and spoilage—and whatever else a cook in charge of a kitchen has to allow for."

"Would it be *all* the business girls?"

"Not all at the same time, certainly not. We'd schedule them in twos or threes. They would take notes and go back to class and type up their reports and make their calculations. Would you be willing to show them how you run your kingdom?"

"Just so it's not around the meal times."

"Oh, certainly not, we'd work out the most convenient times for you. Are you willing to try?"

"I never heard of anything like it, Dean Fox, but I'll do my best."

"Thank you, Florence." The dean stood up from her desk, and the cook promptly vacated the wing chair. "We'll be in touch as soon as I've arranged things."

Above the dean's desk hung the Lovegood College coat of arms, anonymously embroidered by someone who knew an impressive variety of stitches. Even Winifred Darden could not furnish the name of the accomplished needlewoman whose work had predated Winifred's own arrival. ("When I came here thirty-one years ago, it was hanging on *that* wall where the sun was bleaching out its colors. It shows to much better advantage on the shady wall behind your desk.")

The school's motto was ESSE QUAM VIDERI. "To be rather than to seem." The dean's first impulse had been to move the coat of arms to another shady wall and replace it with art more to her taste. Above her desk at Saxon Hall had hung winter and summer versions of a stately colonial home. She had bought them in an antique shop and reframed them in handsome oak. When asked by an early visitor whether the house in the pictures had been in her family, she had thought "why not?" and from then on had equivocated. "No, I found them in an antique shop, but they remind me of my grandparents' house."

She'd had no qualms about transferring the dour portrait of Horace Lovegood looking choked by his double cravat to an outside waiting room wall. But days and weeks went by, and the embroidered coat of arms still hung in its pride of place. It seemed to have set its will against hers. *I was here long before you were and will be hanging here long after you're gone.*

ALTIORA PETO was the Saxon Hall motto. "I seek higher things." Most people in Susan Fox's previous life, including herself, had been striving fiercely to live the reverse of the Lovegood motto, to seem rather than to be. And yes, there had been a time to seem, a time to climb, digging in with your fingernails, beating out the others, staking your claim on "higher things," preening your seem-worthy-self atop your pinnacle. Until the fall from grace into the dreary lowlands of humiliation and self-hate. Florence's recent colloquial use of the verb *to carry* evoked a droll image of herself, Susan Fox, trudging down life's great highway, lifting her skirts to cross the Mason-Dixon line, hauling the proven wing chair on her back.

5

"In the Middle Ages, a *fiefdom* was the estate or domain of a feudal lord," said Miss McCorkle. She dictated rapid-fire from her five-by-eight notecards, and the girls wrote as fast as they could in their notebooks because that was the way she ran her classes. The more words from Miss McCorkle's brown-edged cards you corralled into your notebooks, the easier Friday's quiz would be. "However, in modern usage it has come to mean an area over which somebody has control."

Lovegood College itself was a collection of little fiefdoms. Miss McCorkle controlled what went on in her Quonset hut, which had been meant to serve as her temporary classroom only until Lovegood's new wing was finished in 1947. But she stuck with her Quonset hut, approving of a trek through the outdoors for young bodies, the mental stimulation of putting on a wrap and leaving one place for another. The hut was a reminder of the one-room school-house of her childhood. On extra-cold days she kept two kerosene heaters going and wore her McCorkle tartan scarf wound around her neck until, heated by her own teaching, she tore it off like a dancer removing a feather boa. To hammer a concept into their souls, she startled them with inventive scenarios. ("When you lose track of what has gone before, or don't bother ever to learn it, you might as well fling open the gates of your city and invite the barbarians in for tea.")

Meanwhile, over in "the new wing," as it was still being called a decade later, Dr. Phillips, PhD, presided over his Bible fiefdom (Pop quiz on 1 Samuel: Q. How did Samuel answer the night voice three times? A. "Here am I." 1 Samuel 3:2. Q. How did Samuel answer after Eli advised that the voice might be the Lord calling him? A. "Speak, Lord, for thy servant hears." 1 Samuel 3.9)

And the beautiful Miss Petrie, MA in English, who had them for both Literature and Composition, was perhaps reading aloud to her classes in her mournful cello voice, and Dr. Alistair Worley, PhD in psychology, was leading the girls in animated discussion of how today's mimeo topic, still smelly and damp off the machine, had relevance to their lives: struggles of famous characters with discordant personalities and divided selves (St. Augustine, Tolstoy, Paul Bunyan, Persephone), or juicy highlights from Freud's analysis of Dora—and an unforgettable session on the subject of virginity sparked by an assigned magazine story whose last line read: "But there was one thing Queenie missed." Dr. Worley offered free evening counseling sessions to any girl who volunteered to type up his stencils and run them off on the machine.

A front-facing downstairs room in the main building was home to the math and science classes of Mrs. Eloise Sprunt, who had studied to be an architect but married her professor instead. She had been won over at first sight by the classic lines of Lovegood's old brick building, had gone to the trouble of looking up the architect's 1858 drawings, and found, of all things, an attached sketch of the proposed school. (*"After Hart House, Richmond, built 1610."*) There in the old sketch were the same double-sash windows as the ones in her classroom, the same front elevation, and the four Doric columns. Lovegood's architect had been inspired by a Stuart mansion, not a Georgian one, as she had first assumed. Now widowed, her children in their thirties, she lived in a smart downtown apartment she had remodeled herself, and walked to work. Any girl who had the temerity to protest that she'd never been good at math or science earned the "Sprunt scrunch," a facial expression somewhere between pity and scorn. In her twelve years at Lovegood College, Mrs. Sprunt had yet to fail a student in either subject, including trigonometry and physics. She trusted in their hidden reserves, once she got them past the old shibboleth that math and science were "men's subjects."

6

Merry Jellicoe knew she looked forward, more than she should have, to sinking into the dark embrace of her bed after Lovegood's lights-out bell. Stretching her legs beneath the cool sheet, she first rejoiced in having gotten through another day. Then she would view the eastern night sky outside her window. She prided herself on having offered Feron the first choice of beds, though she had known she was running a serious chance of losing the window.

If it was a moon night, she could calculate, thanks to Ritchie and his compass, where it would be hanging in the sky at home. If there were only the stars, she would arrange the constellations as they would appear above Jellicoe's distinctive five black barns. When it was overcast or raining, she had her home visions for that, too.

Except for church camp, she had never slept away from home. And Ritchie had been with her at church camp, so when she was feeling choked with homesickness there, she would head over to the junior division "to check on my little brother."

In her first days at Lovegood, she went around with the choking feeling. As she had confided to Dean Fox in their conference, she did her best to hide it from others.

"A person my age should be over being homesick," she told the dean.

"Missing your home usually indicates you've been happy there."

"We're very close as a family. There's only the four of us, but we do a lot of things together. All of us work on the farm during the busy season. My younger brother and I will take over Jellicoe Enterprises one day. That's why I was sent here instead of Meredith, where Mama went. I'm named after her college, you know, but Lovegood has more advanced business courses."

"Yes, we can be proud of our business school. It's too bad more girls studying liberal arts don't cross over and partake of the business courses. Who among us couldn't improve herself with the basics of accounting, not to mention shorthand?"

"I love my stenography class. Every day, I master more of the symbols. It's like, I don't know, being prepared for a secret society."

"An inspired comparison. What other courses do you like?"

"Oh, Literature and Composition. I love Miss Petrie. Everybody does. When she reads *Paradise Lost* aloud you can hear a pin drop. And in Composition, she shows us how a great short story got that way. It's nothing like my high school English classes. And I guess I like History because Miss McCorkle has such an original way of making you remember things."

"I hear from Feron that you two are getting along well."

"Did she say so? Oh, I'm so glad! I've never met a person like Feron."

"How do you mean?"

"Well, she has complex ways of expressing herself. To make her point, she will often say the exact opposite of what she means and count on you to pick up on it."

"That's called irony."

"Oh, is it? And when you get to know her she can be so funny. Not ha-ha funny, but a dry, kind of sideways funny. She's more complicated than any other girl I have known. The more you're around her, the more you realize you don't know. I just hope I don't seem too uncomplicated to her."

"Having heard from each of you now, I'd say it's a good match."

Merry didn't believe Feron had any idea of her homesickness. Now Ritchie was the complete opposite. He loved being away from home and at twelve was making plans for traveling the world. What made him different? Did people who weren't homesick carry their home inside them? And then there were people who wanted to forget the home they came from. She knew Feron must be one of these.

Feron was as usual reading with her flashlight under the covers after lights out, which was an honor code violation. The illuminated bedclothes rising from the bed across the room reminded Merry of the caterpillar tents that infested the Jellicoe cherry trees every spring. Not that the creatures were given much time to get on with their cycle. Ritchie loved blasting the tents with a high-powered water hose and shrieking, "Die, wormies, die!" She preferred a long pole with nails to rake away the cobwebs.

Her roommate's habit divided Merry's heart. By not reporting Feron, wasn't she an accessory to the crime? But if she warned Feron that she was going to have to report her if she didn't stop, it might unbalance their good match, as Dean Fox called it. It might arouse Feron's anger or disdain.

But concerning this particular night, Miss Darden had tipped off Merry to something Feron didn't know. *And I have to make sure she doesn't spoil what's going to occur.*

"So glad I happened to catch you, dear," Miss Darden had said to her earlier that day. Though it was pretty obvious Miss Darden had been waiting for Merry to come out of accounting class. "I want to let you in on something that's going to happen after lights out tonight. Feron is going to be tapped for the Daughters and Granddaughters Club. They're the only organization allowed to roam around in the dark and surprise the inductees. Because there aren't that many girls to be tapped. And, being what it stands for, it's an honored tradition."

Occasionally in the past, some nocturnal tappings had gone awry or been spoiled. For example, one roommate who didn't get tapped went to pieces. "It was the final straw," Miss Darden said. "From the first day, this girl had felt she didn't fit in at Lovegood, and here was her roommate being carried off in the dark by song and candlelight to one more thing that excluded her. Even when we explained it was a club for those whose mothers or grandmothers had attended Lovegood, she wouldn't be consoled and dropped out soon after. And then what to do about the two roommates playing poker for cash by candlelight? That was a tricky one. Both were caught violating the honor code. What was to be done? Well, they went on and tapped the daughter, but both girls were brought before the honor council."

Then there had been those humiliated daughters or granddaughters brought to the ceremony with their hair in rag curlers or night cream smeared on their faces. If only they could have been warned!

"When I arrived as dorm mistress in 1927, there were only three girls in the club, but ten years later the number had doubled, and that's when it occurred to me the event might need a covert 'Warner,' and that I was the ideal person for the job."

Feron didn't use night cream or curlers, Merry told the dorm mistress.

"I still don't understand about the club. Was Feron's mother or grandmother—?"

"It was her paternal great-grandmother. Her uncle's and her father's grandmother, Sophie Sewell Hood, was in Lovegood's third class, the class of 1875. She dropped out after her first year to marry."

"Just like my mother," remarked Merry, inwardly making adjustments to her image of Feron. Not just the solitary girl without parents or a home, but also the descendant of a girl who had lived somewhere in this old building and whose name was still remembered.

"Feron, please turn off your flashlight. Do it now. Do it for me, please."

To Merry's surprise, the phosphorescent tent immediately disappeared.

"I was finished reading anyway," came the nonchalant reply through the darkness.

Soon Merry heard Feron switch into her sleep breathing. Merry slipped into a reverie in which she traced shorthand strokes on her bottom sheet. Then came a soft knocking at the door, and she opened her eyes to a cluster of girls, lower faces lit by candlelight, standing around Feron's bed. Someone hummed a pitch and five or six voices sang scarcely above a whisper:

> *Mothers, embrace thy daughters*
> *And bring them up with gladness;*
> *Guide their feet to walk steadfastly,*
> *Shrinking not from strife or sadness*
> *Now we walk unseen beside you,*
> *Faithful spirits always guiding.*
> *Motherlove abides forever.*

Feron was now being raised from her bed. One girl wrapped a shawl around her, another girl lit a candle, and, after some murmuring, the group departed the room with Feron and her candle in the lead.

And here was her roommate being carried off in the dark by song and candlelight to one more thing that excluded her, Miss Darden had said about the girl who felt left out. Though she herself was blessed with family and home and had never felt particularly excluded anywhere, Merry could imagine how that poor girl had felt.

7

Lingering on the lawn till early dusk . . .
Midst friendship's gentle bonds . . .

—Mary Louisa Summerlin
Class of 1918

F eron, does it ever feel like a dream to you?"

"What?"

"Being here. On this same lawn, in front of this same school, like in the pageant. It feels like we're in the poem, the class poem of 1918. I wonder what happened to the poet?"

Feron's fingertips tapped calculations onto the cool grass. "She would be in her upper fifties by now. Her life would be, not over, but *set, congealed*—like Jell-O."

"I love the way you compare things. But maybe she died of cancer or something. No, I shouldn't have said that, your mother . . ."

"My mother didn't have cancer. She fell against a radiator and died of a brain hemorrhage."

"Oh, Feron, how awful. Was she alone?"

"It happened while I was at school and my stepfather was at his flying school. There was a postmortem, but that was because I had been upset and told some people Swain could have hit her and then left for his work."

"*Hit* her?"

"With Swain, hitting was like part of any conversation. He was small and thin as a whiplash, but he could easily knock you across the room."

Years ago she had teasingly called him "Swine," and had a dead front tooth to show for it. The tooth was still a dull white, but it didn't match the others. Uncle Rowan said they would get it capped, but there hadn't been time before school started.

"But left her to die?"

"Well, no, when she died, Swain was up in the sky giving a flying lesson. The verdict was that she passed out and hit her head on the radiator. I retracted my accusation about him hitting her and leaving the house, and I apologized to him. I had to go on living with him because I was still a minor. Or as he liked to put it, I still 'belonged to him.'"

"Was she a fainter, your mother?"

"No, but she was often unsteady on her feet. She was an alcoholic."

"Oh, Feron, you've had such sad troubles. The worst that's ever happened to me was my dog, Sam, dying. But listen, did you believe he might have?"

"Might have what?"

"Well, hit her and then left the house."

"I must have wanted it to be what happened. Then he would have had to go to jail, and I would be free. That is, as soon as I turned eighteen, I would be free. I dreaded having to live with Swain in the house without my mother. Even when she was so drunk she couldn't stand up, she had a sort of restraining power over him."

"Neither of my parents drink, but Mama gets these dark periods during the winter months. She can't stand being around people, including us, and she spends lots of time by herself in this room at the top of the house. Once it was a hayloft, and you can see where someone has plastered over the loft's opening and put in a plain little sash window."

"But what does she do there?"

"Nothing, as far as we can tell. There's just an old chair with the stuffing coming out and a table and a blanket. As soon as he could talk, my brother Ritchie started pestering her about it. What did she do in there? Until one day she told him she had to go into that room to put herself back together. Ritchie was still little enough for that idea to really frighten him. If Mama needed to do that, it must mean if you opened the door, you would find her in pieces."

"But what about the cooking and things?"

"Oh, she takes care of all that. In the autumn after harvest she does a mammoth canning, and we have all the fruit and vegetables we can eat until she's feeling herself again. Daddy takes care of the grocery shopping. Or Mr. Jack, our manager. But, Feron, this is just our little family side-story, no one gets hurt and Mama always comes out of her room. But then you *did* have to live with your stepfather, didn't you?"

"I did until I ran away."

"You have really been tried, Feron. You and I are the same age, and you have been tested in ways I probably can't even imagine."

Merry waited. Here was an ideal opportunity for Feron to reveal some of the things that Merry couldn't imagine. But Feron didn't reply. And by now Merry knew her well enough to understand it was going to be one of Feron's nonreplies.

8

Miss Petrie often began both her Literature and Composition classes by reading aloud.

From *Paradise Lost*, she read

> *from morn*
> *To noon he fell, from noon to dewy eve*

or

> *Thick as autumnal leaves that strow the brooks*
> *In Vallombrosa*

Her mournful cello voice enhanced the cadences, and the cadences luxuriated in her voice.

In Composition class they were studying the short story. Miss Petrie stood in front of them, fingering the brooch on her blouse, and read aloud a story about a New England minister who wore a black veil over his face, about an Irish boy who got to the bazaar too late, about a poor Russian girl who lived with a medical student and stripped naked in a cold room so he could make chalk marks on her ribs and teach himself anatomy. The girls never knew where Miss Petrie was going to take them. They gave themselves over to the spell of her voice and observed what she wore and wondered what her own story was. Her almost-too-thin body was perfect for her clothes: dignified well-cut skirts that floated when she walked, her large assortment of old-fashioned blouses. There must have been some great disappointment. Her curly black hair was laced with silver threads, but she was too young to have lost a fiancé in World War I. Miss Petrie and the sunny-natured gym teacher, Miss Olafson, shared an apartment and drove to and from school in Miss Olafson's Jeep.

Miss Petrie had just finished reading today's story about a young Russian soldier on a train, coming down with typhus. When he wakes up at home and learns that his beloved sister died nursing him, his consciousness registers the terrible news, but then he can't overcome his own animal joy at being alive.

At first the girls had been bewildered by their teacher's selection of stories, until, in the discussions afterward they realized that (as Feron put it to Merry later) Miss Petrie was leading them toward an acceptance of being left in uncertainty.

"I want each of you to write a story for next time," she was announcing.

Hands flew up with questions.

"It can be anything you want. Either based on a personal experience or you can make it up. Or it can be a mixture of real and imagined. A story starts somewhere and ends somewhere. No, you don't have to share it with the class, it will be just between you and me. Try for five hundred words, that's about two-and-a-half handwritten pages. No, it won't be graded, it's to familiarize you with the practice of writing a story."

* * *

Merry did her homework in bed. She stepped into a pair of boy's pajamas (outgrown by the twelve-year-old brother who slid down bannisters), plumped up her pillows, and set to work. The *fluency* of Merry's attack on assignments was disconcerting to Feron: it was like someone had turned on a switch and Merry started writing, and when she finished the assignment, the switch was turned off. Frustrated by the facile tempo of Merry's fountain pen, Feron decamped to the library and did her work at a long back table under a green-shaded lamp.

Her story, "Bus Trip," was going to take place during a long bus ride. She could smell those bus smells, most of them unpleasant, and feel the sense of endangerment that had ridden with her like a noxious seatmate.

But feeling queasy and endangered was not a story. Her character was on the bus, but what happened before she got on the bus? More important, what happened *after* she got on the bus? In the typhus story the soldier was on a train, coming down with a disease, and that was something beginning to happen. In the typhus story the soldier was on his way home to infect his sister. The sister dies and that is an ending.

What had happened in real life after Feron was aboard the bus was not a story she would ever dream of handing in to Miss Petrie.

"Now, tell me if what I'm going to ask is an imposition, Feron."

"How will I know until you ask it?"

"Will you read my story and tell me if it's acceptable enough to hand in to Miss Petrie?"

Feron had been loitering on her bed, putting off her trek to the library. Her story had reached an impasse, and Friday was Miss Petrie's class. "Sure, I'll read it."

"But you have to be honest." Merry, in yet another pair of her little brother's pajamas, was already en route to Feron's bed. "If it's terrible, you have to tell me. Promise."

Feron accepted the pages. The title was "Lingering on the Lawn."

Oh, God, she's written about us, Feron thought, glancing down at her roommate's fluid penmanship. "Look, I can't read with you standing over me."

"Want me to leave the room?"

"No, I'll leave."

"Please, Feron, don't keep me in suspense too long."

Feron locked herself in one of the bathroom stalls. No, it wasn't about the two of them. Well, it was and it wasn't. She skimmed the two-and-a-half pages so she could see where it was heading and then calmly began again.

Two girls were sitting on the lawn, wondering aloud what the future held for them. One was dark-haired and "complicated," and the other was blonde and "ordinary." The worst thing that had happened so far to the ordinary girl was her dog dying. The dark-haired girl had lost both parents and was living with an uncle. She had moments of looking "haunted." The ordinary girl loved the school and during her second year composed a poem in its honor. It became the class poem. Then it turns out that this is the winter that World War I has finally ended, and everyone is rejoicing. But unbeknownst to her feverish self, the ordinary girl will not survive the Great Flu Epidemic of 1918. She is tossing on her deathbed and remembering when she and her best friend lingered on the lawn and talked about their futures. Only, in her happy delirium she thinks she is back at school and the whole thing is really happening again.

*   *   *

"Okay, you wanted the truth. Here it is. It's a success—"

"Oh, Feron! Really?"

"Wait, I haven't finished. You have to let the reader know right away we're in the year 1918, otherwise we assume it's the present. Also, 'ordinary' doesn't really suit someone who is going to be the class poet."

"What would be a suitable word?"

"Oh, radiant, cheerful, optimistic. Optimistic might pack the most wallop, since she's going to end up dying."

"I'll have to copy over the first page, but I think you're right."

"How did you know so much about the flu epidemic?"

"While Miss Darden was doing our room check, I asked her whether people still got typhus in 1918. She said influenza would be better for my story because everyone was dying of it that year. She had a younger sister and an aunt who got it. The sister died, but after the aunt recovered she described how it felt."

Feron had discovered something new about herself in the bathroom stall. *She was goaded by someone else's success.* First came the sting of envy, then an inner call to arms, which forced her over some barrier that was always reminding her she was tainted, and no matter what she did she would never be good enough.

Later, when Feron was asked what had made her become a writer (*Do you remember a special moment or person that started you off?*) she had fished up Miss Petrie, floating reliably near the surface, complete with long skirts, mournful voice, and anecdotes. "It was this English teacher we had in junior college. She had the most beautiful voice. Like a cello. She read to us from Chekhov and Joyce and other great writers. And she taught us . . ." Here Feron had learned to pause, as one pauses when formulating a fresh thought. "She taught us to accept being left in uncertainty."

Still later in life, when Feron had accepted aspects of her character that could still made her shudder or cringe, she heard herself
easily acknowledging to someone who had asked the old question,
"Oh, yes, I can tell you the moment it started. I was in a bathroom
stall at my junior college. My roommate had asked me to read her
story and tell me if it was good enough to turn in for the assignment.
I read the story and it was a success. For what it was. Then jealousy
woke up in me like a sleeping animal and I thought, 'I can do this.
I can do it better.' I guess you could say the jealousy woke up my
competitiveness. I have always been stimulated by a competitor.
Though this leads me to another question: Can two people be called
competitors when only one of them is competing?"

At the long table under the green shaded lamp in Lovegood's library,
Feron began "Bus Trip" over again.

Nora, on her way to a new life, was traveling long distance on
a Greyhound bus. Spreading out her belongings on the empty seat
next to her, she arranged her face to look as unwelcoming as
possible to anyone who might have the nerve to ask, "Is this seat
taken?"

Twice a week, Miss Olafson gave tennis lessons to Feron Hood.

It was an "extra" for which the uncle had laid out an additional
$100 a semester, the college and the instructor splitting the fee.

"How much tennis have you played, Feron?"

"Not much. Well, none, to be exact."

"Great!"

"Great?"

"You have no bad habits to break. Try this racquet. How does it
feel? It should have a nice heft, but not feel *weighty*. Today I'm going

to hit balls to you over the net. Try to hit them back, but if you miss one, let it go. I have a whole bucketful here."

The gym teacher had the most streamlined figure Feron had ever seen on a woman. Her tanned upper arms curved sleekly where most females, even young ones, had flab. She bounced from foot to foot in her tennis shoes, and you could see the muscles in her calves take on different shapes. Her white-blonde hair was cut so it flopped when she moved, but the neck was shaved like a boy's. She was always in a good mood and had a wonderful, startled laugh, as if you had surprised her. Feron imagined the evenings with Miss Petrie in their shared apartment. Did they talk about their students? Who cooked, or did they take turns? If her name should come up, what would each of them say about her?

Bus Trip
By Feron Hood

Nora boarded a Greyhound bus that she hoped would take her as far away as possible from the life she was leaving behind. Choosing a window seat midway down the aisle, she spread her belongings over the empty seat beside her and composed her face into an unfriendly mask to deter anyone from daring to ask, "Is this seat occupied?"

Across the aisle was a teenage boy with acne, shoveling peanuts from a greasy paper bag into his mouth. In the row ahead of her sat an old lady who coughed on an average of every two minutes. It was an apologetic cough, as though she expected someone to cry out, "Shut up, old lady. I'm trying to sleep."

It got dark. Dark felt safer to Nora, but the steady rocking of the bus combined with the exhaust fumes made her queasy. There was a pale, dark-haired man in a dark coat who kept going to and from the toilet cubicle in the rear. Nora kept her head down each time he passed her seat. On one return trip he paused long enough for her to be preparing a rejection if he asked to sit down. But then he continued up the aisle again.

Nora was at the point where the reasons for her escape had started intruding on the present reality of it, when a woman teetering back from the toilet swayed and fell into the seat beside her.

"Oh, dear, I'm so sorry. I lost my balance. These bus rides are exhausting, aren't they? And boring! Don't you agree? I hope you are on your way to a destination happier than mine."

It was the strangest conversation. Nora was aware of herself speaking back in the intervals, but it was as if she only provided a sounding board for the woman's monologue. At first the woman had seemed younger, but as the passing traffic lights played across her face, Nora saw that she was probably in her forties and the worse for wear. The alcohol from her breath drowned out the exhaust fumes coming from the bus. She spoke quickly and breathlessly, like she was reciting from a list of grievances that had been saving themselves up for a listener.

"I ask myself, at what point did you take the wrong turning? Was it my first marriage? My second? On the other hand, the rot may have set in earlier. Much earlier! When did I start lying and beguiling my way through life? Was I born a liar and a beguiler? I'm not a churchgoer, but I know some people believe in 'original sin' and some others believe in 'predestination.' Either way, you don't have a chance, your fate is decided already. But since I don't belong to any church, does this mean I am excused because I didn't know better? My first husband got me pregnant before he was my husband. I soon kicked him out and returned to my parents' house with 'the wages of my sin,' my baby daughter. Then some years passed and I knew I would die of boredom and claustrophobia if I didn't get away from my parents. Oh, by the way, my first husband taught me to drink. He was a master of the bottle. Husband number two, when he came along, he didn't drink or smoke. I did both so there were two strikes against me from the start. He was a sanctimonious bully. You had to play by his rules. He hit me, he hit my little girl. I tried to protect her, but it wasn't easy. Then he stopped hitting her. But he couldn't keep his hands off her in a different way.

"So, dearie, huddling over there so confident and untried in your window seat, I wish you good luck on your journey. May it land you somewhere happier than mine did. Now I think I'm steady enough to make it back to my own seat and take another pull from my little pint of oblivion. When I wake up, I'll have a headache and won't remember a word of what I said. I won't even remember you!"

Dear Feron,
"Bus Trip" left me with some questions but continues to resonate in my mind. Your sensory details are first-rate. I smell that bus. I feel the slight nausea from its steady rocking. I see the other passengers, the boy eating peanuts from a greasy bag, the old lady with the "apologetic cough." (Very nice.) And the sinister dark-haired man in a dark coat.

But when the inebriated woman, returning from the toilet, falls into the seat next to Nora, I am completely gripped. And the skillful way you set up the exchange they are about to have, ruling out the prospect of back-and-forth dialogue, is ideal for this scene. (And the woman's list of grievances "that had been saving themselves up for a listener" was also a wonderful touch.)

Her monologue is sad and distressing. I thought the whole "original sin"/"predestination"/"am I excused?" questions she asks were astute, and her parting words, about forgetting everything in the morning, is all too realistic. Few writers, even the seasoned ones, can portray a fully human drunk person. It is so easy to fall into satire or disdain.

However, "Bus Trip" in its present form is not a story. I don't know Nora's background, other than it was something she wanted to leave behind, and I don't have any hint of where she's going. If you were to work more on the story, you might include that information without destroying the organic form. Though, mind you, I'm not certain of this!

But as for the woman who collapses beside Nora, you should be proud of creating such a poignant human being in such a short passage. I hope you will keep writing. You seem to have a natural gift!

Maud Petrie

9

The population of Pullen, North Carolina, was a little over three thousand. Any able-bodied person with the right kind of map could walk its landlocked area of 3.2 square miles in an hour. Pullen came into being in 1867, when lots went up for sale around a new railway station. It was chartered as a town in 1873, and was still called "The Railway Town."

Feron Hood came into being in 1940 because her mother-to-be was sitting on a porch in Pullen playing bridge with her girlfriends when a navy ensign swung by on crutches. He would return to his base as soon as his broken ankle, caused by a stupid move on the tennis court, healed. In passing, he asked the bridge players who was winning, and Feron's future mother said, "Come up on the porch and see." The future mother's father was a railroad man, recently transferred to Pullen.

Since Pullen had become Feron's home address, she gave more thought than ever before to this fluke meeting of two people who had seen fit to part company in less than a year. What had been the attraction?

Looks? Looks had to be described right off the bat in magazine stories. All the main characters needed to have looks. The "good" female was usually blonde and blue-eyed and the "good" male was dark-haired and dark-eyed. It was an agreed-upon formula. (Even in Merry's "Lingering on the Lawn," the good "optimistic" girl was blonde, and the "complicated" girl was dark.) Both Feron's progenitors were at the attractive end of the spectrum, though neither possessed startling good looks. Of course Feron had no memory of her father, only a snapshot her mother reluctantly showed her, but she could recall thinking as a young child how pretty her mother was. Before the alcohol started showing.

Availability in a boring town might have been a factor. Now that Feron had become acquainted with Pullen's 3.2 square miles, she thought this was a distinct possibility.

When she asked Uncle Rowan why her parents had gotten married, he said, "Oh, honey, it was a wartime romance. Or, wait, pre-wartime. We hadn't entered the war yet, but your father had joined the navy." When she put the question to his less diplomatic sister, Aunt Mabel curtly replied, "They had to."

Feron lived at Aunt Mabel's because Uncle Rowan said it was proper and his bachelor house lacked the amenities.

"Why didn't he ever marry?" she asked Aunt Mabel.

"He did once, down in Mexico, when he was three sheets to the wind. The girl's Catholic family had it annulled. Now he and Blanche Buttner have the perfect setup. They've been 'engaged' for fifteen years. They court at her antebellum house and she avoids his. You've seen it. Shirts in their laundry wrappers stacked on the sofa, a lemon and a tin of sardines in the Frigidaire, dust in the corners overlooked by his slapdash cleaning woman."

Feron had liked Uncle Rowan at once. When she had first climbed the wooden stairs to his office, put down her suitcase, and announced who she was, he had stared hard at her, said "You're one of us, all right," looked about to cry, then pulled himself together and asked if she'd had breakfast.

He was a large, raw-boned man, with hound-dog cheeks and a sparse moustache. His hair was mostly white and brilliantined. He rocked rather than walked because his long legs seemed to want to go their separate ways. He was generous to a fault ("He likes people to think he's richer than he is," said Aunt Mabel).

"Oh, honey, he never did take care of himself" was Uncle Rowan's answer when Feron asked him how her father had died.

"He drank himself to death," Aunt Mabel said. "The liver can only take so much, and he started while he was still in short pants. I still miss Woody. Pity you didn't get to know him. He was the sweet one in the family. Our oldest brother, Simon, died so long ago we sometimes forget to include him. He was just twenty-three when they gave him a spinal in the operating room and he never woke up. Woody was also the best-looking brother. We all have the long cheeks and droopy eyelids, but on Woody the proportions were just right. You favor your uncle Rowan more than you do your father."

Feron slept in the front bedroom, formerly the master bedroom of Aunt Mabel and her late husband. "I always hated this room," Aunt Mabel remarked casually as she helped Feron hang her clothes in the closet. Aunt Mabel slept in a small back room overlooking the garden.

Perched on the dresser's starched antimacassar in Feron's bedroom were framed pictures of Aunt Mabel and Uncle Dave on their wedding day and little Davey, age three, who now worked as an engineer in Seattle, scowling at a ball he held in his lap.

Among family pictures in the living room was a stout woman in a dark dress standing in front of a fence. Her forehead was creased, and she looked miffed about something. Her right hand braced her hip, and her left hand was curled in a fist. This was Mabel's grand-mother, which meant she was also Feron's uncle's and her father's grandmother. This was the woman Sophie Sewell Hood had become: Feron's frowning great-grandmother, who got her into Lovegood's Daughters and Granddaughters Club.

"Can you remember what your grandmother was like?" Feron asked Aunt Mabel.

"Granny Hood. We children called her Old Witchie Crosspatch. Our parents would threaten to send us to stay with her when we were bad. She was a hard woman."

"How 'hard'?"

"Well, she didn't have much use for people, even her own kin. She preferred her goats and chickens. She made us drink goat milk, and if we even *thought* about being bad, she said we'd have to sleep in the henhouse."

"Did you ever sleep in the henhouse?"

"No, but I still can't pass a henhouse today without feeling scared. And I'd rather die than drink another glass of goat milk."

"What about her husband?"

"He had died so long ago none of us remembered him. Grandfather Rowan was said to have been 'easygoing,' but that can mean any number of things, can't it?"

"So he was named Rowan, too."

"Yes. They had one child that lived. They named him Marcus. That was our father. I'm surprised you care about this family stuff, since you weren't a part of it growing up."

Feron decided not to mention the Daughters and Granddaughters club to Aunt Mabel, who might question her right to be in such a club when Feron hadn't even grown up knowing the Hoods.

She lay in the double bed that didn't seem wide enough for a married couple and thought about her father and mother. Were they both already drinkers when her future mother had called, "Come up on the porch and see"? Had her future mother already had a few cocktails that day? Feron had grown up smelling her mother's alcohol breath. Her stepfather, Swain, who needed to be sober for flying, found her mother's habit disgusting and said her whisky smell kept him from sleeping. Maybe her father and mother had been drunk when they started her.

Or maybe bored and drunk.

During Thanksgiving break, Feron walked the blocks of the town, which was laid out in a grid: uptown with courthouse, stores, law offices, library; then the "good" street, where Aunt Mabel lived, paralleled by a second-tier street, where Uncle Rowan lived in a bungalow with his packaged shirts and his lemon and sardines. Farther down came the not-so-good white streets and, last of all, the houses of the colored people. Then there was open field, and on the far side of the field was Pullen's cemetery. Feron visited her father's stone—how sad, he had barely lived to the age of thirty-four—and the stones of the other family members. There were lots of Hoods, going back to 1800, and a great many Pullens, which wasn't a surprise.

Feron had kept her surname, but her mother had paid for it. When Swain was officially adopting her, he put up a fight to replace Hood with Eckert. Her mother stood up for Hood ("She's already Hood to her friends and it has a nicer sound, it suits her.") until Swain knocked her down and caused another miscarriage. After that, the name change wasn't mentioned again. That Feron's mother never carried a pregnancy to full term Swain construed as her secret wish not to have his child.

For such a little town, Pullen boasted an excellent library. It had the newest books, protected by clear plastic book covers. On its shelves were several volumes of Chekhov's stories. Wishing Miss Petrie could be looking down from above, Feron sat down at a long table and picked and chose among the stories. She went for the ones whose titles or openings attracted her. The titles themselves were short, a person's name or a universal subject that could take place anywhere, at any time: "Anyuta" (the one about the naked girl and the medical student Miss Petrie had read to them!), "The Doctor," "The Schoolmistress," "In the Court," "The Runaway," "A Misfortune," "A Story Without an End."

You never knew what the people in his stories were going to do or what life was going to do to them. A lonely schoolmistress is being driven home in a cart after picking up her salary, and a prosperous, handsome acquaintance in a four-horse carriage stops to talk to her. He is past his prime and smells of alcohol, but it crosses her mind that if she were this man's wife, she could save him. Later in the story, after a mishap with the cart in an overflowing stream, she and the cart driver are stopped at a barrier waiting for the train to pass. Standing on the little platform between the two first-class carriages is a lady who has rich hair exactly like the schoolmistress's late mother. This floods the schoolteacher's heart with memories of when she was young and lovely and safe in a bright Moscow room among her own people. Remembering every tiny detail down to the family aquarium with its little fish, she presses her hands to her temple in an ecstasy of nostalgia and begins crying. At that moment the prosperous alcoholic man pulls up beside her in his carriage and she imagines a happiness she never had. Her dreary years as a school-mistress seem like a bad dream and she greets him as an equal and a friend. Then the prosperous man in his four-horse carriage crosses the tracks and goes on his way, her ecstasy vanishes, and presently the cart driver announces they are home.

"With Chekhov you just can't predict" she imagined saying in a private conference with Miss Petrie. And then maybe adding, if the mood was right, "I guess I was thinking of Chekhov when I was vague about Nora's past and future in my story. You taught us to accept being left in uncertainty, but maybe I went a little too far."

If Chekhov had written a story called "Inquest," it might have opened with the coroner's summation: there had been no foul play in the case of X's wife's death. The widower, who had wept through the entire proceedings and won everyone's sympathy, would murmur to the girl as they left the court: "I am going to forgive you for starting that crazy rumor, but as long as you're a minor in my house, you'll toe the line or I'll commit you to an institution." As they are walking away, onlookers comment on the plight of the unfortunate man. "Bad luck to be stuck with that snooty stepdaughter who ruined his reputation. Did you notice, during the entire proceedings she didn't shed a single tear?"

A story called "The Bus Trip," in the Chekhovian style, might open like "Typhus," with the main character traveling on public transportation. Only instead of being aboard the smoking carriage of the mail train, like the young lieutenant coming down with typhus, the runaway girl would be aboard a Greyhound bus, still in shock from having stolen Swain's hidden roll of cash and committing blackmail in writing. ("If you come after me, I will tell all the things I *didn't* tell: how many times you wished Mother dead, the time you caused her miscarriage, the time you ruined my tooth, and about the nights you came into my room and stuck your filthy hand up my nightgown.")

Yes, there was a boy eating peanuts, you could smell the oil from across the aisle; yes, there was an old lady with an apologetic cough; and yes, Nora spreads out her belongings on the empty seat to warn off any potential seatmate. There was no inebriated woman with her sad and distressing monologue. Instead it was "the sinister man" who went back and forth to the toilet at the rear of the bus. In this version of "The Bus Trip," he pauses after three or four trips and asks if he may join her. He's striking in a sharpish way, with eyes too deep-set to show their color and an unusual pallor under the short black haircut. He wears an open-necked white shirt that looks new under a formal black coat that is too large. He tells her he has been out of circulation for a while and hasn't had much civilized conversation.

"What makes you think I am civilized?" Nora flippantly challenges. Already removing her things from the empty seat.

How would Chekhov end this story?

Perhaps there would be a brief attraction followed by the two going their separate ways after the bus ride, like the schoolmistress and the handsome alcoholic in the four-horse carriage. A "could-have-been" ending. Or maybe the strangers would decide to combine forces (his being a man, her stolen cash) against a city that neither of them was prepared for "until they were both on their feet." Chekhov would leave them in their shabby lodgings, alternately clinging to each other and finding fault. (One day Feron returned from a walk and found him with his head in the sink, dyeing his hair black. "But now it looks fake." "It will make it easier to get a job.")

Uncle Rowan was taking Feron out for Thanksgiving dinner without Blanche Buttner, who traditionally spent that day in the church kitchen, cooking and serving a Thanksgiving meal for anyone who showed up at the Food Hall.

"Mabel, won't you change your mind and come?"

"No, thank you, Rowan. I always hated Thanksgiving. I'm going to have some cornbread and buttermilk and take a nice nap while I have the house all to myself again."

At the Greek restaurant they were settled into their reserved booth with much fanfare, and the owner's entire family stopped by to pay obeisance to Uncle Rowan and make a fuss over his niece.

"Don't tell your Aunt Mabel this," Uncle Rowan said, when they were alone again, "but when the four of us were growing up, we called her 'the tactless wonder.' Mabel managed to make anything that came out of her mouth offensive to someone. So one day your father took her aside. 'Listen, Mabel,' he said. 'You're never going to get a husband if you don't learn to gush.'

"'*Gush!* I wouldn't know how,' she said.

"'I'm going to teach you how,' Woody told her. He said, 'Now, I'm going to be you and you'll be someone you've just met on the street. Now, say something.'

"'Say *what?*' Mabel asks.

"'Just make the sort of comment normal people make when they meet on the street,' Woody told her, 'and remember you're *someone else.*'

"So, being someone else, Mabel says, 'It's an overcast day.'

"And then Woody, being Mabel, says, 'Yes, it is a little overcast, but now for me it's a great day. And you know why? Because I happened to run into you!'"

"I wish I had known him," said Feron. "I don't have a single memory of my father."

"Woody was the sweet one in our family. He had his faults, but he could be so funny. He was always making us laugh."

"I wonder if he and my mother were happy, if they liked each other."

"Well, honey, there was surely an attraction, or they wouldn't have, you know, married."

"Aunt Mabel said they had to get married."

"Aunt Mabel tends to expect the worst of people. You came along about the time you were supposed to come along. It's just too bad Woody didn't live long enough to know *you.*" Uncle Rowan took off his glasses and made a big to-do about polishing the lenses with his pocket handkerchief. Feron could see he was trying to hide his annoyance at having been caught off guard.

"Why did the restaurant owner say you were a saint?"

"I've helped them out a little from time to time." Uncle Rowan pronounced it "hepped." "That nice young son of his you met used to have a wandering eye. It's easily fixed but it costs money. And I helped with the daughter's college and a few other things."

She tried not to feel jealous that Uncle Rowan had paid for another girl's college before he knew her.

Uncle Rowan asked about her friends.

"My closest friend is my roommate, Merry Jellicoe."

"Where's she from?"

"Hamlin."

"The Jellicoe of Jellicoe's bright leaf tobacco?"

"Yes."

"You two get along then."

"She's easy to be with. And I can trust her."

"No small compliment. Do you have any beaus?"

"I haven't been on a date yet. I thought you knew."

"Knew what?"

"First-year Lovegood girls have to have written permission from their parents to go on dates."

"I don't recall anyone asking me for a written permission."

"I haven't missed it. Merry doesn't date either."

"I'm not a tyrant. I would have signed if anyone had asked."

"It's just as well. I like the safety of all the rules and regulations for first-year students. I can focus my mind and bring up my grades."

"Well, I'm glad you're getting on, honey. You're not disappointed about the tooth, are you? The dentist thinks it's better if we wait for the long Christmas break so you can go back to school with the porcelain crown, and not have to worry about displacing a temporary."

"I've lived with this tooth since I was fifteen. Another month is nothing at all."

"I hope I never meet that man." Through his polished glasses Uncle Rowan glowered toward the far end of the restaurant at his invisible adversary. "But you're okay now."

10

The snow fell hard and fast on Lovegood College. A thick white scrim turned the century-old oaks into silhouettes of themselves, the three-foot-high boxwood hedges were level with the snow-covered lawn, and the Doric columns seemed to be growing out of the snow without their brick bases. Where was Mr. Sikes and his snowblower? The high double doors of the front entrance were impassable. Sikes should have been on the job hours ago.

"Nevertheless," Dean Fox informed someone just behind her, "this snow is exactly what this school needs."

"Why so, Susan?"

"It's time for it to start with a clean slate. As I did."

"If you had been patient, no clean slate would have been needed."

"You would still be entreating me to be patient if I hadn't cracked."

"—throwing rocks at my window!" The irresistible laugh.

Oh, God, she was dreaming. This was a dream. But she had to finish this dialogue. Susan Fox willed herself to stay in her dream.

"Not rocks. Gravel."

"All right, gravel. But the cursing . . . and the biting! Dear Susan, why couldn't you have waited?"

"If I had waited, you would still be saying 'Oh, dear Susan, please wait a little longer' and compounding your little treacheries."

"When you attacked that policeman—!" Again the laugh. The complicit, intimate laugh she believed to have been inspired by herself alone. She could still go weak in the knees from wanting him. But inside her own dream she now understood that he had laughed like that with each of the others.

Was the presence fading? "One more thing," she said, "then I'll let you go. Were you lying only to me, or were you lying to yourself, as well?"

When Dean Fox looked out the tall sash windows of her college suite, of course there was no snow. Not a flake had fallen since her arrival last year. It was now a mild mid-December day, and two floors below, Mr. Sikes, in a light work jacket, rode the tractor-mower in swaths of his own design on the winter lawn. Bud, his young assistant, scything weeds that had sprung up around the trees, had tied his jacket round his waist.

Everything in Dean Fox's living quarters was of her own choosing: the color of the paint, the curtains, the upholstery fabric on the furniture. She had only to say. The Lovegood trustees wanted her to be happy. She was their great acquisition.

A few things she had brought from her old life, purchased in those early days when she had had every reason to assume she would be fading honorably into her dotage inside Saxon Hall's noble walls: a handsome oak dresser with a round bevel mirror, an English walnut writing desk, and the chair Florence said she had "carried" to her new job.

"I wish I had your skills," she had exclaimed as Eloise Sprunt led her through her own uptown apartment, which the widowed math and science teacher had renovated herself.

"You have elegant living quarters already. Lovegood's high windows and ceilings aren't doable anymore. But if you ever do go looking for an off-campus residence, I'll be glad to look over the sites with you and offer suggestions."

Am I afraid to strike out on my own, she had asked herself that afternoon in Eloise Sprunt's apartment. The Lovegood trustees had given her the choice. They would find her off-campus lodgings of the type she preferred. But if she chose to stay at the school, they would fix up the suite to her heart's desire. She intuited that she would be more in control of her surroundings inside the school that wanted her.

It was one thing to be a widow of means and the mother of grown children, returning to trade on architectural skills like Eloise Sprunt, and another to be a spinster in your midforties with nothing to show for it.

They called it "the snitching hour." Every week the dorm mistress came to the dean's office, and they "went over the girls." Not all hundred and fifty girls, just the reportable ones who had caught the dorm mistress's attention. The dean spread a cloth at one end of the rosewood conference table and provided the carafe of Madeira, the glasses, the plates, and the napkins. Winifred Darden, famous for her sweet tooth, brought the choicest offerings sent by the mothers. Lovegood's Christmas recess being a week away, today's haul was a bonanza.

"Shortbread, lemon pound cake, brownies, and Patsy King's mother's devastating fruit cake into which she starts injecting bourbon with a hypodermic needle in August. Oh, and cheese straws!"

"Goodness." The dean, who had gained fifteen pounds since coming to Lovegood, watched the skinny dorm mistress laying out the spread with the disciplined slowness of greed held in check.

"What about Stubbs? Is she still sleeping?" Pouring the Madeira.

"I'm afraid so. And since someone informed her she might have mono, she feels entitled."

"Sore throat? Swollen glands?"

"Nurse said no."

"How are her grades?"

"Falling. She failed her last chemistry test. Mrs. Sprunt thinks she can pull her through if Stubbs comes back restored after the holidays."

"Let her sleep for another week. Meanwhile, I will write to her parents for a clean bill of health from their doctor. What about Trask and Wooten? Are they still poisonous to each other?"

"As far as I can tell, they've retreated into a sullen standoff. Both like their room, they just wish the other person wasn't in it."

"Can they maintain their standoff till the end of the school year?"

"I'd bet on it. Isn't this fruit cake wicked? Patsy King's mother has outdone herself. I'm feeling high already."

"What makes you bet on it?"

"Trask's boyfriend is transferring to Wake Forest, and she's begging her mother to let her transfer to Salem Academy. It's more expensive, but they want her to be happier than she is here."

"She told you that?"

"Many of them confide in me, you know. My omnipresence in their lives is a sort of camouflage. They don't see me as threatening. I told Trask she would have to get her grades up or they wouldn't touch her, and that she'd better start playacting the part of a cheerful, outgoing girl."

"How did she take it?"

"She liked the playacting challenge. And it will be a challenge for Trask."

"Good work. Who else is on your list? A little more Madeira?"

"I shouldn't, but why not. There *is* something else, but I hesitate to bring it up . . ."

"If I know you, Winifred, that sounds like a preface to a real problem."

"Well, it concerns Dr. Worley."

"Dr. Worley?"

"He gives free counseling on Tuesday nights to girls who type up the stencils for his Psychology classes."

"Yes, I know that. What? Are more girls showing up for free counseling than he has time to give?"

"No, it's something else."

The dean's eyebrows went up. She decided against a second piece of the whiskey-logged fruitcake.

"I was above them on the stairs, out of their sight line, and Ginny Rogers was saying she almost threw up when he forced her to kiss him."

"This is *Alistair Worley?*"

"Well, I didn't know that . . . yet. And the other girl, I don't know who she was, said, 'Everybody knows he's like that. He tells you the psychological reasons that you act the way you do, and gives you advice about things, and then comes the payoff.' And Ginny Rogers said, 'You mean *you* did it?' And the girl whose voice I didn't recognize said, 'Well at least he soaks them in Polident. You can taste it in his mouth. And when I go back upstairs, I gargle with Listerine. Everybody knows that's part of the deal.'"

"She said 'everybody knows'?"

"Yes, my heart sank when I heard that. You wonder how many is 'everybody.'"

The dean took some more Madeira herself. "I am going to have to think this through, Winifred."

"I dreaded telling you and having to upset you just before the holidays. But I know you well enough that after you think it through, you will make the right executive decision."

11

F eron, you never—I wanted to ask, but—"
"Wanted to ask what?"

The roommates were returning from Cobb's Corner, a seedy store three blocks from Lovegood. They had to step carefully over upended slabs of sidewalk where old tree roots had broken through.

"Your story. You read mine, but you never let me read yours. I showed you my note from Miss Petrie, but you didn't offer to show yours."

Both were sucking grape-flavored Tootsie Pops. The store was popular less for what it stocked than what it offered: a permitted destination Lovegood girls could walk to and from during daylight hours with the sense they were venturing outside Lovegood boundaries.

"That's because mine was never really finished. Miss Petrie wrote that it wasn't a story. And it wasn't. It isn't."

Though alerted to Feron's "lay off" voice, Merry pushed it a notch further. "But I would be interested. I don't even know what your story was about."

"I just told you. It wasn't a story. I knew it when I turned it in. And she said it wasn't a story. It had some good sensory details, but I didn't reveal enough about the main character for it to be a story."

"But still. I would have liked . . ."

"Okay. It was about a girl running away on the bus. Only I neglected to reveal why she was running away or where she was headed. And this drunk woman loses her balance and falls into the empty seat beside her and tells horrible stories about why she's a drunk and her life is ruined. Then she tells my main character she's going back to her own seat to have another nip from the bottle, and she says, I won't remember a word I said in the morning and what's more I won't even remember *you*. And that's the end of my nonstory."

"Oh, Feron."

"Oh, Feron, what?"

"It sounds compelling. What you said about the end, it sounds like a Chekhov ending."

"I must admit, that flicked through my mind when I turned it in. Maybe she'll think it's like Chekhov. But she didn't. Now, with you, she said it was engaging from beginning to the end and that the fever dream part was convincing and it was masterly the way you stayed inside her point of view right up to her last breath."

"But it was you who helped me improve it!"

"All I did was suggest putting 1918 right at the start and thinking of a better adjective than 'ordinary' for your main character."

"Well, anyway, Feron, thank you for trusting me enough to tell me about your story."

"How many times do I have to say, it was not a story. What a terrible sidewalk this is! Why don't they have it fixed?"

"Cobb's Corner won't be here next September. These entire three blocks are coming down, including all the trees that caused the damage."

"What?"

"The contractors and the architects still have to turn in their bids, but this whole area we're walking through already belongs to Lovegood College. Next summer they're going to break ground for new buildings, a cafeteria and a gym with a swimming pool."

"Where did you hear that?"

"From Miss Darden."

"Old Motormouth herself."

"When the architect draws up the plans—after we decide on one—Dean Fox will throw a big reception for the girls and the old girls and the trustees. It's not a secret, Miss Darden says, it's only that the plans aren't far enough along to excite everybody."

"But she told *you*."

"I'm not everybody. She likes to talk to me about the school because she knows I'm interested in that kind of thing."

"What kind of thing?"

"Oh, the history of things and how they change over time and sometimes turn out the opposite of what was planned."

"Like 'Lingering on the Lawn.'"

"What? Oh, you mean my story."

"She expected to graduate with her friend, and they were making plans for the future, then suddenly she's back on the college lawn with her friend and wonders how this can be. But it's a fever dream from the flu that's about to kill her. By the way, don't let this go to your head, Merry, but in 'Typhus' we stay inside the young soldier all the way through his fever but then he recovers. You carried it one step further than Chekhov. You followed her over the threshold into death."

"Only I didn't get very far over that threshold."

"But you furnished us with a glimpse. I can't think of another story, by *anybody*, who does that."

*   *   *

Susan Fox had chosen to stand for this interview so that when the small, impeccably turned-out Lothario approached, he would find himself having to look up at Lovegood's five-foot-nine dean.

"How are you, Dr. Worley? How are your classes going?"

"The girls are enthusiastic. We examine a wide range of human behavior. I try to keep them on their toes."

"I heard about that magazine story that went over so well. 'But there was one thing Queenie missed.'"

"Modern young women like to decide for themselves whether or not they are missing out on . . . well, on certain old traditions."

"Such as remaining a virgin until your wedding night." Good. She had raised a flush on the psychology teacher's cheeks. "And your melancholy biographies—only, you call them something else."

"Discordant Personalities and Divided Selves. We spend several weeks on that topic. Famous cases. Tolstoy, Paul Bunyan, Persephone . . ."

"Now I would have liked to sit in for your Persephone class . . ."

"Why is that, Dean Fox?"

"Well, it seems to me that having lived with the King of Darkness, she could never feel at home above ground with all the beautiful flowers. Because now she knows that all beautiful flowers die. And, also, there's something about her underground consort that she longs to get back to—but no, Dr. Worley, I'm not going to let you psychoanalyze me. I asked you here to discuss those evening counseling sessions you've been giving the girls."

"It's just the girls who volunteer to type the class stencils. A messy job. It's my payback. If they have a problem they want to talk over in the confidentiality of a professional setting, I'm available on Tuesday evenings."

"The sessions, they're how long?"

"I generally keep it to a half hour. Sometimes forty minutes, depending on how many have signed up."

"And when a session is over, what then?"

"I'm not sure I understand, Dean Fox."

"The session is ended, the girl stands up, or both of you stand up, and then what?"

"We say goodnight, and the next girl comes in."

"But after you two stand up and say goodnight, and before you open the door for the next girl, does anything else happen?"

The visible alarm of a boy caught out. A half-century-old balding Lothario. His wardrobe, like the clothes-conscious male teachers at Saxon Hall, tended toward English tweeds juxtaposed against gaily adventurous ties. Today a floral pattern against navy blue. Dr. Worley wore a gold signet ring on his left pinkie. No wedding ring.

Time to strike.

"Any exchange of affection is what I mean, Dr. Worley."

"These girls are affectionate. They come from homes where spontaneous natural feelings are expressed."

Wait it out. Let him squirm.

"I suppose there may have been . . . occasional kisses. But we're talking about fatherly-type kisses."

The psychology teacher was one of Lovegood's prized two PhDs, the other being Dr. Phillips, the religion teacher.

The Lovegood Board of Trustees, to which she reported, consisted of nine men and one old widow of a trustee who never expressed an opinion.

"Well, in the interests of all concerned, I'm going to ask you to discontinue your evening sessions after we return from the Christmas break."

"Have there been . . . complaints?"

"Let's just say it has been brought to my attention. Look, Dr. Worley, I know you'll agree that the last thing either of us wants is for the generous gift of your time to come under a cloud."

Pause. Wait.

"So many things get misconstrued these days. The sessions were something I thought would be of help—and I daresay they have been of considerable help to many of these girls, but, as you say, the last thing we would want is for my . . . gift . . . to come under a cloud. Consider the Tuesday counseling sessions at an end. As of this meeting."

"I'm sure every one of those girls is the wiser from having experienced your sessions, Dr. Worley. What will you be doing over the Christmas break?"

"We'll be going to Sea Island. It's a tradition of my wife's family. What about yourself, Dean Fox?"

"I am going to try the mountains this year with my recently widowed friend. Both of us are New Englanders and are longing for some snow."

"You and your friend won't be disappointed. I hope you are staying at some rustic mountain inn with a four-course breakfast."

"We are, we are, Dr. Worley. Thank you for asking. Well, Merry Christmas."

"Merry Christmas, Dean Fox."

"When we meet again, it will be a new year. I wonder what it will bring?"

The previous year, her first Christmas break at Lovegood, she had slipped up. Having given a Thanksgiving luncheon for the teachers the day before everyone departed for the holiday, she had announced to the dorm mistress that she might just spend Christmas in her lovely quarters and have some time to herself.

"But you can't do that, Susan. The college closes down for the Christmas break. Florence Rayburn goes home, and so do the rest of the staff."

"But what about you, Winifred? I assumed you stayed. I had thought we might explore the city, you could show me the sights."

"Oh, no. I always go down to my cousins in Fayetteville. They are all very kind to me."

"Well, why shouldn't they be?"

"Oh, I don't know. I often wonder what they think I am. I'm not sure it's anything close to what I think I am. But enough of this old maid talk."

So last year, the dean of Lovegood College and her imaginary friend, the widow from New England, had found last-minute accommodations at a charming boarding house in Beaufort, walking distance to the sea.

During her tenure as dean of Lovegood, Susan Fox added so many realistic touches to her widowed Christmas friend that she felt she could have recognized her in the dark. She knew what this friend took in her coffee, what shampoo she used, her foibles and prejudices, her pet expressions, the secrets of her late marriage. When the time came to kill her off because the dean had found living friends to share holidays with, Susan Fox knew what hymns had been sung at her friend's funeral, and why, and what scripture had been chosen, and why.

12

Well, Feron, looks like all the Hoods are using the Christmas holidays to refurbish ourselves. You'll finally be getting your tooth crowned, Aunt Mabel is booked in to have her operation, and I'm headed up to Duke to get a series of electrocutions to restore my mental balance."

Which meant that Feron would be staying with Uncle Rowan's fiancée in her antebellum house in the nearby town of Benton Grange.

Blanche Buttner's household was in another galaxy from Aunt Mabel's. It offered new comforts and graces, but amplified Feron's growing awareness of her compromised upbringing and her social lacks. She liked the appointments of her upstairs room overlooking a garden of gloomy statuary, though the room got no sun until late afternoon. She liked having a bathroom all to herself for the first time in her life. She liked the breakfasts laid out for them by the cook every morning. You edged your way along a serving table and lifted the lids on silver dishes, and there were scrambled eggs kept warm over a flame, there were oatmeal and biscuits, either sausages or bacon, and warm stewed fruit. The first stage of Feron's dental work had been completed: Swain's damaged front tooth was now drilled down to a sharp little point no one would ever see and covered by a temporary crown until the permanent one could be fashioned from a mold.

Blanche was "statuesque" to her friends and "buxom" to people like Aunt Mabel. Following a breakfast of tablespoon-sized helpings of egg and oatmeal, one slice of bacon, stewed fruit, and black coffee, Blanche in her quilted kimono with a dragon crawling down the back retired to her sunny office to sit at a desk with pigeonholes and make phone calls and take care of her correspondence. This took at least two hours. Personal letters, thank-you notes, club accounts—she was treasurer of at least four clubs—and business pertaining to Buttner Oil and Gas, founded by her grandfather and whose stock she still held. After that began the many-layered ritual of Dressing for Lunch, and around noon she would depart for whatever luncheon she was attending that day. Returning about 2 P.M., she would shut herself in her downstairs rooms for a "refresher" nap. After that, she and Feron would drive to town for necessities, which at this time of the year meant shopping for Christmas presents.

Left to organize her own routine, Feron spent more time than she thought healthy dwelling on her own insufficiencies. Being in Blanche's house only reinforced her certainty that she would never catch up in ways that mattered because she lacked the proper foundations. She was doing well at Lovegood and had no unfinished schoolwork. Her teachers liked her, probably because she exceeded what they had expected of her. The other students seemed to respect her, but maybe that was because she was usually with Merry, who would always pass on anything they said. Girls saw her as "reserved," "mature," or "unusual," Merry reported back.

"But those aren't exactly compliments, are they?" Feron said. "They could go either way."

"I'm sure they were compliments, Feron. Otherwise they wouldn't have said them to me."

During the Swain years, she had been a straight A student because she escaped into studying. Her one close friend in high school told her she came across as "too aloof," but that friend had moved away. After her mother died, Feron's grades hit bottom as she tried and failed at her short-sighted attempt to escape Swain.

There was a nice writing table in her room and even a telephone, but since she would be spending the last week of the holidays with the Jellicoes, it seemed pointless to write, and Hamlin counted as a long-distance call from Benton Grange.

Benton Grange had a different layout from Pullen and was not as easy or as satisfying to explore on foot. Its streets radiated from a central monument to a violent and bloody battle won by the Confederates that had given Benton Grange its status as a town. On this site a century earlier, there was only Mr. Benton's large house and farm buildings. In the last months of what they were still calling "The War Between the States" in these parts, a regiment of Confederates had used the Grange as an arsenal until Sherman's Union troops arrived and routed the winners.

The house and buildings formerly known as the Grange were situated on either side of the monument of a general on his rearing horse. They served as a hospitality center and a Chamber of Commerce for Benton Grange. Next came a park cupped by a semi-circular road of fine old homes, including Blanche's. The privileged semicircle then fanned out on one side into less impressive spokes. Along one spoke was a hardware store, a beauty parlor, a drugstore, and various shops, some of them good enough for Blanche to patronize. You could walk up and back on that street, looking in the windows, then go to the next spoke over, which was a dusty road with a supermarket, a furniture store, a filling station, Blanche's Catholic church, and some fields, after which came a row of Negro shacks, then more fields ending in the entrance to the newly built interstate highway. Or you could skip that spoke and take the one with the school, two protestant churches, each with its own graveyard, a well-manicured funeral home with an operating fountain in front, then another creek, this one smelling of chemicals, and then sudden green and rolling landscape and beautiful young specimen trees and shrubs surrounding the new Sylvania plant.

For Feron's lunch, the cook left ham or cheese biscuits wrapped in wax paper, fresh fruit, cookies, and a pitcher of iced tea. Feron was left to wonder what had happened to the morning's leftover bacon or sausages, until enlightened about the Catholic church's soup kitchen, founded by Blanche's mother, where all their uneaten food went right after breakfast, dropped off by the cook.

"What did Uncle Rowan mean about 'a series of electrocutions'?"

"You've heard of electroshock therapy, haven't you?"

"Sort of."

"Do you know what manic depression is?"

"Merry Jellicoe's mother goes into this dark period every winter, and sits by herself in an old hayloft. But in the spring she's herself again."

"With Rowan, it's more like flashing periods of activity and then a sudden plunge into listlessness and melancholy. When he's in his up periods, he has all the energy in the world and believes he can do anything. When he feels the depression coming, he hides it as long as he can, then he goes up to Duke and checks in for a few weeks."

"I've never noticed Uncle Rowan seeming depressed."

"That's because he didn't want you to notice. Self-control can go a long way, though fewer people choose to make use of theirs these days. The long days of summer are usually good for him, then in autumn he begins to sink, if he's going to, and then by November he books himself into the psychiatric wing."

"He met me in the early summer. If I had arrived in November, I wonder if he would have asked me to stay."

Blanche laughed. She was driving them down the spoke that led to the supermarket. "As a matter of fact, he proposed to me at the summer solstice fifteen years ago. But that has worked out quite well. Rowan and I are each other's mainstay and always will be. But, surely Merry's mother doesn't sit in a hayloft all during the winter months."

"Oh, no, it has been turned into a room on top of the house. Merry says you can see the lines where the opening used to be."

There was one awful thing Feron did during her stay with Blanche. They had bought a Christmas present, a really nice bed jacket that could pass for a silk shirt for Aunt Mabel, who was recovering at home with a practical nurse after her female surgery. "What time shall I suggest we drop by?" Blanche asked Feron. "I'd like to phone over there first."

"Oh, you go ahead without me," said Feron.

As soon as it was out of her mouth and she saw the surprise and distaste Blanche was struggling to conceal, she wished she could pull it back. This was the Feron speaking out of her former life, when she had nothing left to lose and resented every little thing they asked of her, and made a point of refusing as much as she dared. ("Do you want to ride with us to the store, Feron?" "Well, could you at least make a list of the things you'd like to eat?")

A deadly moment passed.

"Rowan expects this of you," said Blanche. That was all she said.

On Christmas morning, Feron was to find an embarrassing number of gifts for herself under Blanche's tree. Every one of them showed careful choosing. A portable tabletop radio with an antenna. A silk scarf with swirls of turquoise and green and yellow. A pair of black leather gloves. A fifty-dollar gift certificate from Blanche's favorite Benton Grange shop. Feron gave Blanche a box of subtly striped man-sized linen handkerchiefs—Blanche deplored the ladies-sized ones where you found yourself blowing your nose on lace. Blanche gave Uncle Rowan a cashmere cardigan in a cranberry color, and Feron gave him a paisley necktie, which Blanche had chosen. Uncle Rowan gave his fiancée the Caron perfume she wouldn't buy for herself because it was immorally expensive. Then they all had Christmas dinner at the Greek restaurant, where they were much fussed over, and Blanche drove her own car back to Benton Grange to get ready for her church's Boxing Day party for the poor. Uncle Rowan took Feron to visit the recuperating Aunt Mabel, who told Feron "not to tell Blanche," but she was exchanging the bed jacket for something more to her taste. Then he drove Feron back to Benton Grange. Having been alerted by Blanche, she deduced from his few heavy sighs that he was controlling his low spirits as best he could. He was probably counting the minutes until he rejoined the company of his laundered shirts on the sofa and the lemon and olives in the refrigerator.

13

Jellicoe Farm, December 26, 1958

Why are you making up your bed for her, Merry Grape?"

"Because my bed has the nicest view."

"What's wrong with the view of the curing barns? Don't you think they look spectacular with their new coats of paint?"

"Waking up in a strange place and seeing five black barns between her window and the horizon might seem like a bad omen to Feron."

"I don't see why. I wish I had them outside my bedroom window."

"Feron has a darker history than we have."

"Oh, how?"

"I told you. Her parents are both dead. She ran away from her stepfather, who beat her."

"Why?"

"For him, beating was just part of their family conversations, she said."

"That's hilarious. I love that!"

"Now, move, so I can tuck in the top sheet."

"I just had this thought."

"What?"

"The curing barns are beautiful when they're empty and closed up. And the fields are beautiful when everything's been cut down and carried away. But when people are empty and flat, they're just dead."

"You have the strangest thoughts, Ritchie."

"Strange interesting or strange scary?"

"A little of each."

"Is she going to like me?"

"Yes, I think so. Feron likes things not easy to figure out."

"What a weird name. Like a feral cat or something. Why would anyone name a girl that?"

"There was this character in a movie her mother saw, and she liked the sound of it."

"A girl character?"

"I assume so. It sounded odd to me at first, but now I think it suits her perfectly."

"Mom and Dad should be taking off in his plane soon. You know, don't you, that you can learn to fly years and years before you get your student pilot's license. I know a lot already."

"You do?"

"I've been at the controls of Dad's Cessna a lot. You'd be surprised the things I can do already."

"Just as long as Dad's sitting right beside you."

"I bet they had a luxury buffet lunch at the Greenbrier, and they're getting ready to leave for the airport. It will be getting dark when Mr. Jack takes us to meet them at *our* airport. And then we will make them open their Christmas presents as soon as we get home."

"They may be tired. We should maybe wait till tomorrow."

"But your friend Feral is coming tomorrow. I'll bet the first thing she asks is why would anyone want to paint their barns black."

"Let that be the last time you utter that nickname."

"But if she were my *sister*, I could call her Feral, right? Just like with you. When I was little, I couldn't pronounce her name, so I called her Feral and it stuck."

"You just uttered it two more times. Let that be it, okay?"

"Sorry, Merry Grape."

"And you can explain to her how the black traps the heat and gives our leaves that famous Jellicoe crackle."

"Hey, wouldn't that make a fabulous radio pitch? It would come after the auctioneer winds down his chant, like in the Lucky Strike ad. Then we could have another guy, like on *The Shadow*, say in a really deep voice: THAT FAMOUS JELLICOE CRACKLE."

"Actually, that's an interesting idea, Ritchie. Tell it to Dad."

"Listen, tell me something. What do you really think about Mr. Jack?"

"Mr. Jack? Other than he's Daddy's manager, I can't say I ever think about him at all. What on earth made you ask that?"

"Because he just parked in front of the house. He's not supposed to pick us up to go to the airport for two more hours. And he has that look he gets when nobody's looking."

"I wonder what he wants. What look?"

"It's different from when he's with any of us. It's like another person has taken over."

"You've been reading too many of those fright comic books."

"No, it's something I've noticed. I just never got around to saying it until now."

"Well, there's the doorbell, Ritchie. Go down and see what he wants."

Left alone, Merry walked to the door of her room, "became" Feron, turned around, and, as Feron, looked at Merry's room. Feron heard Merry saying, "This is your bed, Feron, it looks out over our orchards."

And she, being Feron, would say what? Oh, what a nice view. Or just "Oh."

That first day when Merry had asked which bed she wanted, Feron had said, "You got here first. You should be the first to choose." Merry had been sure she would take the window, but Feron said she liked corners.

Now I've given her my bed, which is both in the corner and looks out over our orchards. Knowing Feron, she might say nothing at all. She might not appreciate this room. She might not appreciate our family. But how could she not?

You never can tell with Feron. Sometimes she looks at me like I'm too simple to be believed. But other times she looks at me like she's counting on me above all others to keep her intact. It didn't take very long to figure out that she was more complicated and had suffered more. The family things. The dead front tooth, which she brought up herself and how she got it. I had of course noticed it right away, and it was like she wanted to protect herself from having to hear me ask, oh, what happened to your tooth? Which I would never have done, of course. The odd thing was, seeing the tooth was what made me realize how handsome she would be if the tooth was fixed.

Why, Merry wondered, was she so anxious for Feron's approval of her family and home? Why had Feron so easily slid into their friendship?

What did Feron see in her? Once Merry asked her mother why she never had to make overtures to get new friends. ("I don't usually have to go first because they seem drawn to me." Her mother had said, "One of the finest things about you, Merry, is that you have attractions you don't seem aware of. At least you don't behave as though you're aware of them. Oh dear, I hope I haven't spoiled you by telling you this.")

When Merry had first seen Feron in the parking lot, before she knew they were going to be roommates, her impression was of an aloof girl at odds with something or somebody. It didn't seem to be the man she was with; there was a silent ease between them as they unloaded her stuff. Merry had first assumed they were father and daughter. She was a frowning girl with a stoop. The stoop may have developed because nobody ever corrected her posture or because she thought she was too tall for a girl. She had shocked Merry when she said her small weasel stepfather could send a person sailing across the room. Up until then, Merry had pictured Swain as a lengthy filled-out fellow like their Mr. Jack.

Feron seemed to prefer Merry's company to anyone else's. The only person they both admired was Miss Petrie. If they were younger, you might call it a shared crush.

Merry felt Feron must be getting something she needed from her, but Merry hadn't figured out what. Maybe Mama would be able to shed some light on this when she saw them together.

"Merry Grape!"

"What?"

"Mr. Jack wants us downstairs."

"I'll be down in a minute."

"No, he says *right now*!"

PART TWO

14

1968, New York City

When Feron would wake yet again from what she called "the visit to Merry dream," she would lie in bed in whatever apartment she was staying and demand of the empty room: "Am I going to keep having this dream till I *die*?"

The Merry dream continued to evolve during the decades, stretching into Feron's old age. The early ones had started with Feron aboard the bus, on the way to visit her roommate in the days after Christmas, a visit that in real life had never happened. Or, Feron was already in front of the Jellicoe house, and they were standing in a row like a family of paper dolls waiting to greet her.

In later years, Feron would dream that Merry watched over her or guided her. Or sometimes that they were horsing around in a devil-may-care way they had never achieved in life.

In the most distressing dream, Merry had published a book about their friendship, which had won all sorts of prizes, and Feron burned with envy and wondered why she had not written this book herself. When she woke from this dream, she would demand of herself, "*When* am I going to outgrow this envy?" She would recall Merry's unnerving fluency when she applied herself to her homework, how she had settled down on her bed in her brother's pajamas and started writing out Miss Petrie's assigned story as if a switch had been turned on.

What if, after your death, you were fated to carry your dreams into eternity, like a backpack fused to your soul?

Then Feron reenters whatever time period she happens to have awakened in and marches herself through the debriefing. On the day Feron was to arrive for her after-Christmas visit, the Jellicoe parents crashed their plane flying home from the Tobacco Growers' convention at the Greenbrier. Merry never returned to Lovegood; she had to take care of her twelve-year-old brother and run the tobacco farm until he came of age.

Now it is fall, going on winter, of 1968. Feron's husband, Will, is dead. Aunt Mabel is dead. President Kennedy was assassinated in Dallas five years ago, the same year as Will's death. His brother Robert was assassinated this summer in Los Angeles, two months after Martin Luther King Jr. was assassinated in Memphis. Uncle Rowan has been reelected mayor of Pullen and is still engaged to Blanche Buttner. Merry has published a story in the *Atlantic Monthly*. During her first year alone in New York, Feron committed to paper a sort-of novel about her brief marriage, titled *The English Winter*, had it typed professionally, and sent it to seven publishers before she lost heart. So far, Feron has published nothing.

"The Curing Barn," by M. G. Petrie. This had leapt out at Feron the previous spring, when she had been putting herself through her monthly ordeal of paging through certain magazines at the branch library in mid-Manhattan to see what was being done by her contemporaries.

My God, Miss Petrie had written a story. M. was certainly Maud, and the G. must be her middle name, which they had never learned. No, wait a minute, the story was about a sister and her younger brother during the first curing day of the tobacco season. What was going on here? All it said on the contributors page was "M. G. Petrie lives in North Carolina." No gender, but with the tobacco and the younger brother, Feron was sure M. G. was Meredith Grace. But why the last name of their English teacher? It didn't make sense.

Unable to sit calmly at the library table and read the story through, Feron went out and bought the *Atlantic Monthly* so she could agonize over "The Curing Barn" in the privacy of the East Side apartment she was currently housesitting.

On a hot, dry August day, the sister, in her early twenties, and her teenage brother, along with a crew, are getting the ripe tobacco leaves ready to be hung upside down in the curing barn. The sister is outside in the tying shed instructing some new women recruits in the art of tying three aligned stems, or "hands," of leaves to a six-foot-long tobacco stick. The workers loaded these sticks on a V-shaped structure, which was then passed, person-to-person, inside the barn, where someone straddled a network of high rafters and guided the sticks to their upside-down hanging places. The person straddling the rafters was the long-legged teenage brother, Randolph. The sister, who is telling the story, is nameless. There is enough back-and-forth among the workers to familiarize you with the process of tobacco curing and some witticisms and hijinks from the boy balancing on the high rafters.

Then there is a time shift to a future harvest ("cropping"), when they are stacking the sticks in the barn for the drying process, and the sister is guiding two college girls in the art of tying the leaves. The girls are earning good summer money, but also, thinks the sister, they are pleased with themselves for mixing with "farm people." The boy is no longer in the picture, and you realize that what you are reading now is the present tense of the story. And in this present tense, the sister allows herself to remember the first time six-year-old Randolph was allowed to take part in the curing. His job was to pick off "lugs" before they got woven onto sticks. He delighted in screaming, "Out you go, luggie!" every time he snatched out an imperfect leaf.

And at last the nameless sister forces herself to look up at the rafters and remember how as a young man Randolph proudly straddled the beams and to acknowledge what this story has been building toward. The brother has died in Vietnam, and the sister has been rerunning memories of the curing barn in order to cure herself.

Feron remembered locking herself in a bathroom stall back at Lovegood and reading Merry's "Lingering on the Lawn" in order to judge whether it was "acceptable" enough to hand in to Miss Petrie. Feron had reported to Merry that it would be a success if she alerted the reader sooner that the story opened in 1918 and not the present, and advised her to find a better adjective than *ordinary* to describe the class poet, which was the Merry-character.

Funny, "The Curing Barn" followed the same pattern as "Lingering on the Lawn." You realized at the end that what had been taking place was already over and the person was dead. If "The Curing Barn" was autobiographical, then Merry had sacrificed college in order to raise a boy who would become fodder for an unpopular war. Oh, God, the brother on top of the parents! Poor Merry.

But how had Merry gotten into the *Atlantic Monthly* ten years after the canceled visit in the last days of 1958? ("I have shocking news," Blanche Buttner had said, putting down the phone. "I am so sorry, Feron, but you won't be taking the bus to visit the Jellicoes.")

Surely Merry must have suffered the humiliation of having her work returned in the dreaded self-addressed envelopes. Or not? If Merry still kept up her unnerving *fluency*, maybe on her first try she had sent "The Curing Barn" off to the *Atlantic* and received a return acceptance. Maybe, oh God, there were more M. G. Petrie stories awaiting publication.

"The Curing Barn" was the kind of story that contained death yet left the reader feeling complete. You understood that the sister had kept faith with her tobacco barn reruns and found a way to contain her grief. Her loss was simply part of the ongoing human drama. The American flag covering the brother's footlocker at the end signified the kind of "coverings" that a human being could live with.

Was it that Feron's work lacked any "covering" element? The characters were always grasping to understand what was happening to them, but the endings were unsatisfactory. "The ending is unclear" was the single personal note scrawled on one of Feron's seven printed rejection slips. (At the time, Feron had derived an atom of comfort that the person must have read to the end. Or at least skimmed.)

She had not come up with any "clear ending" to the event in her life chronicled in *An English Winter*. She had known while writing that she was trying to capture things she wanted to remember, but she hadn't seen beyond that. Like the sister in Merry's *Atlantic* story, she had been moving forward slowly, allowing herself to recollect what was acceptable in bits and pieces after Will had died from a fall off a Northumberland cliff in January 1963.

After "The Curing Barn" had ambushed Feron in the branch library last spring, it would have been perfectly possible to pick up the phone and dial "information" for an M. G. Jellicoe listed in Hamlin, North Carolina. Within moments she could have been connected to her old Lovegood roommate. But Feron had been a fickle letter writer during the time when Merry needed to hear from her the most, and Merry did not make it to Feron's wedding in the spring of 1962. She had a conflict: Ritchie was playing the major role of Stage Manager in his high school play, *Our Town*. She sent Feron a covered silver serving dish, which was embarrassingly expensive, considering their lapsed friendship.

After reading M. G. Petrie's story in the spring of 1968 ("an *Atlantic* First," accompanied by a striking pen-and-ink drawing of an open barn with tobacco leaves hanging upside down), Feron opened the box with the rejected manuscript of *An English Winter* and grimaced at the task ahead. She stared at the title page for a minute, then resolutely crossed out *An English Winter* and wrote *A Singular Romance* above it. Tomorrow she would buy a new legal pad and begin again.

Good old Meredith Grace. Depend on her to wake up the sleeping demon of competitiveness and goad it into action. Perhaps the best way to start, Feron had decided on the weekend morning she began afresh, was just to write steadily across the page, one line after another, using the easy language you'd use if someone happened to ask you: "How did you come to marry that particular man?"

He was a professor at the university. He was older. The requirements for his course were intimidating. I considered dropping the course because I couldn't risk any more bad grades my second semester. One reason I didn't drop it was because I would never learn why he thought individuals in the period from 950 to 1150 A.D. had been reaching toward the highest feelings human nature were capable of, but sadly didn't make it. What were those feelings, and why not? The other reason was that I shrank from the picture of myself going up to his desk and asking him to sign my transfer slip. As he had done with those other dropouts, he would sign it with a frosty smile and without bothering to look up at the person.

* * *

Halfway through the first legal pad, she had relaxed enough to switch into third person and become someone both herself and not herself. At the end of the fourth legal pad, after researching England and Durham more than absolutely necessary, she had come to the scene where she needed to get them in bed. In real life and in her novel, they were spending the night with his mother before their transatlantic flight. They were upstairs in Will's old room, and the husband was leaning forward over the sill, looking at the stars above his mother's garden, and she was standing behind him with her arms around his waist.

Astonishingly, writing about this young woman pressed against his back awoke in her the powerful longing she had felt at the window. *Yes, he's mine now, we can take our time and do justice to our highest feelings.* After the excitement of the wedding, and the nervousness about tomorrow's journey, she and Will had agreed to stay chaste while they were in his mother's house. It had been her suggestion, one of the wisest acts of her short marriage. She had picked up on Will's anxiety, whether it came from fear of not pleasing her or his reluctance to "make sounds" while in his mother's house.

Will's loss hit her afresh, and she capped her pen. I will never be able to "write him back," so what's the point?

She would start a new legal pad to elucidate their bed life in Durham, she decided.

Dear Merry,

You will probably be surprised to hear from me. I've been meaning to write since last April, when I came across "The Curing Barn" in the *Atlantic Monthly*. Congratulations! I have so many questions. But let me start by telling you something you might not know. My husband, Will, died in January of 1963, we were spending the year in England where he had a fellowship, and he went hiking by himself and fell from a cliff. I don't think I'll ever get over it. I don't want to. Since then I have been living in New York, working at various jobs and trying to write. Do I guess right from the story that you lost your brother? If so, I hurt for you. What a waste, what a loss. I am really curious about the "Petrie" pen name. How did that come about? If you feel like answering this, please send it to my office address, since I don't have my own place yet. I have a sort of editorial position at MacFarlane & Co., a big management consultant firm here. It pays well and keeps my mental energies more or less undiminished so I can do my own writing at night.

> Your Old Lovegood roommate,
> Feron Hood

As she was tipping the stamped letter into the corner mailbox (Meredith Grace Jellicoe, Hamlin, N.C.—was that enough of an address?), Feron thought of the Chekhov story about the little boy who writes to his grandfather in the country to come and rescue him from a cruel apprenticeship to a Moscow shoemaker. He puts a stamp on the envelope and drops it in the box, already imagining himself back with his grandfather and the dogs. But he has addressed his letter only to his grandfather "in the village."

15

After completing her two years at Lovegood, Feron had transferred to the university at Chapel Hill. Miss McCorkle had
guided her through the application mazes, and they had landed
a full-tuition scholarship for her. All she had to do was keep up
her grades. But during her first university semester, Feron had
ruined her 3.9 Lovegood average. Both Geography I and Ethics I
had sounded like subjects she wanted to know more about, but it
turned out the geography class was about topography, not travel,
and the ethics class was about systems of language, not "what
should I do?" She had squeaked through with a C-plus and a
C-minus, but the scholarship allowed her a semester's grace
period to redeem herself. She must be on her guard against future
stupid mistakes. For her history requirement, she was most drawn
to Anatomy of the Russian Revolution, perhaps because of
Chekhov, and a little less so to Introduction to Medieval England.
However, an introduction to something sounded less threatening
than the anatomy of something, and she had a head start from
her European history classes at Lovegood. Miss McCorkle,
admitting her bias regarding the Middle Ages, had shamelessly
lingered in that period, slighting the Renaissance and hardly
touching the Industrial Revolution.

Professor Avery had his back to the room, writing on the board when Feron entered and took the last empty seat. A slender-built man, wearing loose corduroy trousers and a tweed jacket, he was so intent on his task he seemed unaware that his classroom had filled to capacity.

By the time he turned toward the class, two students had left their seats and hovered nervously beside his desk. He had a spare, introspective face behind heavy black-rimmed spectacles, and his retreating hairline disclosed an older man than he had appeared from behind.

"Ah, you must have been reading the writing on the wall," he said. He signed their transfer slips, dispatching them with a frosty smile.

"Anyone else? If not, I'll go over the class requirements I have written on the board. If anyone else is having doubts, now is the time to transfer. There will be a midterm exam, a final exam, and one term paper. Each will count for a third of your grade. The exams will be on what we have covered in class or material I have assigned you to read outside class. Your term paper should aim for fifteen hundred words, which is about seven typed pages, double spaced. I will be handing out a list of possible subjects very soon and will meet with each of you privately to discuss a subject congenial to you. I advise you not to procrastinate. The paper is due before the final exam. Any questions? Yes?"

"But, sir, you don't allow points for improvement. Three shots and that's it? Shouldn't a person's improvement count for part of the grade?"

"You are Mr. . . . ?"

"Tribby."

"Well, Mr. Tribby, if you aim high, work hard, and keep up with the assignments, you can certainly count on the kind of improvement you'll be able to measure for yourself. As for the 'three shots,' that's my grading system and I've found it usually works well. If any of you has hesitations about how it might work for you, now is the time to transfer out. Don't be shy. You have a week in which to find yourself a more compatible class."

A spatter of nervous giggles erupted. By fits and starts, half a dozen more students, including Mr. Tribby, rose and shambled forward.

Having signed all their transfer slips and closed the door after the last departing student, Professor Avery counted heads. "Twenty-four. I ordered twenty-five textbooks. I'm getting better at this. They are waiting for you over at the campus bookstore. The class meets twice a week, and by next time I want you to have read the introduction and the first half of the first chapter, which comes to about forty pages. Do yourself a favor and don't leave it for the last minute. The author packs a lot into his sentences, but it's worth it."

He began to lecture without notes, strolling back and forth in front of the room, mostly addressing the air in front of him. His accent was southern, but different from Uncle Rowan's. It was softer and missing the *r*s.

He asked how many had heard the phrase "dwarfs standing on the shoulders of giants." When no hands went up, he explained it meant that we discovered things by building on the discoveries of those who went before us.

"The phrase itself—*nanos gigantum humeris insidentes*—is attributed to Bernard of Chartres, a twelfth-century philosopher. However, we wouldn't know this if one of Bernard's students, John of Salisbury, hadn't written it down."

Now he was talking about something called The Great Conversation, which was the term for the references and allusions made by scholars to the works of their predecessors. Abbreviating and condensing, Feron scurried after his phrases, but his agile switch into Latin had gone by too quickly for her.

"Which returns us to John of Salisbury, an English philosopher and churchman, whose fame is based not only on what he knew but all the famous people he knew. He studied with the best scholars of the early twelfth century, including Bernard of Chartres, whom I've just mentioned, and the great Peter Abelard, whom many of you have heard of, probably because of his ill-fated love affair with Heloïse, but they conducted their correspondence for the rest of their lives, he from a monastery and she from a nunnery. I've placed several copies of their letters, translated into English, on the reserve shelf, in case any of you are interested.

"Then John came back to his native England, where he served as an aide to the Archbishop of Canterbury, Thomas à Becket. He became a friend of Pope Hadrian and a thorn in the flesh to King Henry II, who'd had Thomas à Becket murdered—

"No, please don't try to write everything down. You'll be hearing all these names again. I am simply giving you an idea of how the giant/dwarf succession works through time."

Slamming the cap on her fountain pen, Feron sank back in embarrassment. She was sure he was referring to the frantic speed-writing she'd taught herself in Miss McCorkle's classes so as not to miss anything of significance for the Friday quizzes. Her zeal probably struck a university professor as slightly comic.

He told them they would be concentrating on the period between 950 and 1150 A.D., and in the next class they would begin to consider how European medieval civilization was formed by the absorption of attitudes and ways of life from previous civilizations.

"The key word here is 'absorption.' Yes, okay, you can write that down. After you've read your first textbook assignment, you'll know more about how absorption works down through the centuries.

"Though we may feel we're self-made and self-contained, every one of us in this classroom is an accumulation of thousands of years of absorptions. How we think, what we value, how we worship, our legal system, our economics, our politics, our social forms, our whole pattern of daily life, much of it evolves from ideas dating back to the ancient world.

"The thing I find astonishing, though it makes me sad, about the period we will be studying is that during this time certain elements of the population were reaching toward what they thought were the highest feelings human nature could achieve. A new respect for human possibilities was in the air. Ultimately they fell short, but there was something in that period that made them eager to try."

He had removed his heavy black spectacles and, while polishing them with his pocket handkerchief, gave the remaining students a near-sighted smile, a marked contrast to his frosty, impersonal send-off of the initial deserters.

"I'll leave you with one more quote by another Bernard from that era, St. Bernard of Clairvaux: no need to write it down, because it is one of my favorite maxims and you'll be hearing it again. St. Bernard said that some of us want to learn so we may be looked upon by others as learned, which is ridiculous vanity; others of us desire to learn so that we may morally instruct others, and this is love; and lastly there are those of us who wish to learn so that we may become enlightened ourselves, and that is prudence. End of quote. End of class.

"No, one more thought. Speaking of love, we will see love, the practice and celebration of love, many kinds of love, come into its own during this time. This is also the period in which the idea of the *individual* began to make itself felt—the idea that there existed such a thing as a *singular* person, inside his own skin, unlike any other person. The beginnings of Western psychology, you might say."

Feron was to come within a hair's breadth of dropping Professor Avery's course. She had gone directly from his classroom to the campus bookstore and bought the text for it, *The Making of the Middle*

Ages; she also purchased the first book assigned for her Modern Novel class: *A Portrait of the Artist as a Young Man*.

Back in her second-floor dorm room she settled into bed (glad her morose new roommate was out; last semester's roommate had transferred to a sorority house) and opened *The Making of the Middle Ages*. By the third page of the introduction, she realized she hadn't taken in a single thing. It was a style of writing she wasn't used to—Miss McCorkle hadn't assigned a textbook. Professor Avery said this writer "packed a lot into his sentences," but for Feron those sentences were too dense and distant. Professor Avery's off-the-cuff remarks had been far more engaging and alive.

She put the Middle Ages on hold and picked up *A Portrait of the Artist as a Young Man*. The English professor had told them this was a coming-of-age novel about a boy growing up, "also called a *bildungsroman*, which is a German compound word combining *education* and *novel*." Miss Petrie had read them a story by this writer, about an Irish boy who gets to the bazaar too late and is disenchanted, both with it and himself.

A Portrait of the Artist as a Young Man opened with baby talk.

> Once upon a time and a very good time it was there was a moocow coming down along the road and this moocow that was coming down the road met a nicens little boy named baby tuckoo . . .

Feron had no trouble beginning this novel, but distractions of another kind interfered. The little boy's father was telling him that story. Then there is his bedwetting, and we go from home to the school playground, where the bully boy shoves him into the ditch and breaks his glasses.

Reading Merry's story in the bathroom cubicle back at Lovegood was the first time Feron had been aware that someone else's success goaded her, but in this instance it was much worse than reading Merry's story about the class poet of 1918 who died of pneumonia.

Feron hungered to be capable of writing something like this. Her own "education," but in Joyce's style, scenes moving back and forth in time, showing the presentness of the past. Stephen is in his cold dormitory bed but also back in his warm home, where his family argues fiercely about politics.

But wait. How old was the writer when this was published? Turning back to the introduction, Feron scribbled numbers in the margin: Joyce was thirty-four, but he'd been working on it for ten years, revising a different and much longer draft with another title and then somehow breaking free into this free-flowing style with its experiences radiating out to form a pattern.

She could remember being very little, being sung to and read to by a grandmother who was always complaining but who had taught her to count by drawing rows of lollipops, and there was a grandfather who took her to the park and smoked cigars, but she wasn't sure whether this was an actual memory or because there was a photograph of her three-year-old self leaning into a plump kneeling man in a fedora with a cigar in his hand. She had been told after his death that she had talked to the paper bands she'd collected from his cigars. Those were the years in Fayetteville, where Grandad, a master mechanic, had been transferred from Pullen by the railroad just before he died. Mother was out a lot in the evenings, making up for her young single womanhood cut short by the sudden marriage to Feron's father. In Fayetteville, there was a big army base with an airfield and a series of admiring soldiers and air corps men coming to the house and taking her off to dances. When Feron turned four, the war ended and two bad things followed. Granny died of an aneurysm, and an air corps flying instructor named Swain Eckert married Feron's mother and took them away to the middle of the country, where he became part owner of a commercial flying field.

Probably it would be wise to drop Introduction to Medieval England. In her notebook she made a column for Leave and a column for Stay. She was working on the Leave column ("won't be able to keep up," "can't afford another C!") when Gweneth, the new roommate, slunk in, collapsed on her bed with a loud sigh, and turned her face to the wall. Feron knew she had a choice: ask Gweneth "are you all right?" and resign herself to a lengthy litany of today's reversals and slights, or continue working on her Leave and Stay columns in silence.

As far as roommates went, Feron had had the best first in Merry, and it was all downhill after that. Cynthia Chasteen had replaced Merry. But Cynthia was already thick with her two roommates on the top floor and sneaked upstairs after lights out to spend her nights with them. Feron had a room to herself for most of her final year at Lovegood because her next roommate, Ione Satterfield, had eloped right after the Christmas holidays after discovering she was getting varicose veins in her legs.

In fact, Feron's year and a half without Merry at Lovegood had been strange to her. She had gone around feeling both overexposed yet more hidden. No longer part of a pair, she had to be seen as herself alone. At the same time she seemed to have gained a mysterious authority. Her standoffishness was interpreted as discrimination. Elected president of the Daughters and Granddaughters Club, she set the members the task of creating an archive, each girl chronicling the family member who had preceded her to Lovegood. The second-year girls just assumed she had grown up with the Hoods in Pullen.

Her first semester at the University of North Carolina she had roomed with Lee Ann Piggotty, whom Feron had privately christened "the paper doll," because Lee Ann changed outfits three or four times a day and seemed to have the inner life of a cardboard figure. Lee Ann had moved to the Pi Phi house, and now there was gloomy Gweneth, who was rather good-looking when she wasn't sighing and crying, but who suffered from the biggest inferiority complex Feron had ever encountered.

Funny how the different shortcomings of her successive roommates had doubled and tripled Feron's appreciation of Merry's qualities. Sometimes she caught herself feeling Merry had died. Then she reminded herself that she could pick up a pen and write to her. But she didn't.

"Are you all right, Gweneth?" Feron had known all along she was going to break down and be human. "Is there anything I can do?"

And while Gweneth launched into her day's recitation of humiliations and hurts, Feron listened with half her attention and leafed through the university's catalog of courses to see what her options were for transferring out of Professor Avery's Introduction to Medieval England. She could get her other science requirement out of the way—biology's squirming things ought to be livelier and more accessible than geography's rocks. Or she could transfer to another history course, one that also counted for a sociology major: American Culture, "a broad survey of American habits, customs, and social norms from 1776 to the present." That might be useful as well as enjoyable.

Certainly it would be humiliating to ask Professor Avery to sign her transfer slip. She wasn't up to it. She couldn't take it. And she would never find out about absorption and the rise of the individual and the various kinds of love. As with the other dropouts, he would sign frostily without bothering to look at her.

If she remained in Professor Avery's class, she wouldn't have to endure this shame. This item belonged in the Stay column.

16

Within a week, there was Merry's letter waiting in Feron's office mailbox.

Dear Feron,

What a surprise to hear from you after so long. Oh, Feron, I am so sorry about your husband, Will. I wish I had met him. It must have been terrible for you, and being in a foreign country and all. Of course, you don't want to forget him, that's how I feel about my brother, Ritchie. "The Curing Barn" is my only published story so far, but I have been writing ever since I had to leave Lovegood. I work on my stories for a long time before they are ready. I have some more in different stages of development. About the Petrie name, Miss Petrie died three years ago at Easter. It's sort of my memorial to her. In a way I write for her. Her faithful letters to me after I left Lovegood right up until she died probably saved my life. It was Miss Petrie who told me about the *Atlantic* Firsts. There is a lot more to tell, but I can tell you in person if you're free for tea at my hotel next Friday afternoon. I'm coming to New York, getting in late next Thursday evening and then I have a six o'clock train home on Friday afternoon. I have a lunch commitment, which is actually the reason I'm rushing up there and back, but could we meet any time after three on Friday in the lobby of the Algonquin Hotel? It's too late for you to write back but could you leave a note for me at the hotel? I've checked my Manhattan map and your workplace looks walking distance from the Algonquin.

Crossing my fingers we'll be able to see each other again.

Yours faithfully,
Merry

. . . hear from you *after so long* . . . Her *faithful* letters to me . . . I have some more, in different stages of development . . . yours *faithfully* . . .

From her apartment-sit on East Fifty-fourth Street, Feron walked the blocks down to the Algonquin (how did Merry know about the Algonquin?). She sat at a desk in the lobby and wrote Merry a note on the hotel's stationery.

"She'll be arriving late evening next Thursday. Jellicoe, Meredith Grace, or maybe M. G. Jellicoe. Or possibly M. G. Petrie. Will you make sure it's waiting for her?"

A young man in a bow tie checked the reservation book. "There's an M. G. Jellicoe checking in next Thursday. Sure, we'll hold it for her."

"Where will you keep it meanwhile?"

"Pardon?" Cocking his head at her.

"I mean, do you have a special place you hold mail for your future guests? I want to make sure it doesn't get misplaced."

"We have this." He brought out a gold-tooled leather folder from under the counter. "See? I'm putting it in right now. So unless it walks off by itself, it'll be in her box when she arrives."

"Thank you." I am twenty-seven years old and a widow, she thought. How old and eccentric must I seem to this desk clerk?

"You're welcome. If you want to make extra-sure, you can always drop by next Thursday afternoon and check that it's in her box."

"That's an idea. I might."

It was Merry tilted forward in an easy chair with no pretense of doing anything other than being on the watch for her friend. Then the tanned and smartly dressed woman was already on her feet, rushing toward her. A stranger would probably take her for a rich woman up from Florida to see a few people and do some serious shopping.

"Feron!"

She wore a black lightweight suit, perfect for the mild November weather, and a black narrow-brimmed hat. What had I expected, Feron thought: a farm girl turned out in her Sunday best?

When Merry was hugging her round her waist, Feron had to bend so their cheeks could meet. She had forgotten how petite Merry was.

"It's been a while." Her own greeting sounded flat and stingy.

"Oh, it has, it has. You're looking wonderful, Feron. The city must suit you."

"You're looking fabulous yourself. I like your hat."

"Do you? The person I had lunch with said he thought hats went out when Jackie left the White House. Then he fell over himself assuring me that my hat was charming. I've saved us these armchairs with the little table in front. Isn't this the most wonderful room? Can't you just imagine all the literary conversations that must have taken place here?"

"How did you know about the Algonquin?"

"The person I had lunch with put me up here."

"The one who said your hat was charming."

"That's the one. Mr. Sterling. He's a literary agent. But we'll get to him later. Now, if we want something to drink, we ring this little bell and a waiter will appear. You can also order a sandwich. Are you hungry? You've just come from work."

"Thank you, no, lunch is on the house at my place of work. As long as we order in and stay at our desks, we have an international choice of menus."

"I've already checked out of the hotel, so we'll have more time before I have to leave for the train. I left my suitcase with the bellman."

"Maybe I will have a glass of white wine," said Feron.

A literary agent!

"Oh, good, I get to ring the little bell. I'll have one, too. I'm going to come right out and say it, Feron. I didn't expect to ever see you again."

"Really?" How else to answer such an indictment?

"Well, we kind of lost touch. I was surprised to get your wedding invitation, but I would have come if it hadn't been for . . ."

"Your brother was starring in *Our Town*."

"You remember!"

"I remember a great deal about you, Merry. Despite my disgraceful letter-writing habits, you're an important part of my history. You're one of the ten or twelve regulars who show up in my dreams."

"Really? Oh, you don't know how much that means—" Merry had teared up at the mention of her brother but now required a folded handkerchief from her purse to blot her cheeks. "I was completely stunned after that awful day. Next month it will be ten years. I felt like someone who had died but had a duty to stay around and preside over things, like old Horace Lovegood in our college play. I had to watch Ritchie grow up and keep Jellicoe

Enterprises in business. And I did do that. Well, up to a point I did. We sent a record crop to the tobacco auctions this year and Ritchie had a secure adolescence, though I couldn't prevent him from enlisting for Vietnam even before he had to. And now there are all these protests, Feron! They're saying the whole war was an evil mistake. But you've had your own sorrow. What was he like, your husband? I remember when I received your wedding invitation, I wondered who William Michael Avery was. I tried to imagine the kind of man you would be marrying. Does this upset you, my talking about it?"

"No, it brings him back. You really want to hear?"

"Yes!"

"He was my professor, he was fifteen years my senior. While I was in his Medieval History class, I worked harder than I ever had to earn his good opinion. This was the second semester of my junior year. It wasn't until the following semester that we ran into each other in the campus coffee shop. It was a Sunday and I was depressed. I've forgotten why. He asked me to drive with him to visit his mother. I was really taken with her and the house and the garden and the way they were together and the way they included me. At the end of the afternoon as we were driving back to campus, I found myself imagining being the daughter-in-law in such a family. And then I sneaked a side look at him and something tipped upside down in me and I thought, how amazing if I could marry this man."

"How romantic."

"Well, that was from my side. It took a while longer before he looked at me sideways and saw more than the hardworking A student in his class who got along with his mother. He was one of those consecrated scholars who lived more inside his subject than he did in the world. I knew I had to be careful or I'd scare him off. Fortunately, his mother started a correspondence with me, so I learned about him slowly, how he'd always preferred his mind to other people, that kind of thing. She and I did most of the groundwork."

This was the place for Merry to pounce: *Good thing you kept up your correspondence that time!* But Merry didn't say it, didn't even think it, probably. Merry wasn't the pouncing type, springing at you out of a forest of undermeanings. ("Merry is easy to be with," Feron had told Dean Fox back at Lovegood. "There's nothing underhanded about her. We're comfortable together.")

"Your wedding invitation . . . I remember being surprised you weren't getting married in your uncle's town."

"It was at my uncle's fiancée's house in the next town over. She took care of everything. She loves organizing events. Blanche Buttner and my uncle have been engaged for, let's see, twenty-five years now."

"Good grief, what's holding them back? They were engaged when we were at Lovegood."

"Well, she likes planning and overseeing other people's weddings, but I think she dreads getting trapped on the other side of them. The wedding was small and perfect. We didn't have it at Blanche's church, because she's a Roman Catholic, so we had it in her beautiful house with the Methodist minister from Uncle Rowan's church officiating. And I was more than ever in love now that I knew Will loved me back. It felt incredible. Even when we were standing together at the altar, I felt that upside-down thing."

"Do you keep in touch with Will's mother?"

"No, she died. Not long after Will, in fact. She was already sick at our wedding, but nobody knew it yet, not even her. Oh, that whole period with Will was incredible. Everyone should get what they want at least once. I tried to write a novel to capture some of the feeling before it was lost."

"You wrote a *novel*?"

"That's what I thought I was doing. It was more like an impressionistic elegy. Only one editor invited me to his office. A nice older man. He said a lot of nice things, but he had to turn it down."

"Why?"

"He said that I needed to put in more, well, intimate scenes between them to make it work."

How expert she had become at making up lies!

"You mean, like bed?"

"Like bed."

"Are you going to do it?"

"Well, that's where I'm up to in my present draft. I still can't see a way. Nothing really fits what Will and I had together. Right now, I'm working on a new opening, something else the editor suggested. He said I should show how they met, right from the start, before they are in England."

"Did you ever read that Chekhov story about the man and the woman with the little dog? It's not one of his stories Miss Petrie read to us in class. I discovered it later."

"They kept seeing each other, that's all I remember. Not one of his typical endings."

"I read it again recently. Reading Chekhov makes me feel closer to Miss Petrie, and it improves my writing. It also makes me feel closer to you and what we had at Lovegood, though I probably shouldn't say that."

"Why not?"

"Oh, I might scare you away. I might as well say it, Feron. Oh, I've already said it, I really didn't think I'd ever see you again."

"Well, here I am" was Feron's lame reply.

"With Chekhov, he can write so little, but it's exactly the *right* little. I mean, 'The Lady with the Little Dog' is a story about a love affair, but there's surprisingly little 'bed' in it. Instead there are these firsthand touches that make it just *their* affair, like her hotel room being stuffy and smelling of some perfume she bought in a Japanese shop. And how he's aware of a feeling of embarrassment between them, like someone has just knocked on the door. Isn't that wonderful? It's so true to life. And at the same time, he's recalling other women, who were false or predatory, and how, when the passion was over, the lace on their underwear reminded him of fish scales!"

"Fish scales!"

"Yes, you wouldn't think of the comparison, but he did, because he's such a well-imagined character. And then there's a description of her face after they've made love. He thinks she looks like a repentant sinner in a painting. And then another great touch is, while she is having a fit of remorse, he is eating a slice of watermelon. Then he comforts her and they end up laughing and go out and sit by the sea, and he realizes the sea will go on perfectly well after they are dead, and that it's our own small thoughts and actions that prevent us from seeing that the world is beautiful and human beings have dignity. That's one way you could do it. Just little details that belong to nobody but them."

"Fish scales and Japanese scent and watermelon! I'm going to stop by the library on my way home. Think of me reading that story tonight, while you're on the southbound train. Tell me about your literary agent. Did you find him or did he find you?"

"He was really kind, but I'm afraid he sees me as more of a prospect than I am."

"Why?"

"Well, he wrote me care of the magazine after my story came out, and they forwarded it. He offered to pay my expenses if I would come up here and talk to him. But he has in mind a book of connected stories about people living their daily lives in a southern tobacco town and all their secrets. Also he thinks I should use my real name and describe myself as the owner of a tobacco enterprise. I told him I'd been working on about a dozen stories on and off, but they're not ready yet. And that my real name and the tobacco farm part were out of the question."

"Why?"

"Maybe if I try to explain it to you, it will become clearer to me. If it doesn't bore you."

"It won't bore me." She would deal with her feelings about Merry's success on her walk back to the apartment.

"What I told him, Mr. Sterling, was that I had to remain M. G. Petrie. First of all, the farm is named after my great-great-grandfather. Jellicoe's bright leaf tobacco is an old concern. A Jellicoe who published stories about people in a tobacco town wouldn't sit well with people at home. I'd be an insider turned informer. I mean, look at 'The Curing Barn.' There are more characters in that story than the sister and brother. There are the other workers. And those workers are somewhat based on real people, though I tried to mix it up and disguise things."

"That's what writers do. Mix up and disguise."

"But if 'The Curing Barn' had come out under my name, those workers would be trying to guess which parts I had stolen from them. Then Mr. Sterling asked why I used the initials. Why not Meredith Grace Petrie? Was it that I wanted to be gender-neutral? If so, Meredith without the Grace could be either a man or a woman. But he didn't push it, and I was grateful. He said whatever made me happy was fine with him. Though he said it would probably come out at some point that M. G. was a woman, and at an even later point, especially if I were to win some prize, people would find out that Petrie was really Jellicoe. But we didn't need to worry about that yet, he said; all I had to do was go back home and write more stories."

"That was a smart thing for him to say."

"Well, here's something I didn't tell him. Jellicoe's has fifty workers on the payroll. Forty-three of them are men. I think one reason I've made a go of it is that those men feel protective of me.

I'm the poor little woman who had this huge responsibility thrust upon her, who lost the last male in the family who was supposed to take over, so it's up to them to take care of me and make sure I keep the business going. I would lose that advantage if they started seeing me as the writer who's going to use them in stories. 'The secrets and sorrows in a southern tobacco town,' the agent said. But I couldn't reveal real secrets, even if I knew what they were. I mean, everyone has secrets no one else should know."

Here Merry stopped, as though censoring herself. She had gone red under her tan.

"Of course they do. Secrets are the only personal assets some of us have." Feron realized this was true as she said it.

"And even as M. G. Petrie, I wouldn't feel free to put their secret sorrows—or what I might guess about them—in my stories. It wouldn't be playing fair."

"Merry, what exactly is it you do to keep the business going?"

"I mostly sit in an air-conditioned office when I'm not out inspecting the fields, which my dermatologist warns me not to do anymore. I had three cancers cut out of my face this past summer. They were all on the forehead, and luckily I can cover up the scars with my bangs—and hats, of course. And, let's see, I make payroll once a week. I enjoy that, I don't know why. Maybe because it reminds me that others have lives that are just as important to them as mine is to me. And I order the supplies and I pay the bills. And I tend to all our correspondence and spend half a day with an accountant who comes once a month from Raleigh. I meet with my manager, Mr. Jack, who keeps the outdoors going. He oversees repairs and maintenance of the heavy equipment, and he's completely in charge of our big harvesting machine, which we're still paying for. He calls it his demanding baby. And he delegates people for all the chores that have to be done every day when you have a crew working for you: like seeing that water coolers are filled every morning, sending workers to the sick bay for heatstroke and minor wounds. He goes up to NC State and meets with soil consultants and comes back with all these figures he tries to explain to me. And now we've got a new problem to deal with. You probably haven't heard of the antitobacco movement, but we have to start thinking about what other crops would be profitable in our soil. I grew up being a little afraid of Mr. Jack, but he's a loyal person and I'd be lost if I didn't have him behind me overseeing things."

"He worked for your father?"

"He was my father's manager. His last name is Rakestraw, but everyone, including me, calls him Mr. Jack. Daddy got him straight out of graduate school. He has five and a half years' more college than I do."

"When do you write?"

"In the evening if I'm not too tired. I curl up on a lounge on the back porch or write in bed."

"At Lovegood you'd crawl into bed and start writing in your notebook. As if you had someone inside, dictating the words. It used to unnerve me. Do you still write by hand?"

"I do. When I get a halfway decent draft, I type it up in the office and then I go through the typescript, reading it aloud. That's when the bad writing really screams at you, when you hear yourself reading aloud. Then I copy my marked-up typescript back into the notebook and begin the process again."

Good God, no wonder it took her so long to finish anything.

"When do *you* write, Feron?"

"Same as you, in the evening. After work."

"What do you do at your job?"

"My first job was in something called 'the Tandem Room.' I worked with a partner. We sat across from each other and read the consultants' reports aloud, correcting the typos and grammar mistakes and then sending them to the higher-up editors who worked on the structure and content. It sounds boring, but I enjoyed my partner. She advised what we should order from the menus; she even taught me to use chopsticks. And she could be so wise about how to avoid bitterness. She'd say, 'I try to stay away from any situation that promises to bring on dissatisfaction with myself.' Her name was Shawna Samuels."

"What happened to her?"

"Oh, she's still in the big Tandem Room downstairs, working with another partner and ordering out Chinese and Italian meals. What happened was, I got moved upstairs to become one of those higher editors. Now I have a room to myself, with a window, and I revise clumsy syntax, move paragraphs around, see if it lacks pace, check that it's accurate, and I send it back to the consultant for more work if the content seems skimpy. Then it goes to the typist, and after that to the editorial director, who adds her final touches and sends it on to be vetted by the top brass before it's delivered to the firm that paid a lot of money to hire the consultant to tell them what they were doing wrong and how they could do better."

"But couldn't you and your friend still meet, Feron?"

"Well, it got complicated. We weren't in each other's orbit anymore. Sometimes we'd meet on the elevator, and it was just so awkward. Neither of us knew what to say. I guess she felt I had betrayed her somehow. Or maybe it was just me feeling bad about leaving her behind. It still makes me uncomfortable to think about it."

"You said in your letter that you could do your job and then come home and write at night because it hadn't drained your mental energies."

"If I'm not too tired. Same as you. MacFarlane pays well and has little perks to make you feel like family. For instance, you can sign up to apartment-sit for employees who are going on vacation or leave. You have to be interviewed by the owner, you also have to get bonded, but a nice place to stay in this town is a gift from the gods.

It's usually for only a month or so, but meanwhile I'm saving all that rent money, and it makes me keep my belongings down to a minimum."

"It sounds ideal. Maybe not for the long haul, but—"

"No, not for the long haul. I'm hoping to have my own place when I save up enough to pay the security and two months' advance rent."

"You plan on staying here, then?"

"The city suits me. I feel invisible when I want to be, observing the human scene. I never fail to see something that takes me by surprise. Also I like to walk, Will got me into that. He'd walked obsessively, ever since he was a little boy, and the doctor told his parents that for many people the brain was stimulated by walking."

"You're not afraid of walking around by yourself?"

"I don't walk at night. Though I often dream I'm walking at night. But I'm always alone in these dreams, so the only thing I have to be afraid of is what I might dream next."

"Oh, Feron, I've missed you so. You say such unusual things. I remember once when we were sitting on the lawn at Lovegood, I was wondering what happened to the class poet of 1918, and you counted on your fingers in the grass and said she would be in her upper fifties. Then I'll never forget it, you said her life was probably not over, but *set*—like Jell-O. I wish we could stay in touch. Tell me where I can always be sure to reach you."

"The surest way would be care of my uncle. Rowan Hood, Pullen, North Carolina. That would be enough."

"Do you ever think of your time at Lovegood?"

"It's more like I carry it with me. It provides a whole sort of reference aura. I mean, my husband, Will, knew exactly who Miss McCorkle was, her staunch work ethic and her sassy figures of speech to make history come alive: he often brought her up. He approved of her. And there's Miss Petrie, of course. I was shocked when I returned in the fall and learned she had left when Miss Olafson got a better job. I never became close to Miss Petrie like you did, but Chekhov inhabits me and that whole notion of Miss Petrie's that in reading or writing you have to get used to being left in uncertainty."

"See? That's what I mean. I don't have someone in my world who talks about 'reference auras' and being more afraid of what you might dream than going out at night."

"Well, you may not believe this, Merry, but you are in my reference aura, too. When I come up against some moral problem, I ask myself what you would do. And, except for Will, I have never felt so at ease with someone day and night. I felt that you were always on my side."

17

Leaving the Algonquin, Feron walked east on Forty-fourth and turned left on Fifth. The big cast-iron clock on the corner pointed to half-past four. Was a person like Merry born with her character, or had it been built up brick-by-brick by people who taught her to choose the good, the kind, and the true?

It was not officially rush hour, but hurriers filled the sidewalks in both directions. I never fail to see something that takes me by surprise, she had told Merry. Just close your eyes for a second, and what do you see when you open them again?

Today it was a domineering old geezer yelling at a young nurse guiding him along the sidewalk. A spruced-up gentleman looking pleased with himself, carrying a bunch of red roses. But, oh no, who was approaching him? It was the lady with the veiled hat and dirty gloves, laden with Lord and Taylor bags. This was Feron's third sighting.

The first had been an actual encounter. Feron had just turned the corner from Fifty-seventh onto Fifth when the lady laden with bags approached her.

"Excuse me, but you look like a nice young lady. My wallet has been stolen and I have no money to get home. Can you help me?"

"Of course! How much do you need?"

"Whatever you can spare."

Feeling magnanimous, Feron placed a ten in the outstretched gloved hand. That's when she saw the gloves were dirty.

The second time, it had been raining, and Feron huddled with others on the porch of St. Patrick's Cathedral. She heard a familiar voice addressing an older man: "Excuse me, sir. I wonder if you could help me. My wallet was stolen and I have no money to get home." "Why, that's awful. How much do you need?" "Whatever you can spare." The woman set down her Lord & Taylor bags to put the bill in her purse, and the man walked away. Then Feron had done a spontaneous thing that turned out to be stupid. Stepping forward, she caught the woman's eye. "Hello again!" Feron said. Giving her a horrified, affronted look, the woman fled the porch into the rain. This time Feron had seen into the Lord & Taylor bags. They contained folded clothes but not those bought today in a store.

Now the woman had accosted the gentleman with the red roses, who was handing her bills from his wallet. He continued talking to her until she excused herself and walked down the block.

Fifty-seventh and Fifth, Fifty-fourth and Fifth? Was Fifth Avenue her territory? What had happened to bring her to her present occupation? Could it happen to me? wondered Feron. But I would never choose waylaying people on the street. How humiliating if someone said, "Get along with you, Granny." If I were going to steal, thought Feron, it would most likely be something more solitary, like embezzling.

"I have stayed off Fifth Avenue for fifteen years," Shawna Samuels would matter-of-factly remark. "As I've said, I try to avoid any situation that brings on dissatisfaction with myself."

Shawna had been right, you had only to look in store windows to see that Manhattan's streets and avenues had a hierarchy based on appearance and possessions. Feron did not need to "stay off

Fifth" because in whatever direction she walked she knew she had a safety net beneath her feet. She was still in her twenties and considered this a temporary job. She had Uncle Rowan. "At least let me help you," he implored, pronouncing it "hep." He had wanted to wire quarterly deposits to a bank in New York.

"Thank you, Uncle Rowan, but I need to know I can do it by myself."

But hadn't she spent every Christmas with him and Blanche Buttner since coming back from England?

When the Jellicoe parents were killed, Merry had no choice but to go home and raise her little brother and keep the family business going. If being authentically self-reliant meant having no alternative, Feron wondered if that made her a fake.

When Will fell to his death in England, walking too close to the edge of the Saltburn cliffs with his mind in the clouds, Uncle Rowan flew over to guide her through the labyrinth of practical and legal requirements. He even phoned Will's mother when Feron said she wasn't up to it. And after Will's body was flown home and buried—his mother following him within half a year—Feron was encouraged, indeed expected, to move into Blanche's spacious Benton Grange house, an eight-mile drive from Uncle Rowan in Pullen, and get used to being a twenty-three-year-old widow before she decided what to do with the rest of her life.

What had really happened on the bus after the pale man in the dark coat asked if he could sit beside her? She knew he was all right when he added, "I haven't had a civilized conversation for a while."

"What makes you think I am civilized?" she had countered.

No one in this world except a person named Dale Flowers knew about those days in Chicago before he pried out of her that she *did* have an option. She had an uncle, didn't she? Her late father's brother? Why didn't she get on another bus and go introduce herself to the uncle? She had nothing to lose. What a paradox, that "the sinister man," who had no options, no long-lost relative himself, turned out to be the generous one. She had used him far more than he had her.

As soon as Uncle Rowan had taken a long look at her and announced, "You're one of us, all right," Feron had excised Dale Flowers from her biography, though she could not wipe out their time together.

"I mean, everyone has secrets no one else should know." Didn't Moral Merry say so herself an hour ago? And blushed under her tan.

If she and Merry had maintained a more "faithful" friendship over the decade, would they have felt easier about exchanging secrets? Though Feron couldn't imagine what kind of secret a person like Merry could have.

An hour earlier with Merry, she had slid expertly into two lies, the one about the Sunday she had met her medieval history professor in the campus coffee shop—"I was depressed. *I've forgotten why*"—and Will Avery had said he was going for his Sunday visit to his mother, would Feron like to go with him? ("Getting off campus might do you good. It does me, sometimes.")

And what a whopper about the nice old editor who said a lot of nice things about *English Winter*! But had to turn it down because it lacked intimate scenes.

And she had been in another state far below "depressed" that Sunday morning in the campus coffee shop. The previous day, Swain Eckert had shown up at her dormitory. He had announced himself to the girl on duty as Feron's father, which he legally was, and forced Feron to listen to him in the visitors' parlor as he enumerated all the ways she and her mother had ruined his life. ("She always did look down on me, but I was her ticket out. She raised you to share her lack of kindness, and both of you were spectacular liars, you lived inside a tissue of lies. As long as you got what you wanted, morals could go out the window. You never bothered to thank me for a single thing I did for you. By the way, you still owe me that four hundred and fifty you took out of my shoebox.")

Swain, dwarfed by the overstuffed parlor chair he had chosen to plop himself into, had announced before they sat down that he was a recovering alcoholic and his visit to Feron—a sixteen-hour drive—was so that he could fulfill Step Eight, "making amends." She was embarrassed that the girl on duty would now think this seedy man was her father. He looked more *compressed* than the person she remembered, though the deep armchair may have contributed to that. His hair must have been dyed; it was never that dead brown before. His jacket and pants didn't go together, and he still wore the awful white socks that he used to insist protected him from athlete's foot.

"You sound like you drove all this way so *I* could make amends," she said.

"I'm sorry if I was hard on you, Feron. I did it for your own good, so you wouldn't grow up spoiled rotten like your mother, but my temper wasn't always the best. I flew off the handle a lot more than I do now and, you know, slapped you around."

"I'd call it hitting rather than slapping. You knocked both of us to the floor plenty of times."

"I don't remember ever knocking anyone to the floor, but if I slapped, that was wrong and I want to make amends."

Swain, having recited this, appeared as pleased with himself as someone who has just performed a noble act. Wriggling up straighter in the armchair, he recrossed his legs and launched into a confession about how unhappy he had been at the time.

"I was twenty-three. I was an honorably discharged pilot, I had the GI Bill for college, my whole life in front of me. And next thing I know, I'm getting married to a pregnant woman who *says* she's twenty-eight, but actually a few years more, and I have a four-year-old stepdaughter. The baby, by the way, didn't make it. The next one didn't and the two after that. By then your mother was a drunk and had turned bitter, and you were not an adult but thought you were."

"This is a lot to take in," Feron croaked, having suddenly lost her voice.

"Living with the two of you was like being somewhere you're not wanted. No, worse, like realizing you're invisible."

"Was that when you started making night-journeys to my room to commit your disgusting liberties?"

"What? Oh, the thing you threatened in your runaway letter. If I came after you, you were going to report something that really would send me to jail. When I read that letter, want me to tell you the first thing I felt?"

She nodded. Her knees had begun to shake.

"I felt relief. Then after I got over my relief, I knew I had to make up a good story to tell people. After living with you and your mother, I had the art down cold. I would start by admitting that, sadly, we just hadn't been able to get along. Not surprising, after you went around saying I'd murdered your mother. Only I didn't say that part, I knew they were already thinking it. You left with my blessing, I would say. I even threw in the four hundred and fifty as my parting gift to get you started."

"How did you find out where I was?"

"Your high school principal stopped me on the street and said, 'Well, it all turned out for the best, didn't it?' The dean of that first college you went to had been in touch with him. I didn't need a detective to keep track of you after that."

"You weren't afraid I'd tell about the other?"

"What other?"

"What I just said. The night visits." Her voice had come back, but it sounded like a little girl's.

"Any night visits, as you call them, were made up, just like your mother's murder."

"What do you mean? I remember them! You creeping down the hall. Holding the latch so nobody could hear you opening and closing my door. Then the shuffle, shuffle in your moccasins across the bare floor to my bed . . ."

"All details of your fantasy. Details are convincing, I've learned that about lying."

"You drove for sixteen hours to make amends, and then leave out the worst thing you did to me?"

"I didn't leave it out, Sweetheart, because it didn't happen."

His horrible endearment used in arguments, sometimes right before a hitting. In this case, from the overstuffed armchair that enfolded him. They had never owned such a chair in the places they lived.

"*Now* who's the liar?" She almost wailed. "Sometimes I'd be asleep and wouldn't hear you when you came in. I'd wake up and find you kneeling beside my bed, your fingers crawling up into places nobody else had touched. One time I yelled out, and you should have seen yourself scurrying for the door."

Amazingly, she laughed.

He was silent. Preparing another counterblow? They stared at each other across the parlor. The dark eyes, which could be brooding or commanding, unfortunately brought back a time in her childhood when she had adored him. He had taken her up in his plane and let her control whether it went up or down.

"Oh, me," he said, uncrossing his legs and working himself out of the deep chair. "Looks like it's time for me to get back on the road. If things had gone better, I was going to take you to lunch. But that doesn't seem to be in the cards, does it?"

"No." She didn't get up.

"I guess you don't want to see me out."

"No, I don't think so."

"Well . . ." He was standing over her now. "Enjoy your life. Enjoy your college. Enjoy your youth. Whatever I did or didn't do, I want you to know I cared about you. I'm sorry everything turned out the way it did."

"I'm sorry, too."

Not turning her head to see him out of the room, she remained seated for she couldn't say how long.

18

The compass went with Merry everywhere. Now it lay inside its case on the pullout table of her roomette, ready to be of service. The train, still in its early departure stages, was meandering all over the compass. She would know when it was headed seriously south from the view outside her window. Then she would take the compass out of the case and hold it waist-high in her lap and take her bearings: more for the ritual of doing something Ritchie had taught her than anything else.

Her other items she had stored in the places built for them. Not a lot of room to turn around in, but at least it was just yourself turning around in it. Whoever had designed this cubicle must have been proud to have fit so much into the allotted space. Pull-down bed when she was ready (she wasn't), little sink for a light washup, and you walked down the hall if you wanted the toilet. Her mind had almost twenty-four hours to call its own.

"It's easy, Merry Grape. This is a genuine U.S. Air Force pocket model from World War II. First I'm going to show you how to take your bearings, and then I'm going to show you how to *find* a bearing. Once you know that, you'll be able to locate the Jellicoe properties from your dorm window."

"But I can't take away your compass, Ritchie. It's your prized possession."

"You're not taking it away. I'm lending it to you. I know how you are. It will keep you from getting homesick. With this compass, Merry Grape, you will always know where you are."

Six years later, as he was leaving for boot camp, he gave it to her again. "I can't take this, Ritchie. You're going to need it more than ever."

"No, I'm not. They'll issue me a new one. By now they've probably developed one that talks to you in the dark: 'No, no! Wrong way! Left, stupid, I said left!'"

How she missed his imaginative wit. He made things come alive, like the scolding compass guiding you through the dark. He could also see right into people. He was a noticer. Like the day that their old life was already over, but they didn't know it yet. "Mr. Jack has that look he has when nobody is looking," Ritchie said, as their father's manager walked toward their front door hours too early. "It's like another person has taken over."

She had said he read too many of those fright comics.

Yet, within the span of that awful day, she had found herself face-to-face with a new Mr. Jack.

"I've put Ritchie out downstairs with one of my Benadryls," Mr. Jack had announced, looming in the doorway of her room. Confused by the upside-down-ness of all that had passed since she was last in this room, Merry was not lying in her own bed because, before her life flipped over, she had made it up for Feron so her friend would not have to look out at the black barns.

"Would you like to try one, Miss Meredith?"

"No, thank you. I think I'll just lie here in the dark."

"Then I'll leave you to it. Unless you want some company."

And she had said, whether from courtesy or not wanting him to feel rejected. "Oh. Okay."

She made room for him to lie beside her, but his feet in their big shoes hung over the end of the bed. To put him at ease, she had made some silly remark about it still being a little girl's bed.

"I know. And I shouldn't be in it," he said hoarsely, and then to her astonishment he laid his elbow across his face and began to sob, with helpless gasps in between, like a child.

She was eighteen years old and had never lain on a bed with a man, let alone a sobbing man. She tried to imagine what would be the most adult thing to do. Should she slip her arm under his neck and put her face close to his and say comforting words as she did with Ritchie? She really hadn't a clue. Neither she nor Ritchie had cried yet. It was all like something beyond a bad dream, and she could have used some reassurance herself.

Then somehow she was holding this big man, his head burrowing between her breasts, his tears soaking her pajama top. She could smell his pungent maleness, also a first for her. The high school boys she had dated would always arrive at her door doused in shampoo and toothpaste and aftershave scents. This man smelled of underarm sweat and soil and burnt grass. He had been "putting the fields down" for the winter when his pager went off.

Dr. Alistair Worley. Why him, just now? The psychology class back at Lovegood where he had them discussing the last sentence of that magazine story. *But there was one thing Queenie missed.* Merry had contributed nothing to that class discussion about what Queenie missed: being a virgin on her wedding night. Merry seldom spoke up, for fear of making a fool of herself. But she remembered thinking during that discussion that *she* didn't intend on missing what Queenie had missed, even if she couldn't picture very well how it would take place when it happened.

The big body covering hers. "I'll take care of you, Miss Meredith."

"Oh . . ."

"Am I hurting you?"

"Not . . . *too* much." Polite to the end.

"Oh, Miss Meredith . . . oh, Miss Meredith . . ."

She had meant to tell Feron more about Ritchie. What a rare human being he was. He had been more than a little brother. He grew into her guardian, her teacher, her beloved compensation for having lost so much else.

Everyone should get what they want at least once. Feron describing herself standing at the altar with Will.

Losing a husband you had loved for less than a year, how did that compare with losing a brother you'd loved for almost nineteen— plus the three posthumous years and counting. But to be fair, Feron also had those posthumous years of loving to get through. Her novel, *English Winter*, how did it start? How did it end? What were the bed scenes she hadn't put in?

("I just had this thought," Ritchie had said, only hours away from their turned-over lives.

"What?"

"The curing barns are beautiful when they're empty and closed up. And the fields are beautiful when everything's been cut down and carried away. But when people are empty and flat they're just dead."

"You have the strangest thoughts, Ritchie."

"Strange interesting or strange scary?"

"A little of each.")

Had Ritchie been one of those lucky people who got what he wanted at least once? It seemed to her he had gotten it twice. He had passionately wanted the part of the Stage Manager when his high school drama group put on *Our Town*, and he had gotten it. He had passionately wanted to enlist in the air force even before the draft, and he had done it. ("Now they'll teach me to fly and I'll see the world and I'll be able to go to college without us having to pay for it. I'm all set, Merry Grape. Now all I have to do is live.")

I meant it today when I told Feron I hadn't expected to see her again. Will I ever hear from her again?

She did seem happy for me about the *Atlantic* story. But writing a novel about a lost husband has to be demanding. She said to think of her stopping by the library to consult the Chekhov story with the good bed scene in it. I hope it helps. But, oh, Mr. Sterling, I'm afraid you wasted your money on me. A book of connected stories about people's secrets in a southern tobacco town. Where would I start? I certainly wouldn't begin with mine. I have drafts of other stories about secrets. One is about Maud Petrie, from her point of view. I am a minor character in it, visiting her apartment, the one she shared with Miss Olafson, after I had left school, and seeing the single bedroom and the one bed. And having her see me understand. Yet, speaking of people's secrets, Mr. Sterling couldn't sell such a story even in 1968, should I offer it. He wouldn't risk his reputation by sending it out to magazines. Feron was baffled why I would take Petrie as my pen name. I neglected to tell her our favorite teacher had left me all her books, and I didn't tell her about Miss Petrie and Miss Olafson's relationship. Maybe she had figured it out for herself long before I did. I loved Maud Petrie. Not the way she and Miss Olafson loved each other, but my heart took her in.

Feron said that besides Will I was the only other person in her life she had felt comfortable spending all day and night with.

I can't remember ever seeing Feron cry. My first sight of her in the Lovegood parking lot, before I knew she was going to be my roommate, she looked at odds with someone or something. That look has not changed. I saw it on her face after I had hugged her. She still has the stoop and the at-odds-with-someone look, and it didn't occur to me until after we sat down at the Algonquin today that the dark front tooth was gone. She had just gotten her crown when she was coming to visit us on that terrible day that turned my life upside down.

I think of Feron and me lying on the grass in front of Lovegood College, and me, the untried me, saying blithely, "The worst that's ever happened to me was my dog, Sam, dying."

19

1976

The Castle, the inmates called it. Having abided by its rules and customs for a third of his life, he had been set free with gate money, job training skills, and a set of civilian clothes. The black double-breasted overcoat, prewar Brooks Brothers, had pleased him until he saw his antiquated plate-glass reflection bobbing up and down like a scarecrow among the newer overcoats on today's streets.

He had two seats to himself on the bus. Directly across the aisle an unfriendly looking girl spread out her belongings across the empty seat beside her. She didn't want company either. People kept walking to the back of the bus. That's when he realized buses must have toilets now.

At the next terminal he looked out the window and saw the restless line of new passengers waiting to board. And soon enough, a woman attached to a little girl eating a moon pie stopped beside him and looked accusingly at the empty seats on either side of the aisle. "Mavis, you sit beside the young lady and I'll sit next to the gentleman."

"I want to sit next to you," screamed the child.

"Well, you can't, Mavis, because there aren't two seats together."

Frowning at the unavoidable, the girl across the aisle had begun dismantling her barricade.

He was on his feet, scarecrow overcoat folded over his arm. "No, please. You two sit together. I'll join the young lady."

"If that's okay with you," he addressed the frowning girl, who answered him with a shrug.

—opening of *Beast and Beauty*, by Feron Hood. Knole, 1976.

Lovegood College
Office of the Dean
October 2, 1976

Dear Feron,

Congratulations on *Beast and Beauty*. Now Lovegood can list a novelist among its alumnae. And thank you for your generous donation to set up the Sophie Sewell Hood scholarship for an incoming first-year student. And last but not least, thank you for inscribing a copy of your fascinating novel to me. It is rare to receive so many gifts in a single package!

I remember you well from the beginning of that 1958 term when Miss Darden and I were discussing possible roommates for you. Winifred Darden died last spring (stroke, but mercifully no lingering). Winifred embodied a spirit of Lovegood that was in place long before I arrived. Her graciousness made my job smoother, often without my even knowing it at the time. How delighted she would be by the Sophie Sewell Hood scholarship. She and I often discussed how fast things were changing all around us and how we must hope and plan to accommodate the Spirit of Change without forfeiting Lovegood's values. On good days, I think we've been moderately successful. On other days I feel like someone waiting for both shoes to drop.

I read *Beast and Beauty* the day it arrived. It's the perfect length, and the black and red cover art, those two lovers going up in flames, is compelling. Eloise Sprunt (still teaching math and science) has it now, and we are going to compare notes after she's finished. I like that they are never given names. It creates the mood of a tale. The man is an unusual character. One fully expects he will take advantage of the girl, but it turns out she takes advantage of him. The outcast is kind and generous and becomes the agent of her freedom. I had remembered the fairy tale all wrong, I realized after I went over to the library, which now has its own building on campus. The beast in the fairy tale was also kind and generous (except when he loses his temper with the father). I imagined pairing your novel with the fairy tale for class discussions. The erotic scenes wouldn't be acceptable in an 1878 classroom, maybe not even in a 1958 one, but here we are, halfway through the 1970s and in the midst of a feminist revolution.

Since your time here, the campus has sprouted five new buildings: a science and business building, a sports center with basketball court, indoor tennis courts, and an Olympic pool, the new library, a new dorm with en suite bathrooms, and a dining hall with conference rooms. The dining hall stands on the site of Miss McCorkle's old Quonset hut. She also still teaches full time, only she is now Mrs. Radford. He is a retired high school history teacher, and it's a first marriage for both of them. It is quite a love match. You should see them crossing the campus arm in arm. Our enrollment has doubled; there are currently fifteen members of the Daughters and Granddaughters Club, and Lovegood still remains one of the dwindling number of junior colleges for women, where, if you recall the pageant song, "removed from strife . . . they may seek the mental life."

In four years, I will step aside as dean, though the trustees are working on an honorary title complete with housing so they can keep me close by as a figurehead, but with no power. "Sort of like the Queen of England," as one of them said. Lovegood has made leaps of progress, but the postwar times were conducive, and things probably wouldn't have been all that different if someone else had been dean. Though when I tell them that, they say I am just being modest, and perhaps they are right.

Do keep in touch, Feron. I was going to put you on the mailing list for our handsome quarterly brochure with all the updates, but saw someone had put you on it already. I will bet anything it was our Winifred Darden.

With Warm Regards,
Susan Fox
Dean

PART THREE

20

1979

A week from today, the new decade would begin, "the eighties," and whatever it would bring. For the first time, Blanche Buttner and Feron attended the Steeds' Christmas party alone. Uncle Rowan had died on the job in late August. Finishing out his fourth term as mayor, he had flown to D.C. to meet with his friend the congressman to secure Pullen's water rights. The state capital had been curling its tentacles around a wider circumference of small North Carolina towns in commuting distance from the capital, and Pullen didn't wish to partake of pumped-in water from some shared system. Driving himself home from the Raleigh airport, he stopped at his favorite barbecue place, ordered seconds, had a stroke, and was borne away to the hospital, where he never regained consciousness.

Feron had of course flown down from New York to be with Blanche for her first Christmas alone. Driving them home from the airport, Blanche said, "If it's all right with you, Feron, I'd like to attend the Christmas parties. Rowan would expect it. He's only been gone four months, and people will be wanting to talk about him. And we'll be his living ambassadors." Blanche the fiancée had quickly and efficiently transformed herself into Blanche the widow.

This Christmas, "the Steeds' party" had become "General Steed's and Marguerite's party" because the past year had taken Mrs. Steed as well.

And as Blanche had predicted, everyone did have something to say about Uncle Rowan: Rowan Hood the young lawyer, who'd saved their farm from foreclosure; Rowan the pilot, who'd taken his old girlfriend, now in her seventies, up in his Piper ("he turned the plane upside down and liked to scared me to death"); Mayor Hood ("Honey, he'd've been elected by a landslide for a *fifth* term . . . he had the weather eye to see what Pullen was going to need before we knew it ourselves"). Several men who'd been partaking liberally of the general's bourbon alluded to parties "with wild girls" at the young lawyer's house, and the night, years later, when Mayor Hood stood out on his lawn with his arms crossed and stared down the drive-by shooter who had phoned ahead to say he was coming to kill him.

This year's fashionable parties in New York would be showcasing the latest in furnishings and catered foods, while in Pullen tables and chairs stalwartly stood in their original locations, and the hosts faithfully offered the same dishes that had graced their tables fifty years before. Maybe if she had been raised in such a structured world, Feron would have run screaming for the exits long ago. But she was charmed by these traditions she had never lived inside.

As her fortieth birthday approached, she visualized her life to date as a stack of colors. Infancy and early childhood with grandparents and mother was colored gray, not the soft dove gray of a young mouse, but the ashen gray of grownups' extinguished dreams. Age four to almost eighteen with Swain and her disintegrating mother were a brownish-yellow, like brackish water with snakes in it.

The bus ride episode had a layer all to itself. At first it was colored the lackluster black of Dale Flowers's hair color out of a bottle. However, in the early seventies, after her writing teacher at Columbia, Alexy Cuervo, had shamed her into abandoning "middle-class fiction" and assigned her to "modernize" a fairy tale, the bus interim in her life took on the red of the tumbling figures on her book jacket and her own brief taste of success.

The Uncle Rowan rescue and the innocent years at Lovegood Feron had colored white. She alone knew that it was a fake white because of what it covered up. Like the crown that eventually covered the front tooth ruined by Swain.

The green layer from the days of Will still lay like an ache in her chest, first the awakening green of Will's mother's garden to the misty-green of Yorkshire during their short marriage.

How many more layers and colors was she destined to travel through? If someone offered her a preview of the stack of her remaining life-colors, would she accept out of curiosity or turn away in horror?

"We haven't met." A man with a December tan was extending his hand to Feron. "I'm Thad Hood. We almost met at Uncle Rowan's funeral back in August, but you were so deep in conversation with that sublime little woman in the black hat that I couldn't bring myself to barge in. Actually, I'm your first cousin. Your father and my father and Uncle Rowan were brothers. My father, Simon, died when I was a baby, you've probably heard about that freak spinal when he was having his appendix out. When I was in my terrible teens, Uncle Rowan saved me from dissipation and ruin and probably jail, but that's another story. And you're his long-lost niece who writes books and lives in New York."

"So far, it's just the one book, but how nice to have a cousin. How is it I never met you before?"

He was her least favorite type of handsome man. You could see him checking himself over with approval in front of the mirror before setting out for this party.

"I just retired from the navy. Twenty years away from Pullen, and I return to find it exactly as I left it. Which makes my wife, Lou, ecstatic. We've had her family's old house moved out to the country on a flatbed truck, and she stays inside it, in the middle of a twenty-acre field, pretending our last two decades in beautiful, exotic places were just a bad dream. You're widowed, aren't you? Or should I not have brought that up?"

"I've been a widow for almost seventeen years, so I'm pretty used to being one."

"Listen, I want to talk about Uncle Rowan. Can I bring you some refreshment from the table?"

"The eggnog would be good."

"From the teetotaler's bowl or the spiked bowl?"

"Oh, spiked, please."

Marguerite Steed approached. "I saw you looking at the dolls. The one in Japanese costume is new since last Christmas."

"They really are exquisite, Marguerite. I am so sorry you lost your mother."

"We both had big losses this year, didn't we? This town won't see the likes of your uncle again."

Marguerite was unaware that she had been a walking symbol for Feron since Feron first laid eyes on her sixteen years earlier. It had been July 1963, when Feron was newly widowed. She and Uncle Rowan were having an early supper at Howard Johnson's. In came a proud trio, an elderly couple and a serene middle-aged lady whom the hostess reverently seated at the best window booth. Uncle Rowan jumped up. ("I'll just go over and pay my respects.") He had begun his campaign to be elected mayor of Pullen. "That's General Steed and his wife. And that's their daughter, Marguerite, who has one of the finest collections of dolls in the world. She has won all kinds of prizes. Every Christmas they open their house, and there are these priceless dolls in glass cabinets."

My God, Feron had thought. Surely as a young woman, Marguerite Steed must have had other plans for herself than becoming a middle-aged doll collector still living with her parents. Feron had spent the first months of her widowhood in Blanche Buttner's stately house, but seeing the general's daughter had been her wake-up call. It was time to get out of here and be off on her own.

"I keep my more personal ones upstairs," Marguerite was saying. "I could take you up after this crowd thins, if you're interested."

"I would love that."

Her new cousin returned with two glass cups of eggnog.

"Uncle Rowan was the nearest thing I had to a hero. If he hadn't been available when I was seventeen, I might have ended up in jail. He showed me how to tap better outlets for my energy. Which we can all use at seventeen. Uncle Rowan himself had the kind of energy that could have taken him as far as he wanted to go, but he chose not to leave his pond."

"Would you have known my father?"

"I was a little tyke when Uncle Woody passed, but from what I've heard he was a sweet fellow, kind of a dreamer, not, well, as *strong-minded* as Uncle Rowan. By the way, who *was* that sublime little woman in the black hat at his funeral?"

"There were *several* black hats on the scene that day, but I think you're probably referring to Merry Jellicoe. She was my roommate at Lovegood College. Not for very long, because her parents died in a plane crash and she had to drop out of school and raise her little brother. And then he was killed in Vietnam. So she's down in Hamlin, running the family tobacco business by herself."

"That little slip of a thing?"

"That little slip of a thing. She saw Uncle Rowan's obituary in the *News and Observer* and came over to the funeral, which touched me. I hadn't seen her in ten years."

Thad Hood produced a card from his wallet. "Next time you see her, which I hope won't be ten years from now, please give her this card and say I'm your cousin and if she ever needs our services."

THAD S. HOOD

SURVEYORS AND APPRAISERS

NO PROPERTY TOO SMALL OR TOO LARGE

"You're in luck," Feron told him, slipping the card into her jacket pocket. "I'm having lunch with Merry tomorrow."

"What are you planning on doing with Uncle Rowan's house?"

"I haven't made up my mind what to do with it."

"That's exactly what Blanche Buttner said about the little airfield he left her. 'Thad, what am I going to do with an airfield?' she said. I had my own quandary about the rental property he left me. I didn't have the heart to kick out the old couple who had been renting the house for twenty years. And *then* I realized that had been his intention all along. He knew he could count on me to let them fade away in comfort and afterward convert it into a showpiece. It's a Queen Anne cottage, way too big for them. It would make a fabulous restaurant if zoning permitted. Well, who knows? By the time they vacate it, the zoning might have changed. Now, in your case, I advise finding some responsible renters—for now."

"How does one go about finding responsible renters?"

"Oh. I can help you with that." He said "hep," just like Uncle Rowan and handed over a second business card. "Call me when you're ready. Get it cleared out, redo the floors, put in a modern kitchen and—how many bathrooms are there?"

"There's a full bath upstairs and a half-bath downstairs."

"Is there enough space to *make* it into a full bath?"

"I think so. I'd have to check. I'm staying with Blanche over Christmas."

"Rowan's house hasn't had anything done to it since Great-Granny Hood lived there."

"Was that Sophie Sewell Hood?"

"Why, yes, but I never thought of her as anything but Great-Granny Hood. She was something of a virago, but she could cook. I doubt if Uncle Rowan ever once cooked a meal in that kitchen. It would be worth the outlay if you're looking for prime renters. Pullen's in commuting distance to Raleigh and the Research Triangle. If you rented it for two hundred fifty, you'd make back your investment in two years. I could help you with that, too."

When the party had shrunk to a clutch of Blanche's faithful friends and a few old-timers gathered around the general, Feron followed Marguerite Steed upstairs to see the more personal dolls and confronted herself in a long pier mirror hung between two windows on the landing. She was not petite, and the winter light was unflattering. Though she had been described as "very personable" in her MacFarlane & Company file, and Will's mother had told him (which he of course reported to her) "Feron has the kind of looks that will mature well," nobody would ever refer to her as "sublime."

Marguerite's upstairs dolls in no way resembled the ones on display downstairs. For a start, there was not a single porcelain doll. Once, when Feron had been racking her brain for a story someone might publish, she had pounced on the tale of a middle-aged woman who lived with her aged parents and collected porcelain dolls. The woman was a porcelain doll herself. As long as she stayed inside her parents' house, her porcelain youth and beautiful equanimity would last. Unable to imagine an ending she liked, Feron had abandoned the idea.

Unlike the downstairs dolls, these figures, settled in the window seats or on the floor, were uncanny, a few downright ugly. There was an evil-looking clown, a primitive woman made of straw, and a large sad doll in a hat and ragged coat, carrying a worn suitcase. Marguerite was telling how she belonged to a doll club. "We exchange photos and sometimes trade or buy from one another. The straw doll is a nineteenth-century Mexican 'Kitchen Witch.' They kept it in their kitchens and called it 'La Última Muñeca' ... And look at the expert stitching on my little housewife fleeing Nazi Germany—she's a copy of an Edith Samuels doll, the Israeli doll-maker: I couldn't afford the real thing. And this tacky little thing in pink satin and lace with the outrageous yellow hair is the first doll I ever bought with my own money ... it's a Sparkle Plenty doll. Do you remember the *Li'l Abner* comic strip?"

Feron asked if Marguerite's parents had seen the upstairs dolls in their own house. "Mama would come in here sometimes. Once, oh, when I was about twelve, we tried to make a schoolgirl doll, with clothes and bookbag, but it was an amateurish failure and we destroyed it."

Feron was looking forward to laughing with Uncle Rowan after the party about Marguerite's weird upstairs dolls until she remembered that he was gone.

21

Merry had suggested lunch at the Neuse River Café.

"It's midway between Benton Grange and Hamlin. There's a bar, so the lights are kept low and the food is plain but good. Probably your uncle will have taken you there."

"No, he would meet his cronies there, but Blanche didn't like it. She thought their Board Game was obsolete and morbid."

"Oh, then we'll think of another place."

"No, no, no. I'd love to see it. I want to see the Board Game."

They made a date for twelve thirty, the day after Christmas. It would be their first sit-down meeting since the Algonquin, eleven years before.

Feron left Benton Grange too early because she was still uncertain of herself behind the wheel. Uncle Rowan had left her his 1974 Oldsmobile 98, and before she returned to New York after his funeral in August, Blanche had taught her to drive, losing her equanimity only once, when her student sailed through a stop sign. The last time Feron had seen her lose it was over twenty years before, when Feron had tried to wriggle out of delivering Aunt Mabel's Christmas present. ("Oh, you go ahead without me.")

Feron's neglect of Merry had become a chronic drip-drip of guilt on her conscience. After Merry's prompt and affectionate thank-you letter following their Algonquin meeting, Feron's procrastination in answering lapsed into a failure to answer. Then time went by and Feron made no further contact, though Merry was often in her thoughts. When Feron read in the news that tobacco companies could no longer advertise on radio or television, she wrote a sort of wry condolence letter to Merry, but disliked the tone and decided not to mail it.

Merry remained a constant figure in Feron's dream life, and she continued to serve as a moral compass when Feron felt she needed direction: "Would Merry do this, would Merry consider it wrong?" (Take MacFarlane & Co. office supplies home for her personal use? Co-opt a perfect idea from someone else's writing, changing a couple of words so you wouldn't be caught plagiarizing?) However, Feron didn't necessarily feel obliged to follow what the compass told her.

How could you feel so bound up with the idea of what someone meant to you, yet feel no urge to get in touch with the real person? After all, Merry wasn't dead. She was at the other end of a letter or phone call. She wasn't even in another country.

Feron hadn't sent her a copy of *Beast and Beauty*. She had deliberated over it as she had done with the tobacco letter, then concluded it might seem like a boast or a reproach: Well, I've been busy, as you see. How are all your stories you write and read aloud to yourself and then rewrite again coming along?

As soon as Feron had spotted "the sublime little lady in the black hat" coming through the church door at Uncle Rowan's funeral, she began practicing lines of excuse and apology she wouldn't need to use. When they were face-to-face, Merry hugged her and behaved as though it had not been eleven years since she had written Feron and received no reply. She had actually apologized to Feron for showing up! ("I wasn't sure whether it was my place, since I had never met him. I can't stay long at the reception because we're right in the midst of harvesting, but I thought you might be pleased to see me.")

As she was departing, to get back to her harvesting, Merry had said, "Feron, next time you come down here, let's meet for lunch."

"I'll probably be back at Christmas. I'd love to meet for lunch."

"Well, my number's in the phone book. If you still want to meet at Christmas, you phone me."

And Feron had phoned.

"I can tell you what you don't know about yourself, when you're ready to ask." Her mentor and former teacher Alexy Cuervo liked to challenge her. So far, Feron had resisted his offer. Alexy Cuervo, teacher, mentor, or evil genius? Sometimes Feron felt as though she had made a contract with the devil: the writing teacher at Columbia who had told his students the first day, "Write anything you want, but don't bore me with the conventional."

"Sir, could you define what you mean by 'conventional'?"

There was a student like that in most classes. Like the one in Will's Medieval England class who had protested, "But, sir, you don't allow points for improvement." After which he transferred out of Will's class.

"Certainly," replied Cuervo. "What I'm looking for is something more than the utilitarian narrative which narrowed minds perceive as a sufficient picture of reality." He was a small, rather delicate man, yet they cowered before him.

How glad Feron was that someone else had asked the question!

Nevertheless, she had amassed ninety pages of *A Singular Romance*, and he was being paid to teach an MFA course, and teaching included having to read his students' writings.

She went to her first tutorial armed to defend her conventional novel-in-progress. But Cuervo was respectful. I must have misread him, she thought, confronting his black-browed pointy face regarding her from above his customary white guayabera with dark ascot and the turquoise cufflinks he always wore.

"Will you be surprised," he began in his tripping Spanish cadences, "when I tell you I read all of it? Yes, it is conventional. It could have been written a hundred, a hundred and fifty years ago. But I was curious, because you had caught something, oh, strange, different, about this odd trio, the mother and son and the young woman. If she continues with this, I thought, she should take more chances."

"What kind of chances?"

"You have more strangeness in you than you are aware of. I would urge you to cultivate the strangeness. You can glimpse the undersides of people's lives, what is going on beneath the realistic narrative."

"But do you think I should go on with it, my novel?"

"It has a propulsion, it may be leading you toward something you don't yet know. Writing can do that. But perhaps you could use a short sabbatical. I will set you a task, like someone sets the hero a task in the fairy tales. He's known as the donor figure, so I will be your donor. Go to the library and browse through Vladimir Propp's *Morphology of the Folk Tale*. Don't try to read it, just see which ideas jump off the pages for you, his theories of character and narrative structure. And investigate some fairy tales. I want you to write me a story, set in the present day, based on a fairy tale. Think of it as a class assignment."

"When is it due?"

"When you feel you have fulfilled your task."

Feron had taken a seat in a booth facing the parking lot of the Neuse River Café so she could watch for Merry's arrival. What kind of car would she drive? How would the "sublime little lady" be dressed for lunch with her old roommate?

But she got diverted by the Board Game—Blanche was right, it was obsolete and morbid—also ridiculous to an outsider like herself. Her placemat had a map of the battle lines (Blue for the Confederacy, Red for the Union) of the last month of the Civil War in North Carolina. If you wanted to play the game, there were directions at the bottom of the placemat. You got up and went to the board, which covered most of a wall, and pushed buttons and knobs, like with arcade games, and *changed the results*. Of course, to play you needed a thorough knowledge of the battles and what circumstances might have changed the outcome, but people down here seemed to have memorized the history, backward and forward, of what they called "The War Between the States."

"Oh, Feron, I'm sorry. Have you been waiting long? I thought we said half past twelve, but then I wasn't sure, so I tried to get here by quarter after twelve so I wouldn't be horribly late if it turned out we had said twelve."

"I got here early. I'm new to driving and allowed myself time for mistakes. You look radiant, Merry. What's your secret?"

Merry, an easy blusher, colored up.

"Well, probably because I'm rested. This is the one time in our year when there's nothing we have to do. In January we will start burning the undergrowth of last summer's harvest and preparing the seedbeds indoors. Then we wait till April to transplant the seedbeds into the fields. The transplanting was always my favorite part, even as a child. I wish Daddy could have seen our brand-new transplanter; it looks and sounds like a giant mosquito spreading its wings across the fields."

Shedding a black suede fleece-lined coat, she slid into the booth, tossing in her tote bag first. She was still petite. A paisley scarf of mingled pinks, reds, greens, and black was banded low on her forehead to push back her hair. She wore a maroon sweater dress with a string of black pearls. Any stranger would take her for the stylish lady down from the city and me for the country woman in twill pants, tweed jacket, and turtleneck, Feron thought. Though Feron didn't think she qualified for "sublime," the woman across from her did have that quality of *containment* that Feron had noted back in their dorm room on the first day, as though God had taken pains to color all of her inside the lines. However, there did seem to be more of the containment, or indwelling, or whatever it was. *Was* there more of it, or had it just become more solidified?

The waitress was prompt. "How grand to see you again, Miss Jellicoe. What will you all have?"

"Do you have any specials, Patty, or is it too soon after Christmas?"

"We have a *special* special because of the Christmas leftovers. The cook made this delicious turkey chili. I had some earlier and I recommend it. We also have bass, brought up this morning from the coast. You can have it fried or broiled. It comes with French fries, coleslaw, and hush puppies."

"Now I'm sorry I ate breakfast," said Merry. "Patty, this is my friend Feron Hood. We roomed together at Lovegood College. Feron's a writer. She lives in New York now."

The New York part didn't seem to impress her. "Would you by any chance be kin to Mayor Hood from Pullen?"

"He's my uncle. I mean was. He died last summer."

"Oh, everyone knows that! Mayor Hood was one of our favorite customers."

"I'd like a cup of the turkey chili and two of those hush puppies from the other special, if that's allowed," said Merry. "Feron?"

"I'm sorry I ate breakfast, too. I'm staying with Blanche and she sets out a sideboard breakfast every day. But I'd like the bass, broiled, with all the trimmings, only small portions."

"Got it, ladies. Bring you some iced tea or something stronger while you're waiting?"

"Iced tea," said Merry. "Is that okay with you, Feron?"

"We have sweetened and unsweetened."

Merry wanted sweetened, which Feron would have liked, too, but in recent years she put on pounds if she didn't watch it. So far, bargaining had worked: small portion of fries versus no sugar in tea.

Merry patted around in her tote bag and extracted a hardcover copy of *Beast and Beauty* with its handsome red-and-black cover of lovers swirling around in flames. She laid it like a statement on the table between them.

"Now, Feron, I want you to sign this, and make it to me, and anything else you feel like saying."

Now I need to come up with an explanation, thought Feron as she turned to the title page and began writing slowly. I need an excuse for never sending her one.

She wrote,

> To Merry, my friend (I hope) of twenty-one years.
>
> Feron

Still without her credible excuse, she closed the book and slid it back to Merry, who opened it and read the inscription.

She shut the book and smiled. That Merry-smile with no under-meanings behind it. "Yes, we are friends, Feron, and I love you just as much. Maybe more, because of all the thoughts I've had about you over these twenty-one years."

Feron regretted she hadn't signed "with love" above her own name. "Do you know how I found out this book existed, Feron? I still didn't know about it when I came to your uncle's funeral last summer. But in September when I was taking a girl up to Lovegood for orientation week—our accountant's daughter—I was introducing her to Dean Fox, and she couldn't wait to bring it up. She assumed I had read it when it came out three years ago, and asked if I knew how you could write so knowingly about someone just out of a military prison. I said I meant to read it and would write her when I had. By the way, this is her last year as acting dean. You wouldn't recognize the place, or, no, I shouldn't say that, it's just that so many nice things have been added to what was already there. They've bought up all the land around the original acreage— remember Cobb's Corner?"

"That derelict store with the tree roots and the stale Tootsie Pops."

"Well, now that's the new library. Remember, the old one was inside our building. You liked to go there, while I did my homework mostly in bed."

Their food came. It was much better than Feron had anticipated, having taken Merry's "plain but good" at face value.

"That is the most beautiful scarf," Feron said, mostly to keep herself from gobbling.

"It's one of my mother's. She loved scarves, and so we always knew what to get her for birthdays and Christmas. I wear a lot of her things. They don't go out of style, and with the farm and all I don't have the time to shop."

"Is that ruby ring your mother's also?"

"They're actually garnets, but yes it was. We've had it sized to fit my skinnier finger. Feron, this is my wedding ring. I married Mr. Jack after harvesting season last fall. Are you surprised?"

"I don't know what I am. And you still call him Mr. Jack?"

Merry colored again. "We're working on that. It's something that happened over time, Feron. I've known him practically all my life. We were children when Daddy brought him home. I was eight and Ritchie was two. One day he was just there to stay. There he was, building his own house on our land. Daddy admired him because he had a graduate degree and knew all about fallow fields and soil chemistry, and he worshipped Daddy. He had come looking for a job, and Daddy was flattered that this young man had thoroughly researched Jellicoe Farms, down to statistics and crop histories, and told Daddy it was the place of all places he wanted to be."

"How much older is he?"

"Jack is fifty-six. We are sixteen years apart."

"Do you have a photo of him?"

"Not with me. How stupid of me not to bring one. He's a big man. Six three. Gray hair, what's left of it. Scars all over his forehead, like me, where basal cells have been cut out. So he wears a baseball cap most of the time. Like I wear hats and scarves."

(Is he attractive? Are you attracted to him? Is it sex? Have you been his lover for a while? You're forty, do you still mean to try for babies?)

"I think you'd appreciate him, Feron. Like you, he keeps himself to himself. His parents and grandparents were tenant farmers. Which makes him uneasy in social settings, though he comes across as distant and proud. Some people like him, some don't. But they respect him, because he knows more about the things they care about most than they know themselves.

"But, Feron, you know what? It was something you said at the Algonquin that influenced my decision to marry."

"Something *I* said?"

"You were talking about marrying Will. How you felt when you looked at him when you were exchanging vows. And you said you felt—do you remember?"

"I remember how I felt, but I don't remember what I said at the Algonquin."

"You said, 'Everyone should get what they want at least once.'"

"You're saying you wanted him?"

"I was what *he* wanted. For years and years. And I had the power to give him that one thing."

"But what about the others?"

"What others?"

"Other men. Other boyfriends. Between when you were eighteen till now."

"I *saw* other people, but Feron, you have to remember that at eighteen I became Ritchie's guardian and had charge of Jellicoe Farms until Ritchie came of age. And I saw Mr. Jack every day. It was strange. I was his boss, but he knew the business inside out and I always ran things past him. And we were sort of substitute parents to Ritchie. We went together to see him in his school plays. We took turns driving him places until he could drive himself. And Ritchie went through periods where he found Mr. Jack useful. Boys need men for men things."

Merry was studying the garnet ring. One faceted center stone encircled by smaller ones. Feron still wore her gold wedding band on her right hand.

"Jack has known the people I loved best. He can tell me stories about Daddy and Mama and about Ritchie that I would never know otherwise. And we're working for the same goals. We always were, but now there's the security of knowing if Jellicoe goes under, we will still be partners looking out on empty fields and deciding together what to do next."

"Is going under a possibility?"

"Indeed it is. You wouldn't believe, Feron. When I was growing up, tobacco was king. Now it's a murderer on trial. There's actually a billboard near our farm, it has a picture of a huge pack of cigarettes and underneath it says: How to Kill Several Million People in Your Home State." We've already had offers from three developers. Hamlin is within commuting distance of the Research Triangle, and our acreage could support two large subdivisions, or one subdivision and a golf course and a man-made lake. We could sell and enjoy our riches somewhere else, only we are both work addicts, and we both feel ties to the land. Mr. Jack, I mean Jack, has always wanted to have horses, and we could have a stable and farms growing something else and still do the subdivision. But we need to study up on it more. Neither of us knows enough about real estate."

"Ah," said Feron, digging into her purse and producing the little card:

Thad S. Hood

Surveyors and Appraisers

No property too Small or too Large

"Maybe you need the help of my first cousin Thad."

She was about to add, "He saw you at Uncle Rowan's funeral and said you were sublime."

Then thought, what's the point?

22

Two men, beer glasses in hand, were playing the Board Game. Raucous cheers, groans, some cursing. Finally when one of them graduated to the f-word, Patty the waitress strolled over and murmured something, nodding toward the women in the booth.

She came over to apologize to them. "They get so worked up. I swear sometimes it's like they're back in that old war, fighting it all over again. Can I get you some dessert? Fresh iced tea?"

"I think we'd both like some more iced tea. Feron, what about dessert?"

"We have Christmas fruitcake drowned in bourbon, little minced pies made fresh this morning, and there's always brownies. Everything à la mode, of course."

"No, I'm fine," said Feron.

"Me, too," Merry said. "Patty, would it be all right if we just hung out a while longer? My friend and I have a lot to catch up on. If it gets crowded, I promise we will get right up and leave."

"It's not going to get crowded the day after Christmas, Miss Jellicoe, except for the Board Game squadrons. Would you believe, on a slow day, we make more on that old historical map with its flashing lights than we do with the food?"

"Yes, I believe you. Some of my crew drive over here just to play."

"I'll get the tea. You're sure about the desserts, now."

"We're sure. Thank you, Patty."

When they were alone, Merry asked Feron if the man in *Beast and Beauty* was based on the man on the bus who had informed her about the Irish village.

"I *told* you about the man on the bus?"

"Our first day. It was when you and I were making our beds, and you said your mother had named you after this actress in a movie. And then you told me there had been this man beside you on a bus who told you there was a village in Ireland named Farran, with the different spelling."

"I remember us making our beds, but I don't remember telling you about the man on the bus. As for the movie actress, I've searched and searched and found no Ferons. It would be interesting to know the true story of how I got my name. Where did she really get it? Who suggested it?

"Did I ever tell you what a liar my mother was?"

"You said she was an alcoholic . . ."

"She was also a consummate liar. If I had the time to spare, I would make a list of things she told me and then in a column opposite I would try to figure out what the true story might have been. Fabrication was just her way of life. If something happened and she was reporting it, she would likely make up something completely opposite. Like that Board Game they are so rapturous about over there. Making up a different ending."

"You know, Feron, after all these years I feel I haven't even scratched the surface of what you must have gone through. So, the man with no name in the book, was he based on the man on the bus?"

"The simple answer is yes. I didn't reveal it in any of my newspaper interviews about the book, because I thought it made a better story to leave out the mundane basis and stick with the fairy tale angle. See? I'm my mother's daughter, tell a different story whenever you get the chance. In the interviews I focused on how I came to write *Beast and Beauty*. I took this writing class at Columbia from a former superstar named Alexy Cuervo. Did you ever hear of him?"

"No, but I'm not really up on the literary scene. I didn't even know about *your* book, Feron."

"Well in 1958, while we were rooming together at Lovegood, he became an overnight prodigy with his first novel, *Nito's Garden*, which remains his only novel to date. He wrote it in Spanish and translated it into English, and both versions were published simultaneously. Which made a big stir in itself. It was a weird little novel about a boy who lives behind walls in a South American garden where nobody he comes in contact with reveals to him that he's a monster."

"That gives me the shivers. What kind of monster?"

"That's never exactly revealed because we're always inside his head. But slowly you realize that everyone he comes in contact with has some abnormality that makes them assume they are monsters. He sees them and hears them talk about themselves, but he never thinks he is one of them."

"But if we're inside his head, how do we know he's a monster?"

"Because it's an artful piece of work. The critics salivated over *Nito's Garden*. They called the author a boy genius, and lavished all their academic rhetoric on the little book. It was short, just over a hundred pages, with the imprint of a classy publisher. I looked up the old reviews before I signed up for Cuervo's class. Nito remembers watching conversations between his caretakers before he learned to talk. Then later he matches the meanings to the words and gestures. Cuervo even shows how this can happen by using the example of learning a foreign language. Some reviews said the novel was Caliban's version of *The Tempest* with Prospero and Miranda left out, or they speculated it was a clever allegory in which the young author had portrayed himself and his acquaintances. Others maintained that it wasn't a portrait of particular people but a brilliant aggregate of the vices and stupidities of an entire generation. It helped that Cuervo was an interesting mix—Chilean father and Russian mother—and was striking to look at. He still is today. He's small but perfectly formed with a classical face. Anyway, the celebrity of *Nito's Garden*, or *El Jardín de Nito*, as he prefers to call it, has paid his way through two decades of reputation and grants and lectureships. He's never written anything else. In our first class meeting, he told us to write anything we wanted as long as we didn't bore him with conventional narrative. And here was I, submitting revised pages of my marriage novel to him—a conventional narrative now titled *A Singular Romance*."

"Oh, Feron! What happened?"

"Surprisingly, he liked it. He said it could have been written a hundred years ago, but there was a strangeness about it and I should cultivate the strangeness. Then he said I ought to take a break and write something else. A fairy tale in modern dress. He sent me to the library to look up an expert work on folktales and see which fairy tale called out to me, but while I was actually walking to the library, the whole thing had already formed in my head. The story of a woman living safely in an enclosure with an outcast—another monster, if you like. And she finds herself loving him, as long as they don't go outside."

"I understood that! Many women have felt the same, don't you think?"

"Well, I was on fire. It was exactly what I wanted to write. I gave them names, but Cuervo convinced me to leave them nameless like in the fairy tales. He wouldn't let me name Chicago, either, but anyone who had been there could guess it. I wrote steadily for six weeks, even at work. When I wasn't editing some consultant's pitiful report, I just rolled in a piece of copy paper and typed away. Then everything happened really fast, which made me doubt I had anything to do with it. Cuervo showed it to his contacts, and I found myself with a publishing contract for the great sum of fifteen hundred dollars from the same classy house that had published *Nito's Garden*. When *Beast and Beauty* came out, I had reviews in the right places—again, I chalked it up to Cuervo's string-pulling, but he said that was the way it worked in New York, and I should leave off being a *buscador de alma*—a soul-searcher—and bask in the attention. He said it would be over soon enough. It lasted a little longer than he predicted because of women's lib. Beauty got all she could from Beast, he even liberated her in the right direction. Well, that was one opinion. Then there were some mean ones, which I seem to remember word-for-word. 'Either a cunningly-timed feminist fable or a handbook on how to use people.' And a headline: 'Who Is the Monster Here?' But it sold out its first printing, which was all of two thousand, and there was a film option, which got renewed twice, then abandoned. Oh, and the academics had their say, too. 'Ms. Hood is a practitioner of the grounded surreal.' Cuervo loved that one."

"I liked him. Your beast, I mean. I rooted for him. I knew early on, because you alternated their chapters, that she would probably leave him. I liked her, too, in a different way. She reminded me of you sometimes."

"In what way?"

"Her privateness. When he first sees her on the bus, she is spreading out her things in the seat beside her so no one would sit there. I could picture you doing that. That's not a criticism, Feron."

"What else?"

"Well, she has this complicated place in herself he can't go. I often felt that about you. I felt the way he did. Was he really an ex-convict from a military prison?"

"Yes, he had been released from Leavenworth the day of the evening I met him. But I kept everything generic like in the fairy tales. Specific places never named."

"What had he done?"

"Ran over his sergeant with a Jeep."

"Did he kill him?"

"He crippled him up pretty badly. If he had killed him, he would probably still be inside."

"I know I shouldn't ask, but did the physical part between you really happen?"

"Yes and no. He was unbelievably gallant, maybe unnaturally so. When he found out I was a virgin, he let us do everything but. Or, who knows, maybe he was impotent. In the novel, I let her talk him into it the night before she leaves."

"I cried at that part. When she says she wants him to leave his mark on her so later she wouldn't look back and think it never happened. Was he really an artist?"

"He was a medical illustrator. That was his job training in prison. But he was always drawing portraits of me. Once—I shouldn't tell you this—"

"Please do!"

"We were talking about my virginity and I said, 'I don't even know what it looks like, that thing.' And he sat down with a piece of paper and drew a vagina with the hymen covering it sort of like a cloud will halfway cover a moon."

"I wonder what happened to him. Do you know?"

"I tried to erase him happening to me until—well, until I transported him safely into a fairy tale and secured him there."

"Will you tell me his name?"

"I will not. You can't get all my secrets out of me, Merry."

"Does anyone ever get all of someone else's secrets out of them? I don't think so."

"What about you? Are you still writing?"

"Oh, yes, but I've given up hope of publishing anything again. But I did bring you . . ." From the canvas bag she pulled out a glossy magazine. "This is yours to keep. See? I even made the cover."

Rows of waving gold leaves stretched to the edges of the cover. Superimposed, in white letters edged in gold, was

The Tobacco Issue
The Slave Who Discovered Bright Leaf
by
Meredith Jellicoe

"Well, this sure looks like a publication to me," said Feron, turning to the page Merry had flagged with a sticky note.

"But it's just a state magazine. I didn't even get paid for it. I spent almost a year writing it, and then they cut one third of it. No, don't read it now, Feron. Not many outside the industry know the story of the slave who fell asleep and let the curing fires go out in the barn. His name was Stephen Slade, because slaves took their owners' last names, and he was nineteen years old. For such a mistake in the 1830, a slave could be skinned alive or sold to pick cotton. But he piled charred logs on top of the embers and rekindled a roaring fire, and the sudden intense heat dried all the moisture from the curing tobacco and produced a beautiful unsplotched gold leaf. His owner, Abisha Slade, turned that discovery into a formula for bright leaf tobacco, which caused the flue-cured revolution in the tobacco industry and made fortunes for the Duke and the R. J. Reynolds families."

"So at least Stephen didn't get skinned or sold to pick cotton."

"No, his owner gave him a small farm, and then the Civil War came and ruined Abisha Slade. Stephen raised tobacco on his small farm, lived as a free man until the age of ninety-three, and was buried on his own land."

"What a story. Why did they cut a third of it?"

"To make space for all the advertisements that keep the magazine in business. It *was* long. I counted the words when I was cutting it, and it was originally seven thousand words. I could have made it longer, there was so much material. I felt close to those times because they overlapped with Horace Lovegood's dates, and it was fascinating to compare the two stories going on at the same time in the same state."

"But why do you say you'll never publish again?"

"I'm afraid I let Mr. Sterling down after my fluke success with 'The Curing Barn.' I did send him two more stories, and he couldn't place them anywhere. Too long for the magazines, or nobody wants to read about farming, or they were inflammatory."

"Inflammatory?"

"Both stories are about the end of harvest banquet that growers throw for the seasonal workers. The first was from the point of view of the grower's daughter, who is upset because she helped prepare the food but wasn't allowed to eat with the workers. The second was the workers' version of the banquet. That was the one that was considered inflammatory because the growers came off looking like exploiters. Mr. Sterling asked would I consider cutting and changing some things and I said I'd try. But I lost interest and never did. Every year he sends me a Christmas card with a nice note. He always ends with, 'Remember, I am always here for you.'"

23

Mama's summer starts today!" Ritchie would always shout at winter solstice. Winter solstice had been four days ago. Some years it fell on December 21; on others, December 22. This was a December 22 year.

Just as 1958 had been.

At winter solstice, their mother's spirits began their seasonal climb out of what she called her Slough of Despond. By harvest time in autumn she had sunk pretty low, and November was the bottom. During November and early December, Ritchie kept reminding her, "Not much longer, Mama!"

That afternoon in 1958, when Mr. Jack showed up too early at the house and Merry had been making up the bed for Feron's visit, Ritchie had calculated they were probably in the air heading home from the Greenbrier. "Her mood is already better. I can hear her saying to Dad, 'Can't you already notice the difference in the light?'"

Merry chose to take the two-lane county road home and look at the way things used to be. The new truck's diesel engine hummed along on a baritone note.

"You drive a *truck*," Feron had said in the parking lot.

"It's what we always had. I'm used to having an empty body in case I want to pick up something and carry it somewhere else."

"It's very pretty. Is it hard to drive?"

"No. I've driven one all my life. This was a wedding present from . . . Jack. I probably wouldn't have picked red for myself, but it's a deep red, and he's had this beautiful logo painted on the cab doors."

"A leaf."

"A tobacco leaf."

"Hmm," said Feron. Whatever that meant.

Feron is the most complicated person I have ever known. That late afternoon when we were lying on the lawn in front of Lovegood and talking about the class poet of 1918, I was wondering what had happened to her, and Feron tapped her fingers in the grass, adding up the years. "She would be in her upper fifties. Her life would be—not over, but set, congealed—*like Jell-O."*

She compares things and makes you see more. She turns things around and lets you see another side.

And after she read my "Lingering on the Lawn" story before I turned it in to Miss Petrie. She said it was a success, but I needed to let the reader know right away it was set in 1918. Also she said "ordinary" didn't suit someone who was going to be the class poet. She suggested other words. "Optimistic might pack the most wallop, since she's going to end up dying," she said. That's a perfect example of the way Feron turns things around. Dean Fox said it was called irony.

And at the Algonquin when she was describing how she felt at the altar beside Will. "Everyone should get what they want at least once."

When I was making up my mind whether to marry Mr. Jack, I thought how happy it would make him, after all his years of feeling guilty, then doing it again, then going back to feeling guilty. Why not make things right?

As for myself, I think what turned the corner was rereading that Chekhov story, "At Home," about the young woman returning from her education to the family estate on the steppe. An eligible doctor wants to marry her, but she doesn't like him. Finally she accepts him. She sees how peaceful it would be to stop worrying over some vague future and accept the steppe as her destiny and make the most of what she can do at home.

Miss Petrie may not have been a complicated human, she was too tamped down, all her strength had been used up daring to live with the woman she loved. But she was complicated enough to recognize complicated writers. "She is leading us toward an acceptance of being left in uncertainty," Feron had pointed out.

And today, describing walking to the library to get started on Cuervo's fairy tale assignment and having the story she wanted to write form in her head as she walked: about a woman who found she could love a man as long as they didn't go outside.

Her flashes of insight have influenced my life—or revealed something I would never have thought of myself.

Mama, in her dark days, had her complicated side. She never spoke of what went on inside her Slough of Despond, though Ritchie pestered and pestered her for details. In her dark days she would go up to that old loft room and sleep under some blankets. Did tobacco farming bore her? Did she regret quitting college to marry Daddy? Had she fallen out of love with Daddy? If so, had he known it?

Ritchie would definitely be a complicated person today. He had been growing into it. Maybe he'd already become one when he died in that combat mission.

Feron hadn't changed much. She still had that look of being at odds with someone or something. If you were being critical, you might say that age had frozen that expression in place. She had let her hair grow long and wore it pulled back severely from her face, which made her look schoolteacherish. Merry had been surprised that Feron hadn't dressed for their lunch, but maybe she was taking a vacation from having to dress for her job every day.

The story about the man on the bus had been sort of what Merry had assumed might have happened. But somehow the story about the drawing of the hymen had shocked her more than young Feron having lived with (the nameless convict) for more than a week.

Feron's first cousin on the card. She would call him and ask his advice. Feron said she had inherited her uncle's house, and the cousin had advised making some improvements so she could charge a higher rent.

Maybe, now that Feron owned a house in Pullen, they would live close to each other when they were old. She could imagine it. They would take turns driving to each other's houses and comparing the complaints of their aging bodies. It would be a long, long friendship, catching up on each other's stories over decades.

"You can't get all my secrets out of me, Merry," Feron had warned her.

"Does anyone ever get all of someone else's secrets out of them?" She had countered. "I don't think so."

And I don't.

24

Buttner House
11 Park Crescent
Benton Grange, N.C.

December 26, 1979

Dear Merry,

I read your wonderful article as soon as I got back to Blanche's house. She was out all afternoon—her church has a gift-giving day for the poor the day after Christmas—so I sat on her glassed-in sun porch and read "The Slave Who Discovered Bright Leaf."

It reads like a story. I was hooked by the first sentence when he smells the last thing in the world he would wish to smell, a fire gone out, and realizes he has done the unforgivable, fallen asleep on the job. You got inside his head—his fear, his panic, his envisioning all too well his probable punishments, and then his wild inspiration about the logs. And you stayed with him till he was dying, a free man on his own farm where he is buried today.

You did that with "Lingering on the Lawn." You got inside the girl who would become the class poet and stayed with her till the end, when she is delirious and thinks she's back on the lawn at school with her friend. You stayed in there right up to her death and followed her over the threshold, just as you did with him. (I'm glad the magazine editors had the sense to leave that part in.) Do you remember when we were walking back to Lovegood with our stale Tootsie Pops and I said not to let it go to your head, but you'd carried it one step further than Chekhov went with "Typhus," because in that case the soldier recovers?

When Alexy Cuervo sent me off to look into the morphology of folktales, he said he was being like the person in the tales who sets the hero a task. That person is known as "the Donor."

Let me set you a task, Merry. Mail a copy of the magazine to your agent in New York. Also send him your uncut manuscript. Tell him you have been engaged with this for a while and still feel there's more to uncover about this interesting life. Ask him what he thinks. Would it make a novel? I think it would.

It was great seeing you today. I am glad you still consider me your friend.

Love,

Feron,

Your "Donor" and friend

Now, to seal the envelope of Blanche's elegant gray notepaper and lick a stamp, all of which lay ready for use in the guest room desk drawer.

And run downstairs with this letter and push her good deed through the slot of the sweetgrass mail basket on the console table by the front door.

It's time to get out of here.

She had sounded this inner alarm in these environs before. The evening she and Uncle Rowan were in Howard Johnson's, and an elderly couple with a serene middle-aged daughter came in. "That's General Steed and his wife. And that's their daughter, Marguerite, who has one of the finest collections of dolls in the world." He went over to their booth to say hello, leaving Feron alone with her wake-up call. *Surely as a young woman, Marguerite Steed must have had other plans for herself than becoming a doll collector still living with her parents.*

After she had gone upstairs with Marguerite yesterday and been introduced to the "personal" dolls, which were much more interesting, Feron couldn't decide whether Marguerite was content with her controlled environs, or whether she was biding her time until her eventual breakout.

Feron had spent the first six months of her young widowhood in this same upstairs room of Blanche's stately house, looking down on the shady walled garden guarded by its gloomy statues. Sat at this same desk under the same lamp and jotted fast pages in a notebook. Rushing to "get down" Will as he faded, before important things drained through the holes and the whole marriage seemed like a dream.

Soon realizing that complete sentences and paragraphs and chronological order were not her friends, she had resorted to snatching whatever rose to the surface with a description, an ellipsis, a shard of dialogue catching something Will had said or taught her during walks under the Northumberland skies.

Hail like big white marbles on Haworth Heath . . . then wet snowflakes . . . then sun emerges FOR ONE MINUTE *out of a boiling mass of gray and purple clouds.*

F: Think of all the stuff that *isn't* in Wuthering Heights . . .

w: Think of all the patterns that *are* in it.

F: Why did medieval artists want to be anonymous?

w: They thought of themselves as copiers or illustrators of something that had gone before. They thought it was a higher order of art than trying to be merely oneself and "invent" something new.

Dog misericord in Lincoln Cathedral.

w: The medieval mind focused on the essence of a thing, the modern mind wants to label it. The carver who did this wanted to capture the dogness of a dog, the way a dog would move and act. We would first have to categorize it as "a spaniel," "a retriever," "a collie."

F: If you were a medieval carver, how would you express my essence?

w: I would start with your wary grace of moving. Or your graceful wariness of moving, I'm not sure which. It was one of the first things I noticed about you.

F: Why "wary"?

w: Like someone anticipating a lightning strike or preparing for an assault, but what I love about you is, you keep marching on, your face revealing nothing.

w's SMELL: starched cloth, grass, salt on his neck, soap in the hollow of his ear . . . the arousing gaminess of his underarms.

The curiosity that goes with love. YOU CAN NEVER KNOW ENOUGH *about the other person.*

*   *   *

"You looked like someone trying to be invisible." That was how Beast, aka Dale Flowers, had put it when they were lying together in the rented room in Chicago, exchanging their first impressions of each other.

("Will you tell me his name?" Merry had asked.

"I will not.")

She had said too much, more than she meant to. How did it happen, how had she slipped beyond where she meant to stop? A spike of uncharacteristic generosity (I will surprise this old friend by offering up something really special)? Or did I fall into that old trap writers are always falling into when someone asks, Did that really happen? If you say, No, I made all of it up, it's probably a lie, or a partial lie. If you say, Some of it happened, but I changed some of it around—well, if you say it often enough, one day you may actually lose track of what happened and what didn't. She hadn't reached that point yet, but had certainly breached her self-imposed boundaries.

To give of your private self is dangerous, and you usually regret it.

Did she regret it today?

Yes, yes, yes.

Time to get out of here.

Back to the inconspicuousness at MacFarlane & Company, where she could exist in plain sight, hoard her creative energies, and collect benefits. Back to her present Park Avenue residence of a MacFarlane manager on leave, where she could postpone acquiring things and feel like an untethered artist floating above the high buildings in the night sky. Back to supporters like Cuervo, who had said, "I can tell you what you want to know about yourself. Let me know when you're ready to hear it."

PART FOUR

25

1984

Winifred Darden would say, "The secret acronym for Lovegood's extraordinary endowment fund is 'G.E.T.' As in 'get.' Gratitude, Enclosure, and Tradition. When Lovegood found a place for me, the Dardens, freed of their burden, pooled their resources and contributed abundantly. When girls leave and make something of themselves, they and their kin generously remember Lovegood.

"Now, Enclosure is somewhat suspect these days. But it's absolutely crucial to the mix, because parents still want it. To know your daughters are safely 'removed from strife / where they may seek the mental life,' to quote from our pageant song. Or to put it a different way, think of that infamous fraternity song about dating prospects, whose naughty first two lines concerning the rival colleges in town are followed by 'And LOVE good girls.'

"As for Tradition, that's our ace in the hole. It's like our Doric columns: a classic emblem for donors."

During Susan Fox's early-morning walks across Lovegood's campus, which under her leadership had expanded to twice its size, the late Winifred Darden's informative voice with its gentle humor often kept her company. How wrong she had been upon meeting the dorm mistress, a walking compendium of Lovegood's past, and thinking, oh dear, I'll have to fight this one every step of the way to get anything new done!

Susan Fox dressed for her early walks, and waking students looking out their windows could follow the constitutional of the Dean Emerita, clad in a shawl in cool weather, a cape in winter, a light jacket on the warm mornings.

For the first time since the World War II years, Lovegood College had empty rooms. It was losing prospective students to the four-year womens' colleges in the state. Four-year status must come soon now, and even the die-hard traditionalists were coming around. It is high time, thought the dean, that Lovegood was holding its first baccalaureate ceremony on the lawn. Girls—women!—of twenty-one wearing the green gowns and receiving their diploma from the new president. Who was hardly new anymore, having arrived in 1977.

If anyone had asked her, she could have suggested which new building should be the junior residence hall and which the senior. Regarding suggestions, one must be judicious and wait until one is asked. When the old board members had been planning her on-site retirement, one of them had said, half in jest, "You'll be sort of like the queen." After she found herself with the leisure to read books again, she had looked into both Elizabeths, the present one fourteen years her junior, and found they had vastly more influence.

And then there was the step after that. Vassar College had opened its doors to men in 1969, while she was still dean. That would mean some interior renovations in Lovegood's bathrooms. Again, wait until one is asked. And when and if one is, the term is *urinals*.

Winifred Darden had been alive when the talk of the dean's "queenship" was in the works.

"Winifred, why I am being offered this? Has it happened to anyone before me?"

"Lovegood has never had a dean like you, Susan. We couldn't believe our luck when you agreed to come. I understand perfectly well why they are doing over Dinwiddie House to keep you on the premises. You are classic, like our Doric columns. Seeing you around will set an example for our students and be an incentive for donors."

"A presiding ghost of old Lovegood values?"

"Regarding *those*, we will need all the help we can get. Do you remember when you first came? You would say, 'The world is fast-changing all around us, Winifred. Who knows where things will be in the next ten years?' And now we're approaching the twenty-year mark. Tell me truly, Susan, did you imagine so *much* acceleration, so much change?"

"I can't say that I did. I anticipated some things that never came to pass and failed to sense some that were breathing down my neck. But that's the nature of change, isn't it?"

Winifred would have liked President Brook. (Since he had come to them from his last school as "president," they voted unanimously to retire the title of dean.) Everyone liked him. Lovegood girls— Lovegood *women*—had crushes on him. The Dean Emerita liked him. Devlin Brook was a worthy successor. Carrying on her "lucky to get" qualification, he had been president of a small prep school for boys that everyone had heard of. He had four daughters of his own, he had told the search committee that already favored him, "so I am no stranger to the ways of young ladies." He was a southerner, which was a plus. And a Catholic, which put off several board members until a prevailing one said: "Oh come on, haven't we already been through that with President Kennedy?"

Coming from a boys' academy, President Brook had known about the Anne C. Stouffer Foundation's visionary plan, started by the Reynolds tobacco heiress in 1967, for placing young black men in southern prep schools. He had looked around and discovered the Fairlie Foundation, which, since the early seventies, had been enrolling young black women in state colleges. Lovegood opened places for two of them, but at the last minute they opted for the four-year colleges. She herself would have done the same: Why get settled into one place that had misgivings about your being there, and then after two years start all over again battling a second school's misgivings? But for a while, there had been excitement. Even the holdout board members had been persuaded. Here was Lovegood's chance to set an example of liberal-mindedness (and become eligible for many of the new state grants).

At the end of his first year, President Brook had called on her in her new residence, a block from campus. "Dean Fox, I've come to invite you to be my accessory in fund-raising. I'll do the clubs and the speeches and the footwork and take care of the mailings, if you will host the dinners and teas at Dinwiddie House. If you are game."

"Would I have to prepare the food?"

"Oh, no, no. That will all be catered, and our honor students will be asked to serve."

"In that case," she paused to bestow a touch of ceremony, "I accept with pleasure. But please let me help with the mailings, which I can do quite comfortably from home."

Their combined efforts—yes, she would accept her share of the credit—on behalf of Lovegood's most ambitious Capital Campaign—had surpassed their expectations.

Speaking of the "G" in G.E.T., Feron Hood had published another novel, *Mr. Blue*, and had contributed to the capital campaign fund. She continued to send an annual donation to the Sophie Sewell Hood scholarship established when she published *Beast and Beauty*.

My years at Lovegood shine bright as ever. There, for the first time in my life I felt secure enough to try my wings. It

was while reading a story of Merry's in a bathroom stall that
I decided I wanted to become a writer.

Susan Fox had been honored to be the recipient of such a
personal revelation, even after she came across it in the library,
almost word for word, in a newspaper interview. She wished she had
been secure enough in those first years at Lovegood to seat Feron
across from her in the famous Saxon Hall armchair (which now
graced her study at Dinwiddie House) and follow her former
commanding instincts: "What was it like, to sleep outside in that
Chicago park? How did you keep warm? What were your thoughts?"

However, the initial Lovegood years were her "humbled" years,
when she was seeking to build a new life from the ground up after
bringing the roof down on herself at Saxon Hall. With the young
Feron she had stopped at: "You can count on a discretionary ear in
this office if you ever feel the need to say more about that stressful
period of your life."

Having later read and pondered *Beast and Beauty*, she was fairly
certain the runaway girl never did sleep in a Chicago park, but
under the blankets with an ex-convict, now safely fictionalized into
the sympathetic character of a beast.

I could have gone to jail like the headmistress of the Madeira
School, she thought. Jean Harris was fifty-seven when she shot her
lover. I was forty-two when I broke his windows and bit the policeman,
and was carried away screaming. What made the difference? If I had
gone up to his campus apartment packing a pistol? Not my style. Just
as I never would have penned such obscene foolishness as the famous
Scarsdale Letter. Her rabid handwriting was a neurotic giveaway.
When I told President Brook to leave the mailings to me, I meant
handwritten letters with real ink to five thousand former students and
friends of Lovegood. And as I did my stint (thirty each afternoon in
my study at Dinwiddie House), I would call to mind how many

recipients would recognize the writing on the envelope with the *Esse Quam Videri* crest. Mrs. Camilla Cherrington, my savior in ninth grade, gave me my distinctive cursive. I entered her class writing in a stiff upright with unconnected letters and left it with a facsimile of her elegant, loopy slant because I wanted to copy everything about her. Some people, if they are lucky, meet an early savior who makes all the difference. Does anyone remember me as an early savior? Did Jean Harris have one? Was she one to any of her girls?

Feron Hood's *Mr. Blue* was a short, peculiar work, not as likable as *Beast and Beauty*, nor as satisfactory a read. Though it was beautifully produced, this time with evocative watercolor illustrations that were more conclusive than the story itself. The jacket copy presented the novel as "Feron Hood's feminist retelling of the ancient tale of 'Bluebeard.'" In Feron's story it is the woman who insists on keeping a secret room. The reader meets her as a child of eight, opening the door to Mr. Blue, who has been summoned by her dying father to take over the farm. She is rude to him, tells him to wait outside, and shuts the door on him. The story was set on a large farm, crop unspecific, but the golden leaves waving in the summer sun suggested tobacco. We are in the mind of Mr. Blue, having just had the door shut in his face. He knows the little girl will be made to invite him in, just as she will have to learn to value him, "fear him a little, but respect all the necessary things he could do." She will grow up, still being proud, but the day might come, he thinks, when that proud little face would have to open and let him in. The viewpoints are shared between the two major characters, as in *Beast and Beauty*, and the reader is privy to the imperious little girl's thoughts as she grows into an imperious young woman. She finally accepts Mr. Blue as her husband because she feels it is her fate just as the farmland is her destiny. They will farm it together. She often retreats to her single third-floor room, telling him it is just a place she has to go in order to put herself back together. The room, once a hayloft, is ugly and bare except for an old armchair losing its stuffing, a small table, and a folded blanket. In the illustration you can see the seams where the hayloft opening has been closed in to hold a single window looking out on the fields. Mr. Blue accepts her bid for privacy and never ascends to the third floor. They endure and seem to grow as a couple. Only after his wife's death does Mr. Blue finally enter the room. He is shocked by its bare ugliness. He can't imagine how she would have used this room to put herself together again. He is not only bewildered but bereft, having lost not only his wife but their infant child.

Had *Mr. Blue* incorporated some facts from the life of Merry Jellicoe Rakestraw? The last time Dean Fox had seen Merry, when she accompanied a new student to Lovegood, she announced she had recently married Mr. Rakestraw, who had been her father's manager for many years. But Merry was still alive. She had contributed handsomely to the capital campaign fund, on a check bearing the names of both husband and wife, and, like Feron, had sent annual sums since then.

As she had done with *Beast and Beauty*, Susan Fox withheld final judgment until Eloise Sprunt (still math and science) had read it.

"I loved the illustrations," said Eloise. "Why do books for grownups stop offering pictures? I liked Mr. Blue best. It's the man who gets abandoned in both novels. Of course, in this book, she didn't leave him, she died giving birth, but still . . ."

"Feron wrote that she was uncertain about the ending. She was warned that second novels were destined to disappoint. She knows an older writer of a wildly successful first novel who refused to write a second one."

"After I'd read it, you know what crossed my mind, Susan?"

"Please, tell me."

"I thought, Bluebeard never made an appearance in this tale. It could have equally been called *Mrs. Blue*. The story is about something else altogether."

"How perceptive! I think you are right. You know, he was generous and kind, the way the man was in *Beast and Beauty*. The men in both novels come off better than the women."

"What will you tell her when you write back?"

"Well, I might begin by stealing your comment about grownups needing pictures, too. And I'm going to say I liked the character of Mr. Blue, because, like you, I did. And I might say that although *Mr. Blue* is a more *complex* story than *Beast and Beauty*, its folklore frame suited it. And I will say I am very much looking forward to her next book."

26

It was new in the window of one of those pricey Madison Avenue boutiques that Feron passed on her way to work every day. Center stage between a pair of nineteenth-century jeweled opera glasses and a Chinese porcelain dragon rode a rat in formal morning dress whipping a galloping horse already frothing at the mouth. The rat's yellow buckteeth were bared. Everything was meticulously made: the top hat, the English saddle, the dress shoes in the stirrups, the soft gray vest under the tail coat, the tumbling froth. You even saw that it was a male horse with everything intact. Horse and rider together couldn't be more than six inches high, about the same in length. If Marguerite Steed were standing next to her, she would be able to identify the materials that went into the clothes and explain what hidden structure supported their frenzied flight. On the rucked-up gray velvet beneath the figures was a calling-card-sized price tag in feathered calligraphy.

Rat Race
$2,500

It was the first thing Feron yearned to buy for herself since arriving in New York fifteen years ago. The formal bucktoothed rider and his frothing stallion profoundly impressed her. Constructing each careful item, the dollmaker must have chuckled wickedly. She could see it as one of the rare personal touches she might allow herself in her MacFarlane flat-sits.

Then she imagined sending it back to Marguerite Steed with her cousin Thad, who was in town for a Realtor's convention and was taking her out to lunch today. ("Tell Marguerite this is for her upstairs collection.")

She had been more vexed with herself than disappointed by the reception of *Mr. Blue*, which didn't fare all that badly. It got more attention in "serious" journals and sold more copies because *Beast and Beauty* had given her an outré reputation of sorts. The critics who liked to declare a book "enigmatic" had plenty to work with in *Mr. Blue*.

"You can afford one baffling book," her editor had said. "The students like to carry them across campus—face out. Didn't you do that?"

"I remember doing it with *Nightwood*," said Feron, "and never reading it."

"What? You didn't read *Nightwood*?"

He loved to catch her out like that.

Almost all the reviewers mentioned the art. One of them advised the reader to study the illustrations for the meaning of the story. One quipster declared that the illustrations alone were worth the price of the book.

Feron had prodded herself into writing her second novel. The contemporary writers she measured herself against produced a new one every two or three years. Moreover, she had been goaded once again into competition with her old roommate, Merry. Good old competition! After their lunch at the Neuse River Café, Feron had driven back to Blanche's and read Merry's striking article in the state magazine and hurried off a letter to her friend, assigning Merry the "task" of making it into a novel. That had been in 1979, three years after *Beast and Beauty*. Feron had feared that if Merry still wrote the way she had at Lovegood, line after line with her busy pen, Merry might be halfway through her novel about the slave before Feron even came up with a topic for her second novel.

Her editor had perked up when Feron suggested she try a second modern fairy tale. He had more than recovered his minuscule advance on *Beast and Beauty*, what with its flush of notoriety and the two movie options, though neither was renewed. "If you had gotten out there yourself a little more to promote *Beast and Beauty*, it might have helped," the editor scolded. But he doubled her advance for the proposed *Mr. Blue*, a sum that would have covered the price of "Rat Race" with five hundred dollars left over.

"However, you've got your work cut out for you. Giving a woman Bluebeard's role hasn't been tried, not that I know of. Though it's possible that all the bodies of the writers who tried and failed are piled in a bloody heap behind a locked door."

The editor always enjoyed sending her off on this note of half challenge, half put-down. "But beware," he went on, "the Bluebeard premise might not give itself up gracefully to the gender switch. Do women crave the same kinds of powers men do? Do they have the same things to hide? Are women afraid of the things men are? Are men as curious about the same things women are? I'll be curious to see what you make of your modern tale."

Alexy Cuervo, having transcended her initial assessment of him as her "evil genius," had become her adviser and best friend. "It's time for you to get an agent. One who will mark up the publisher's boilerplate contract and insist on retaining your film rights."

"An agent would just shave off fifteen or twenty percent for himself."

"Who is speaking now, the tightwad or the procrastinator?"

"Probably both. Besides, you got me all the connections I needed better than any agent could have."

"I won't be around forever."

"Well, neither will I, for that matter."

"Look, sometimes the art prevails, sometimes the marketplace does. If you're lucky, there is a fortunate blend."

"Is *Mr. Blue* more art or more marketplace?"

"*Quién sabe.* The readers who liked *Beast and Beauty* will rejoice: 'Ah, here is another fairy tale by Feron Hood. And, look, this one has these beautiful illustrations.'"

"I have a tiny suspicion my editor wanted to promote this artist."

"His style matches your story. His watercolor figures remind me of Charles Demuth."

"Who is Charles Demuth?"

"A late nineteenth-century painter. He illustrated Henry James's *The Turn of the Screw*. He also painted many sailors and circus performers and scenes in public baths. He was a fairly happy homosexual, which was rare in his times."

"Yes, well, I wish I were happier with my ending."

"How would you end it now?"

"That's the thing. I don't know. I was so caught up in being clever and reversing the tale and having it be the woman who forbids the man to go into the secret room."

"You succeeded."

"But she *doesn't* forbid him, she just says it's her private place, and he never goes in the room until after she's dead."

"So you ended up writing a tale that's about a marriage discovering itself, not bloody murder or serial killing."

"But I shortchanged her. It's exactly how those conventional nineteenth-century novels you're always sneering at would have done it. If the woman asserted herself or asked for too much, she had to die."

"Why don't you write a second version?"

"What for? Who would want it?"

"Perhaps nobody. That is to say, nobody who would pay you money to publish it."

"Then what's the point?"

"The point, my dear, is there is the artist and there is the career. If a writer wishes to have a career, he must publish a second book in order to publish a third, and so on, to build his oeuvre. It stands to reason some books in the oeuvre will surpass the others. Every great writer has duds in his oeuvre."

"But you made a splash with your one book and stopped."

"*Nito's Garden* was a prodigy, like myself. We were one bright package that exploded like fireworks on the zeitgeist."

"But why did you stop there? Why didn't you write your second book?"

"I had written my way out of my desperate place. *Nito's Garden* is one of those novels that is in itself a testimony of its need to exist. Nito saved me. Had I not been able to make Nito exist, I would have committed suicide."

"You said, 'if a writer wishes to have a career,' but how can someone not have such a wish?"

"By choosing not to be sponsored."

"What is *that* supposed to mean?"

"You know what a sponsor is, yes?"

"You were my sponsor, right?"

"And the publisher was your sponsor, the business act of the production and publication were your sponsors, and, after that, you are sponsored by the booksellers and buyers, the readers, the reviewers, the admirers and detractors, *ad infinitum*. Sponsors are all the influences outside yourself, or between you and your work."

"Are you saying I could have refused sponsors and stashed my work away in a drawer, like Emily Dickinson or somebody, and died unknown? Which I'm likely to do anyway. But what made *you* seek a sponsor? You said that *writing* Nito's story kept you from committing suicide. But you did write it and translate it, and you still hadn't committed suicide. So what made you need to wrap it up in that package and send it off to a publisher?"

Cuervo, bilingual man of many words, silently opened his palms in a "who knows?" gesture. They were in his Greenwich Village apartment, which he called his beach house, because if you stuck your neck out the window far enough, you could see the Hudson River. Since his debilitating bout with acute bronchitis, he wore woolen gloves with the fingers cut out when he was at home because he claimed he was always cold.

27

Feron had asked Cousin Thad to pick her up at her place of work, and there was a visitor's badge awaiting him downstairs at the entrance desk guarding MacFarlane's bank of elevators. She wanted her colleagues to see this good-looking, soft-spoken southern gentleman who belonged to her family.

She knew she was looked upon as an oddity at MacFarlane & Company. When she had applied for the proofreader's job advertised in the *Times* and the *Wall Street Journal* fifteen years ago, she listed her college degree in English from a good university, so far everything normal, but what made her an anomaly, and possibly worked in her favor, was the fact that she had checked the "widow" box. How had it come to pass that she was a twenty-three-year-old widow alone in Manhattan?

She was hired on the spot by the woman who interviewed her, the same woman who later offered the promotion out of the Tandem Room, where Feron and Shawna Samuels had sat congenially across from each other, taking turns reading the consultants' reports aloud in their proofreaders' lingo ("up" for capitals, "down" for lowercase, "point" for period, "com" for comma). Shawna Samuels had fallen through the cracks at some point, and Feron periodically tortured herself with Merry's question at the Algonquin: "But couldn't you and your friend still meet?"

Cousin Thad arrived punctually at noon. Feron luxuriated in leaving her office on the arm of a handsome, smartly dressed cousin, his hair a distinguished silver now, having introduced him to her colleagues.

In the taxi, he said they were going to his favorite Neapolitan restaurant in Times Square. "Naples was my last tour of duty before I retired. I hope you like Italian food."

"I like every country's food. When I started at MacFarlane's, my co-proofreader and I always ordered in, which was on the house. We had an array of menus: Indian, Chinese, Italian, and she guided me to adventurous items I would never have tried on my own."

"You have quite a setup, Feron. I hadn't realized my cousin was a New York executive."

"I'm hardly that."

"You have a posh office looking out over the water, and how many people working for you?"

"Twelve at present. The number expands with the company. I'm top dog in the editorial department; we even have translators on our staff. If any consultant's report isn't nigh well flawless when we've all finished going over it, the powers on the top floor send it back to my desk with a red flag."

"But when do you write your books?"

"Oh, at night. My day job and my night job draw from different sources of energy."

"That's amazing."

"Many writers do it. Some famous examples are Wallace Stevens with his lifelong insurance job and T. S. Eliot with Lloyd's Bank."

"I recognize T. S. Eliot, but I don't think I've heard of Mr. Stevens."

"He was already a famous poet while he was alive. After he won the Pulitzer, Harvard offered him a teaching job, but he turned them down because he didn't want to give up being vice president of Hartford Accident and Indemnity."

"How do you know all this stuff, Feron?"

"I study other writers to compare my progress against theirs. It's mostly just a matter of jealousy and ambition."

As she asked him to do, Thad ordered for them both, speaking Italian with the waiter. It was peak season for tomatoes, so they shared a caprese rustica salad and, once he made sure she had nothing against squid, a plate of calamari fritti. After which they split the baked ziti Napolitano and the yellowfin tuna with rigatone and alfredo sauce. The waiter suggested the house Chianti.

"You drink wine, don't you, Feron? I thought so. You asked for the spiked eggnog the day we met at the Steeds' Christmas party."

"Did you learn Italian in Naples, or did you speak it before?"

"I arranged to have lessons as soon as I was assigned my command. The navy encourages service members and their families to learn the country's language."

"Did your wife learn it, too?"

"Lou takes a pass on languages, but she can ask for everything she wants with those little phrase books."

"I thought of Marguerite Steed just this morning. I was passing a shop that had a rat doll riding a horse doll, and I considered buying it for her collection and asking you to take it back with you. Then I looked at the price—it was called 'Rat Race,' and it was twenty-five hundred dollars."

"Holy moly, was it made of gold?"

"No, just cloth and other things. Marguerite would have known. It was a work of art."

"Marguerite and I were in high school together."

"But you look much younger. Was she collecting dolls then?"

"She didn't start that till later. In high school she caused quite a scandal in Pullen. She and the music teacher ran away together. Marguerite was a lovely young girl."

"What happened?"

"The general dispatched a search and rescue mission, and they routed them out in no time. Marguerite went back to school, and the music teacher was run out of town."

"I wonder if Marguerite still carries a torch for him and that's why she never married."

"The music teacher was a woman. But, you know, I've sometimes wondered myself."

"How do you like the calamari? Oh, good. Lou says it's like chewing a mouthful of rubber bands. Feron, your exemplary young tenants are moving out at the end of their lease. He's being transferred out of state. That would give us several months to repaint and do the floors, and I have an idea about Great-Granny Hood's old chicken coop where she would threaten to send grandchildren to spend the night. I know a person isn't supposed to ask about a woman's age or her bank account, but if you have anything socked away, it would be a good investment to turn that old coop into a smart little guest house or studio. The foundations are solid. I could get a few bids for you if you're interested."

"I have a friend who calls me a tightwad because I have yet to rent my own place here in the city. MacFarlane's has this setup where personnel can house-sit apartments of other personnel. First I thought it was going to be a temporary arrangement, but the longer I practiced it, the more attracted I became to that way of life and the more in demand I was. It kept me from acquiring things—books, furniture, what people now call 'collectibles'—like the rat riding his horse. If the price tag had said two hundred and fifty instead of twenty-five hundred, I might have rushed right in and bought it—if I'd had my own apartment. To answer your question, yes, I do have a bit socked away."

"Go ahead and do it? Is that what you're telling me?"

"You said it was a good investment."

"You know, when I was in my early teens, before I fell in with the wrong crowd, I had this fantasy of stowing away on a freighter and becoming so indispensable they kept me on. In my fantasy I sailed round and round the world. So I can appreciate the attraction of the unbound life."

"But you *did* sail round and round the world."

"Yeah, well. As a member of the Sixth Fleet and head of an expanding family on the move. Next time you come, you'll have to visit our house. It's chock-full of Lou's collectibles from all over the globe. When will you be coming south again? Have you been back since Blanche Buttner dumbfounded us by bringing home a husband from a cruise?"

"I did go back. The Christmas following their marriage I went back, but it was a huge miscalculation on both sides. I thought Blanche would be hurt if I didn't come, and she thought I would be hurt if she didn't invite me. So the four of us smoldered for three days, and then I changed my ticket and left early."

"The four?"

"Orrin's daughter, the dreadful Daphne. She was staying in my old guest suite, which she considered her quarters, and I was put in a room with a bath down the hall. Daphne hated me on sight. No, she must have hated me from the moment she heard of my existence. She's a person my age, an unhappy, resentful woman, and I guess she looked on me as a financial threat, even though the married couple had signed all kinds of 'postnups,' since they had already been married by the captain of the cruise ship. But don't let me get started on Dreadful Daphne. If I do come back, it'll be to Pullen, not to Benton Grange."

"Why don't you fly down after we've done the floors and the painting. You can sleep in your own house, and we can go over designs for the renovated chicken coop."

"Maybe I will. Not for long. Maybe for the Labor Day weekend, would that be enough time for you to get everything done?"

"Plenty of time. You know who's going to be thrilled to see you again? She talks about you every time I go over to Jellicoe Farm."

"You mean Merry?"

"Who else?"

"How often do you go?"

"As often as I can dream up a business excuse, something I can help them with. Have you met him?"

"No. The last time I saw Merry was the day after Christmas, in 1979. We met at the Neuse River Café, and she announced she had just married Mr. Jack. What's he like?"

"Please. Don't ask me that. I couldn't be objective. He has to be in his seventies, and he's like this old cowboy in faded jeans. And I've *never seen him sit down*."

"You once called her 'that sublime little lady.'"

"Cousin, you've got my number. I'm a victim of unrequited love. Of course, I couldn't imagine life without Lou in it, and Merry seems to dote on her old cowboy. But I like to think she's aware of my hopeless condition and doesn't mind."

"I wrote her a long letter after we had lunch at the Neuse River Café, suggesting she make a novel out of this piece about the slave who discovered bright leaf tobacco. She answered right back, saying it was a great idea and she was going to do it. So I guess I was imagining her down there writing away, and then I waited to hear how she was getting on, only the months went by and now it's . . ." Feron tapped her fingers on the table. "Oh God, it's nine years later, and it was my turn to write."

"You didn't hear about the child?"

"What child?"

"They lost a little boy."

"You mean a miscarriage?"

"No, they had him for about three months. He was in and out of the hospital. A tiny heart that hadn't developed right, even the experts up at Duke couldn't fix it. They both were devastated, but she had to act strong to keep Jack from destroying himself."

"How long ago was that?"

"Let's see. He was born early spring in 1986 and died in early summer."

"How strange she never let me know."

"Well, Cousin, letting nine years go by without answering her last letter might have something to do with it. But she's very loyal to you, you know. Whenever she mentions you, it is always with affection and excitement, as though she might have heard from you the week before."

28

June 12, 1987

Dear Feron,

Last night I dreamed of you. We were lying on Lovegood's
lawn and I was telling you a dream I'd just had. Your expression as you listened to me was as clear to me as if you'd really
been there.

I was telling you how my dream opened with my brother
Ritchie approaching me out of a fog. Then the fog became
the floor of a hospital. Ritchie was wearing his air force
uniform with his pilot's wings. I never saw him wearing it,
but he had sent a picture the day he shipped out.

He was carrying something in his arms, and when he got
closer, I saw it was a little boy. I started running toward them,
but Ritchie put up a warning hand and said, "Stop right
there, Merry Grape, this is a hazardous maneuver and we
have to do it strictly by the rules."

The rules were that I was allowed to look at the boy
without speaking or moving. I have never looked at anything
so hard. I forced myself not to cry because the tears would

blur what I wanted to see. It was Paul, our Paul, but older than when I'd last seen him alive.

Ritchie said, "He can't look back at you, because he doesn't know you're there." Then Ritchie started walking away backward down the hospital floor. I started to call out, please stay a little longer, but I wasn't allowed to speak. As they disappeared into the fog, Ritchie called, "He's with me, Merry Grape. This is—" The voice was fading, but I think he said, "This is the way we do it," but I couldn't be sure.

Now comes the second part, Feron, the part about you. We were lying in the grass, "lingering on the lawn," remember? And I had told you my dream. This is the first time I have ever had a dream within a dream. Have you ever had one? In my dream you had stopped looking at me and were busy digging out something from the grass with your finger.

I started to cry.

"What did it mean, Feron? It's got to mean something."

And you pulled out this piece of jewelry from your digging. It looked like a large medieval brooch. You said, "Don't you recognize this, Merry?" "No, what is it?" "It's an award of recognition from Maud Petrie," you said. Then you leaned forward and kissed me. "I will tell you what your dream means," you said. "Paul is inside your reference aura, and once someone is in it, they are in it forever."

Paul Jellicoe Rakestraw
March 7, 1986–June 12, 1986

Today is the first anniversary of the last day Paul could look back at us. It was in the hospital. He was weak but had a little color in his face, and we were about to get down on our knees and thank God for letting him come through the surgery. Then as quick as someone putting out the light, he was gone. They had warned us it was a high-risk operation. Even if it had succeeded, there would have been more operations in early childhood. He had what is called hypoplastic left heart syndrome, which means that the entire left side of his heart was underdeveloped. His little casket is buried next to Ritchie in the Jellicoe family cemetery.

After I woke from my dream within a dream, I clung to what you'd said in the dream about "reference auras." It seemed to point to a way of trying to live with this unbearable absence. Once someone is in your reference aura, they stay there forever. Couldn't forever include after death? I mean, if someone has died, they are still in your reference aura and so continue to grow in your heart like a living person. That little boy Ritchie was carrying in his arms was about a year old. "This is the way we do it," Ritchie said in the dream, and perhaps this is the way to do it.

The first time I heard of reference auras was when we were meeting at the Algonquin, our first meeting since we said good-bye (not knowing it was good-bye) before the Christmas break at Lovegood ten years ago. I can even trace back the links in our conversation that day at the Algonquin that led up to it. I had asked you if you thought about your time at Lovegood, and you said, "It's more like I carry it with me." And then you said it provided a whole sort of reference aura. You spoke of your husband, Will, approving of Miss McCorkle without ever having met her, and you went on to say that Miss Petrie in her classes had been trying to teach us that we had to *get used to uncertainty in our reading and writing*. And that was when I told you I wished I had someone in my daily life who could talk about things like reference auras.

When Paul was born, I was going on forty-six. Talk about living in uncertainty. That's when I began to go to church regularly. There is an African Methodist Episcopal church not far from us. I had gone there a few times when I was making notes about Stephen Slade's life, the task you had "assigned" me in your generous letter. We didn't tell many people, Jack and I, because we were waiting for something bad to happen as it often did with women my age. There was one scare with some bleeding early on, but then we sailed through the rest of the pregnancy. Of course, we had to dread the bad things that could still happen. The baby could be born damaged in some way. I say the baby, because we were too superstitious to ask for too much, and we refused to learn whether I was carrying a boy or a girl.

And then there was this perfect little boy. It has only been recently that I have allowed myself to look at the photos. Jack has yet to feel up to it. Needless to say, I choose my lookings when I am sure he is going to be out for a while.

In those three short months when we thought we were home free, Jack started talking about the future when Paul had grown to manhood and had taken over Jellicoe. We got into an argument. I reminded Jack that Ritchie had been a grown man when he went off to war, and who knew what kinds of wars this country would be fighting in eighteen years. Not to mention that there might not be any Jellicoe bright leaf allowed to grow. He stormed out, and then it was time to feed Paul again, and that's when I noticed that after he had sucked for, say, half a minute, he was gasping for breath.

I am going to have to continue this later, Feron.

[unfinished, unsent, and destroyed]

29

eron had insisted that she wanted to walk back to work, but it was raining outside the restaurant, so Cousin Thad put her in a cab.

Still smarting from his delicate rebuke, she said, "Please tell Merry I am going to write to her tonight."

"Will do!" he said, sending the driver off with her work address: gentleman to the last.

The last time she had felt this kind of shame had been in 1958, when Blanche Buttner had asked what time they should drop by to give Aunt Mabel her Christmas present, and Feron, slipping back into her pre-Pullen rude, begrudging self, had said, "Oh, you go ahead without me."

That day Blanche had made a visible effort to hide the extent of her surprise and distaste, just as today Thad's countenance had gone through a visible downgrading of expectations regarding his cousin.

Feron's current apartment-sit was on East Fifty-fourth, a favorite venue, it seemed, for MacFarlane employees. Unlike almost all of her other "sits," the spruce headquarters of this single man in the engineering department required no removal of objects at odds with her peace of mind. On the walls were framed reproductions of da Vinci drawings of inventions for the future: a helicopter, a tank, an armored car, a parachute with a little figure dangling, and a flying machine shaped like a giant hawk. The mattress was firm, the flatware was Georg Jensen, the sheets were white, and the towels (faintly smelling of lavender) were brown or gray. Her favorite place was the sturdy oak refectory table, large enough to spread out your work with a meal to one side—or the other way around.

When she took her blue-and-gray Royal portable out of its carrying case, she always set it on a plastic placemat. Though she had never met the owner (one didn't; it was all done through a MacFarlane go-between), she often imagined him floating above her, unsmilingly approving of her behavior among his things.

At twilight, it was still raining as she rolled in a sheet of paper and began to type.

October 21, 1988

Dear Merry,

Today I had lunch with Cousin Thad, and he told me about your little boy. I would have written sooner had I known about it. I cannot imagine the experience of such a terrible loss. I wish you had written me. But why should you? Your last letter to me was your gracious reply to my "donor" assignment letter. Then I guess I kept waiting to hear how you were getting on with the Stephen Slade novel, and before I knew it, nine years had gone by and I still hadn't written back.

Which is no excuse. I will come right out and say it, Merry: I have been a sorry friend.

You came out of a stable and loving background. As I've told you, you have operated as a sort of moral compass for me. (Would Merry do this?) I will spare you my usual screed about a lying alcoholic mother and—I never told you this—lecherous stepfather. Even as I reveal this now, I wonder if I am not just trying to distract you from looking too clearly at my shameful record as a friend. You deserved better. I didn't write to you from Lovegood after you had to drop out of school—fortunately you had good people like Miss Petrie—and the only reason I know you received a thank-you note for my wedding gift was because Blanche Buttner made me write all of them before the wedding, to be mailed afterward by her.

I remember the night of the pageant, when I was hit hard by those words in Lovegood's processional hymn, "I will never, no never, no never, forsake," and you reached over, so naturally, and grabbed my hand. You thought I was sad about my mother, but the truth was I was grieving for something I'd never known and couldn't even put a name to. And though I didn't learn of it till afterward, you saved me from being caught with my flashlight on when the daughters and granddaughters came to tap me for their club.

I ask myself now why I never contacted you when I arrived back in the States as a widow and spent six months with Uncle Rowan. You would have grieved with me and asked the right questions and done your utmost, as you always did at Lovegood, to make me feel *upheld*. From the beginning I have been supported by your belief in me, if that makes any sense to you.

Will was the second person I felt secure spending days and nights with. You were the first.

And now I have been living in this city twenty-five years, and on trips back to Pullen I have never made time to visit you at your house.

I don't deserve you, but you are my first, best, and truest friend.

What was I thinking last night? Feron pulled the unfinished second page out of the typewriter. Spread flat on the refectory table, the abandoned letter did not hold up well in the early morning sun.

What a shameful self-preoccupied piece of crap. Sorry your baby son died, but pity me for being such an awful person. I can see her scanning the typed lines, looking for another mention of her dead child. But then, as always, she would make excuses: "Feron has been tried and tested in ways I can't begin to imagine."

She tore the pages in half and dropped them into the stainless-steel garbage container under the sink.

October 22, 1988

Dear Merry,

Yesterday I had lunch with Cousin Thad, who was in town, and he told me about the loss of your child. I would have written sooner had I known about it. Please know that I grieve for you. I can't begin to imagine such a loss.

I probably won't come down for Christmas this year. Thad might have told you about Blanche Buttner's new husband and daughter. I went last Christmas because I thought Blanche would be hurt if I didn't come, and she thought I would be hurt if she didn't invite me. The four of us smoldered for three days and then I changed my ticket and left early.

Once again, please accept my condolences for the loss of your little boy.

Your Old Lovegood friend,
Feron

October 31, 1988

Dear Feron,

Thank you so much for your thoughtful note. It may make you feel better to know that on the first anniversary of Paul's death, I sat down and began an anguished letter to you, which I never finished and never sent. No friend should have to deal with such a letter. So don't be hard on yourself about not having known.

I wanted to write back the day I received your note of October 22, but Jack and I have been busy from dawn to dusk with last-minute cleanup as we get ready to burn the fields in January. We had a record harvest this year, though who knows how long we'll be allowed to keep up this sort of farming.

We average about one offer a week from someone wanting to turn the Jellicoe acres into a gated community replete with golf course and man-made pond. So far we haven't committed ourselves, though Jack is more willing than I am to let it all go. He had his heart set on Paul taking charge one day. If we were to stop before next season, Jellicoe would have brought 190 years of tobacco to market. Jack talks of starting a horse farm, and we have gone so far as to start construction on some stables on the other side of the west field.

But you haven't been here, so you won't be able to picture the west field.

Cousin Thad drove me over to Pullen one afternoon to see the new guest house and studio, which are beautiful. I could picture you upstairs under the skylight, busy at work on a book. And then maybe after you were done with the day's work, you would drive over to Hamlin, and we could sit on the west porch and talk about writing.

Which brings me around to something I am not looking forward to telling you: the story of Stephen Slade. I began writing it immediately after receiving your "donor" letter. I couldn't wait to fill in the years between 1821, when he discovered bright leaf, and 1914, when he was buried on his own property. It still seemed worth doing after we lost little Paul, and it kept me busy when I might otherwise have lost heart, which would have been bad for Jack, who was worse off than I was.

I never did send the magazine stuff to Mr. Sterling the agent. Why get his hopes up until I at least had part of a novel to show him? First I tried to write it from Stephen's point of view alone, then I decided to add a family of share-croppers who live nearby and become attached to Stephen. So he would have someone to tell things to!

Then the forebodings started. How had I been arrogant enough to believe I could create a life for this historical figure out of the flimsy materials of my imagination? So I took out current books that probed deeper into the experi-ence of black Americans. I got up the courage to attend Ezekiel African Methodist Episcopal Church, worrying I might not be welcome. (Was I ever wrong!)

The Stephen project finally gave up the ghost last year. During my research down at the Tobacco Museum, I came across a small news item on microfiche, "An Old Negro the First to Cure Bright Tobacco" was the headline from an 1886 edition of the *Progressive Farmer*. The reporter had been introduced to the old man at a warehouse tobacco auction. Stephen Slade, sixty-five at the time, was delighted to be recognized, and he regaled his interviewer with the story of how it had happened. ("It kep' on yallowin' and yallowin' tell it got clear up.") The news item ended with the old man saying of his former master, Abisha Slade: "I wish my master was alive and I was his slave."

When I left the Tobacco Museum, I knew my novel had died. I couldn't decide which depressed me more: the reporter's condescending dialect spelling, or the final wish attributed to Stephen. He couldn't possibly have said that, I told myself on the way to the truck. Could he?

And then I thought, maybe he said it because he knew that was what they wanted to hear.

I can imagine you reading this and saying, "So much for donorship!" However, the experience inspired by your donorship has brought me to a church I love, and some of the women in my Bible study group have become dear friends. Like most children, Ritchie and I had Sunday school and Bible study, but it wasn't until I started meeting with the Ezekiel Bible group that I realized for the first time that the Bible had been written and put together by people in need of guidance.

Feron, I can't believe I have gone on like this. Writing to you has made me realize how much I miss you, even though we can go years without seeing each other.

Love,
Merry

P.S. Today being Halloween, Jack asked, "Would a two-and-a-half-year-old boy be wearing a costume?" I said probably. I remembered when Ritchie was very small, Mother made him a baby bat costume. I was about to go and look in old boxes for that baby bat costume when I realized there was no little boy to wear it. That's the way it keeps coming back. Sometime when we are face-to-face again, I will try to describe our little boy to you.

PART FIVE

30

In the nineties, "the sixties" began cropping up in popular culture. Fashions from the sixties were sought in thrift shops (or vintage shops) and "reinvented" by current designers. There were sixties TV reruns, as well as new shows about the sixties or set in the sixties, with overzealous attention to objects like ashtrays (and smoking in the office), and how women wore their bras, pointy and high on the chest.

Debut novels were published by young writers who were praised for their assiduous research concerning the "historical period" they'd chosen. Feron remembered being impressed (and envious) as an undergraduate when she learned that George Eliot had set her masterpiece in the time of the Great Reform Act, forty years earlier than her date of writing. Forty years! What an accomplishment, to re-create a setting from such a long-ago time! Yet actually, forty years before, the fifty-two-year-old author of *Middlemarch* would have been twelve years old, living in that setting and registering things that might never be glimpsed by an assiduous researcher in the future.

Though Feron gave herself credit for some improvement, her envious competitiveness had not slackened in her fifties. She kept abreast of the bright new retro novels, but found most of them overresearched and lacking the "feel" of the decades she had lived through, registering things that might never be researched later.

Cuervo had said that *Nito's Garden* in itself was a testimony of its need to exist: "Had I not been able to make Nito exist, I would have committed suicide."

How many novels out in the world really and truly testified to their need to exist? (Including her own?)

When her novel *A Singular Courtship* was about to go to press, her editor said, "You know, I like this. It's fun to read about intelligent, slightly kinky people. But be warned: readers have been known to punish a writer who switches genres."

Yet as her own fifty-third birthday passed, Feron found herself warily basking in the unexpected appreciation of *A Singular Courtship*.

Why warily? Because sometime after her new start at Lovegood, she became aware of a built-in gauge that sounded an alarm when the pressure of too much elation threatened to overwhelm her. Why had this gauge not gone off before Lovegood? Because in her life with Swain and her mother, there was no need for anything to protect her from the pressure of too much elation? In those days she had habitually acted as people do when there is nothing good to expect from life and nothing left to lose.

And she had continued in that mode after escaping Swain and linking up with the man on the bus. It was only after *Beast and Beauty* had been published that she felt safe enough to look back at that Chicago juncture and dare to imagine where and who she might be if Dale Flowers hadn't shaken her by the shoulders and said: "Think hard. Don't you have any family, any blood relatives you might impose upon?" In their dreary Chicago walkup, *he* was all Feron *had*, and she didn't want to leave him. It was he who pushed her out the door when she came up with Uncle Rowan's name.

Every time another good thing happened to *A Singular Courtship*, Feron would mentally cringe and wait for the gauge's alarm to go off.

A Singular Courtship was set thirty years before, in the early sixties, when she had been in her last year of college, on the verge of beginning her epistolary exchange with Will's mother, who would become the courtier in her son's singular romance.

"I was not prepared for the humor," Cuervo said. "You preserved the strangeness I liked in the original draft, but I didn't expect this humor. Where did it come from?"

"I don't know. I've never thought of myself as particularly humorous, though my roommate back in junior college was always saying I was funny: 'Not ha-ha funny,' she'd say, 'but a dry, kind of sideways funny.'"

"Dry and sideways is good. That was Merry, the tobacco farmer, yes?"

"After I had started the book over again for the umpteenth time, I realized I kept wanting to stay longer with the mother, and I kept putting off the marriage in England part. Then I thought, what if I never get to the England part? They spend the wedding night at the mother's house, but I've always felt comfortable writing the wedding night because in real life Will and I had made a pact to wait to begin our married life after we got to England and were rested. But they discover that their chosen abstinence is erotic for them both. I decided to end the book there, in bed in the mother's house, with the marriage erotically unconsummated. They discover that their chosen abstinence is a turn-on for them both. If readers had gotten that far, they would have known these people well enough to expect that since the courtship had been unconventional, the marriage would be, too."

"*Singular*, in fact."

"Even if I had gone on to write about the English months, the disclosures would have been singular. Doing it. Refraining from doing it. The different satisfactions each brought. Each couple makes up their own route to passion. 'Just little details that belong to nobody but them' is how Merry once described the secret of the lovemaking scene in 'The Lady with the Little Dog.'"

"Your Chekhov and your Merry and Miss Petrie. What a singular *school*!"

"The editor said *A Singular Courtship* might sell better if we had 'romance' in the title. He finally gave up and said it probably wouldn't make that much difference because I was a niche writer and *Singular Courtship* wasn't going to be a blockbuster. He always succeeds in making me feel disposable."

"That's his style. And your niche did expand, didn't it? You were a finalist for the awards and wouldn't even go to the dinner."

"I knew I wouldn't win. And you know how I dread socializing. Every time I open my mouth in public something churlish comes out. I would probably *lose* readers if I went to an event like that. Listen, can I nip out and do some shopping for you before I wend my way home to my present flat-sit?"

"I haven't had an appetite. If I try something serious, it revolts on me."

"Not the beef broth and the Jell-O."

"No, they remain on the party list."

"But just the lemon and lime flavors. No orange or red."

"*Lo mismo, querida.* Gracias."

"De nada, maestro."

Cuervo was ill, they both knew what it was, but he had set the tone of formality, which suited them both. He mostly stayed in bed, wearing a sweater and a cap pulled down to cover his lesions. Feron remembered Blanche Buttner saying once about Uncle Rowan's covert depressions, "Self-control can go a long way, though fewer people choose to make use of theirs these days."

Blanche was now living in Uncle Rowan's house in Pullen. She insisted on paying the topmost rent (quarterly, in advance, through her bank) and repeatedly reminded Feron that she would stay only as long as it was convenient for Feron. Orrin, the man she had wed on the cruise ship, remained at Buttner House in Benton Grange, as did the dreadful daughter Daphne. There was no eviction date set, divorce papers had not been served. "I married the man in full possession of my marbles," said Blanche. "I made the death-do-us-part vow, I'm a Catholic, and he's twelve years my senior. Buttner House is in a trust, so let them enjoy it until I pass on."

She wrote Feron that living in Rowan's old house, which had been his grandmother Hood's before him, felt like being snatched out of an intolerable situation and granted an alternative destiny.

After Rowan proposed, there was some going back and forth about living in his house. I remember (with mortification!) walking through the house, clop-clop in my high heels, examining the closets, and declaring them "too small." I wish I didn't remember his doleful hangdog expression before he covered it with a jolly assurance that we could always add more closets.

Walking around the house—sunset is so beautiful from the larger windows you put in—I often say aloud: "Rowan, you should see these shining oak floors—I wouldn't dream of denting them with my old high heels—and the marvelous new kitchen, would you believe it, I am teaching myself to cook . . . simple things, of course."

And you know, Feron, sometimes I swear I hear his gruff reply. "You? Will miracles never cease?" or "You haven't mentioned the closets,

Blanche." And sometimes I respond: "Oh, Rowan, for my simplified needs these days your closets are way big enough."

Blanche wrote regularly to Feron, and Feron—not previously a reliable correspondent (except in the case of Will's mother)—wrote regularly back. If Feron so much as thought about postponing a reply, Blanche's reproach was as audible as on that awful December day when Feron had been weaseling out of going to Aunt Mabel's: "Rowan expects this of you."

Someone didn't have to be dead for you to hear their voice.

This must be somewhat similar to what happens, Feron thought, when people are raised from the cradle with principles. The voices live on in you, if you choose to hear. Like in the Daughters and Granddaughters refrain:

> *Now we walk unseen beside you,*
> *Faithful spirits always guiding.*

Blanche had promptly read Feron's third novel.

> I don't think I have come across a novel like this before. The thing I loved was, this is the skewed manner in which people actually live their lives. There are many unpremeditated turnings which in retrospect may seem like "fate" to us. A bookish professor sees a downcast former student in a coffee shop and on an impulse invites her to go along with him to visit his mother because it's a nice day. The mother is taken aback when her bachelor son shows up with a young woman. But the mother and the young woman are attracted to each other. As the professor drives the young woman back to campus, she is imagining what it would be like to grow up

in a household of such warmth and civility. And then she looks over at the driver's abstracted profile and feels a little leap of something when she imagines him as her husband. That's all it takes. Then the young woman writes a thank-you note, working to make it charming, and the mother replies to the thank-you note, and away we go.

After I finished your novel, I stayed in the living room until it grew dark. (Wonderful sunset!) And then I set myself to trace my engagement to Rowan. Where did we meet? It was long ago, but where and why? And then who said what and what happened after that? I am still working on this.

Feron had regretted many times throwing away Aurelia Avery's packet of letters. They certainly would have been a great help while she was writing *A Singular Courtship*. Though making them up may have made them better. Feron remembered very well the night she had cut them up in small pieces and buried them in her wastebasket at Blanche's house. Why on earth would she have done that? She had been packing to go to New York and must have felt more guilt about abandoning the dying Aurelia than she wanted to carry with her. She might as well have kept them because thirty years later she still felt the guilt. How could she have hidden behind "incapacitating grief" to convince Uncle Rowan to make the phone calls? Who *was* that twenty-three-year-old person cutting up the letters? As she grew older, Feron's remembrance of callous youthful acts increasingly baffled her or filled her with disgust. ("Oh, no, how could I have?" "What a monster I was." "Was I born that way?")

"The rot may have set in earlier," the drunk woman in Feron's story for Miss Petrie tells the young girl on the bus. How *much* earlier? Would there already be a fine pencil line of rot around the fetus? "Either way," the drunk woman in Feron's story had concluded, "you don't have a chance, your fate is decided already."

Even the drunk woman had been better versed than Feron in the concepts of original sin and predestination.

When Dr. Phillips was leading them through Genesis at Lovegood College, he told them you could also read the fall of Eve and Adam as an allegory. "What was the snake offering them? And what did they gain by it and what did they lose? And if they were destined to beget children marked with their sin through the ages, was human life *always* going to spin on a blighted axis? What, if anything, could you do to reverse the punishment? Or, taking it a step further, what was beyond your human powers to do? And a step beyond that: If you accepted the limits of your human powers, could you still hope for redemption? ("Don't worry, it's not going to be on the test. I'm just posing a theological question. I have a graduate degree in theology, and I'm still pondering it.")

Dear Nora,

The rain kept me from putting the garden to bed, and I was deciding how else I could spend a useful morning when I saw the postman's van stop at my box. I grabbed an umbrella and charged into the downpour. There were two letters. I read Tom's first, saving the thickest one for later, for which I made myself a fresh pot of coffee and settled into the window seat you have become so fond of.

Yes, I, too, was delighted you could stay the weekend this time. The unrushed hours gave us a chance to become more intimately acquainted. Although Tom made himself scarce up there in his attic aerie, I was so grateful that at last somebody besides myself understood that in some very deep place he craves to be left alone to do his work. Even as a child, his powers of concentration were so ferocious and antisocial that his late father, a worrier, insisted we consult a child psychiatrist. Back then, they were few and far between in these environs, but fortunately we had Duke in driving distance, so off we went—only to be told Tom's IQ was prodigious, and if we wanted to change anything in his routine, we might encourage him to stay outdoors more.

Since he was little, he has been an adamant walker. First round and round the boundaries of our backyard. Then, later, announcing he was "in a mood," he would leave the house and walk for hours. His father tried to follow him several times and returned exhausted. Tom hadn't walked far, his father reported, in fact he seemed not to be aware of where he walked, but he set a fiendish pace. The doctor said some people walked to solve problems or get over moods, that brains worked better when one walked. Regarding the antisocial element, the doctor said Tom was an introvert, and trying to change that would be similar to forcing a left-handed person to become a right-handed person. The doctor did advise us to encourage him to play with others his age. I'll leave you to guess how that went!

Then came his long slog through medieval studies; he learned all the languages and ruined his eyes in libraries for twelve years.

When people asked me, 'What is your son going to be when he gets out of school," I started replying, "Old."

—opening of *A Singular Courtship*, a novel by Feron Hood. Knole, 1994.

31

E ven the darkness is not dark to you, the night is as bright as the day . . ."

On the west porch of Merry's house, the Ezekiel Bible group was doing Psalms: four women, including the host, and today's leader, Simone, whose deep and certain voice rolled over your aches and worries like healing balm.

The group numbered six members, but Dedra, a surgical nurse, had been called in to work overtime, and Corinne was attending her great-grandson's graduation from kindergarten.

The west porch of the Jellicoe house still looked out on a pastoral scene: green meadow, grazing horses, new horse barn, all bathed in the golden light of a late-summer afternoon. On the east and south-east sides of the house, the big earth-moving machines had finished their terrible work, scooping away a hundred and ninety years of successful tobacco growing. Next to arrive would be the graders and trenchers, followed by the landscapers, sculpting the broken soil into a "pastoral-seeming" gated community of houses with double garages, a man-made lake, and a nine-hole golf course.

"In your book were written all the days that were formed for me, when none of them as yet existed."

Simone's voice, you wished you could put it in a bottle. Like in that last psalm they had studied: "Put my tears into your bottle."

("Hey, you know what?" Ritchie would have said. "We could package that voice and sell it to a Christian radio station. No, better! Make a CD of Sister Simone reading some fabulous psalms for people to listen to when they are feeling bad.")

Each Sunday, Simone's powerful contralto lifted the Ezekiel choir a few miles closer to Heaven. ("No, wait: at the *end* of our CD, we could have her break into 'Amazing Grace.' It would top the charts, Merry Grape!")

Alda, the trainer who had leased their horse barn, came out of the stables leading the already saddled Nola, a blue roan mare known for her patience with children. And sure enough, here came the rattling Mercedes bringing little Jennifer for her twice-a-week lesson.

This was not what they had planned.

In your book all my days were written before any of them existed.

At children's Bible camp, she and Ritchie had recited the twenty-third psalm with its green pastures, still waters, and the good shepherd who hurried you past the valley of the shadow of death and on to a table laid out with good things all for you. At Lovegood, Dr. Phillips had shared with them a few scholarly facts about the collection of psalms: composed three centuries before Christ—or "Before the Common Era," as it was now called; many were attributed to King David, many more to poets or priests unknown. The book consisted of songs of praise, laments, penitential prayers, supplications, and "some outright vindictive screeds." At Dr. Phillips's last category the class perked up, and he assigned them a choice of maledictory psalms to ponder before the next class.

What were those psalms? She didn't remember. All she remembered was Feron saying something like, "Wishing you could go back and step in your enemy's blood, and have your dog drink it, is, well, *picturesque*, but what would be some more *up-to-date* maledictions?" They had come up with some wonderful little horrors, but again, Merry could not recall a single one. She did recall Feron saying, "Dr. Phillips certainly is in love with the word *ponder*, don't you think?"

Since Jack had moved of his own volition into assisted living at Laurel Grove in the spring of 1990, Merry had spent many hours "pondering" this thing called memory. And overresearching it. She knew more than made her comfortable about "the old brain" and could close her eyes at night and see the X-ray colors of parts of the brain as it shut down. His father had begun losing it a full ten years before Jack's present age of sixty-nine.

One day Jack phoned her from the hardware store and asked her to give him directions how to get home. From there his descent relentlessly progressed until, having seen yet another specialist, Jack told her as they were walking back to the parking lot that it was time they went shopping for a place where he could deteriorate without losing his pride.

"But I can take care of you, Jack. I want to."

"I know you do. But I want it this way. I've ruined your life once."

"How can you say that?"

"I took advantage of you the night your parents died."

"We were both in shock. What happened sort of unfolded out of our trying to comfort each other."

"I robbed you of your rightful future."

"Please don't ever say that again. Don't even think it. And if you feel yourself starting to think it, remember you are Paul's father, and I wouldn't exchange those three months with him for any other future I might have had."

"Search me, O God, and know my heart; try me and know my thoughts: and see if there be any wicked way in me, and lead me in the way everlasting."

Sister Simone, who was from that older generation who still addressed one another as "Sister" and "Brother," closed the Bible on her lap, took off her reading glasses, and, along with the others, closed her eyes.

The silence of a summer afternoon. Which of course was never silent. With closed eyes, your ears picked up the sounds of birds, insects, hum of traffic on the distant interstate, Alda's voice from across the field putting the compliant Nola through her paces. (Little Jennifer, proudly mounted, probably believed she was doing it all herself by her control of the reins.)

This was their time for turning away extraneous thoughts and meditating on the psalm Sister Simone had read. By now, Merry knew the members of the Ezekiel Bible group so well that she could guess at some of the extraneous thoughts each woman was trying to turn away.

She owed these women to Feron. Who had written to her at the end of 1979 that she should make a novel out of Stephen Slade. "It reads like a story," Feron wrote. "You got inside his head—his fear, his panic, his envisioning all too well his probable punishments, and then his wild inspiration about the logs. And you stayed with him till he was dying, a free man on his own farm where he is buried."

It was the longest letter Feron had ever written to her. Anointing herself Merry's "donor," she had set Merry the task of sending the uncut version of her magazine article to Mr. Sterling in New York and telling him she felt there was more to uncover and did he think the story could make a novel.

Merry didn't go so far as to contact the literary agent who still wrote once a year, "Remember, I am always here for you." But she had been excited by Feron's suggestion and began planning ways she might fill in Stephen's life between the night he discovered bright leaf until the day he died and passed over to the other side. Though Feron had praised her for "following him over the threshold," in the article, saying it went one step farther than Chekhov, Merry had grown to regret including such a blatant feat of speculation about Stephen's entry into afterlife. She grew to wish the magazine editor had cut that out, too.

And then came Feron's bewildering little novel with the pictures, *Mr. Blue*, published in the early eighties. Feron hadn't sent her a copy; Merry had found it in a bookstore a year or so after it was published. Who were these people? Where had it come from? What did it have to do with Feron's life? With *Beast and Beauty*, Merry had been able to sense her friend's experience between the lines, even before Feron had elaborated on the real man on the bus. ("I tried to erase him happening to me . . . until I transported him safely into a fairy tale and secured him there.")

But in certain passages of *Mr. Blue*, Merry started to recognize familiar things. Mr. Blue's parents and grandparents had been tenant farmers. He was allowed to build himself a house on the owner's land. He had arrived when the future Mrs. Blue was a child of eight, as Merry had been when Mr. Jack came to work for them. Mr. Blue was distant and proud, but, when you got inside his head in every other chapter (this book had the same alternating point-of-view structure as *Beast and Beauty*), you learned how uneasy he was in society. You also picked up a low-burning resentment, something that was not at all in Jack's nature, but something Merry had strongly sensed in her roommate back at Lovegood. And, like Feron, Mr. Blue often didn't answer you. He guarded his thoughts.

And the crop, that had to be tobacco, though it was never named. ("Keeping it generic like in the fairy tales.") But how well Feron had described its dramatically changing appearance as it grew, the long deep green fleshy leaves, then crowned with yellow-white heads, then the pathetically naked stalks after they had been stripped and dried and sold.

Hadn't she herself use similar descriptions in her magazine article on Stephen Slade? Which Feron had read immediately after their lunch at the Neuse River Café.

And those were definitely tobacco fields in the beautifully strange illustrations. The leaf shapes were accurately drawn. Had Feron simply handed over the magazine to the artist? ("Here, it should look like this field on the cover.")

But Mrs. Blue dies at the end. In childbirth! Child and mother die. There's no one left but Mr. Blue, who owns all the land and is a rich man, like the Bluebeard in the fairy tale. The jacket copy said the novel could be read as a feminist version of Bluebeard. Why? Because she had the secret room? Mr. Blue in Feron's novel is left inconsolable, though he can't stop himself from climbing to the tower room and unlocking the door and seeing what Mrs. Blue didn't want him to see for all those years. A room with a chair with the stuffing falling out, a table and a folded blanket and a single window inserted into a space once big enough to be a hayloft. At Lovegood she had told Merry about Mama's off-limits loft room where little Ritchie had thought Mama went to literally put herself back together. What was *Mr. Blue* supposed to leave you with? Why did it need Merry's family history? Was there something Merry the Reader was too obtuse to see, or was it something Feron the Writer hadn't made clear enough?

The novel had come out two years before Paul was born, which made the childbirth thing kind of weird. Perhaps Feron had assumed if Merry did get pregnant in her forties she would most likely die, or give birth to something horrible, like the monster in Mr. Cuervo's book.

At first Merry hadn't resented the likenesses between *Mr. Blue* and her own family history. Following Feron's creative trail, she felt a pleasant comraderie with her old friend. That girl first seen in the parking lot of Lovegood College, who looked at odds with someone or something, that girl was still there. You could easily imagine her making up a story like *Mr. Blue* thirty-six years later and snatching her friend's family story to make it more interesting. But after a closer second reading Merry realized she felt raided. Feron had appropriated her life without even asking permission. Would she have given the permission? She didn't know. If Feron were with her right now, would she have the nerve to confront her: "Why did you use my family story in your book? And as it is, the story still leaves you hanging. What is the reader meant to take away from *Mr. Blue*?"

"Remember how Miss Petrie led us to accepting being left in uncertainty?" Feron might reply with a touch of disdain. "And how was I supposed to guess you would have any problem with my using your hayloft room story?"

"I can go first, unless somebody else wants to." It was Tabitha, church organist, piano teacher, and mother of five. "Psalm 139 is my favorite psalm, so I was curious about how worshippers down through the ages have translated those last lines, which always reminds me I have a moral life. So I asked Pastor Ford if I could look at some of his books. When he found out what I was up to, he was a terrific help. I could never have tracked down all this stuff by myself."

She reopened her Bible, and the others followed. "Sister Simone read us the King James version: 'Know my heart, try me and know my thoughts and see if there be any wicked way in me, and lead me in the way everlasting.' The New Revised Standard Version is almost the same except it has 'test me' instead of 'try me.' The

Revised English Bible leaves out the heart part altogether. It just says 'examine me and know my mind; test me, and understand my anxious thoughts, watch lest I follow any path that grieves you, lead me in the everlasting way.' The New American Bible, which is the one the Catholics use, says 'Probe me, God, know my heart; try me, know my concerns, see if my way is crooked, then lead me in the ancient ways.' Whereas the New Jerusalem Bible says 'God, examine me and know my heart, test me and know my concerns, make sure that I am not on the way to ruin and guide me on the road to eternity.'

"And those are just four recent translations in modern English from Pastor Ford's study! When you think of all the other ones, from Hebrew then into Greek, and on down, it gives you an idea what the Tower of Babel must have sounded like. No wonder people are always fighting other people over something, even when they are speaking the same language. One single changed word can convey a whole different meaning. 'Test' is not 'try,' or "examine.' And changing heart into mind, that's a big change."

"That's right," the group agreed.

"I want this psalm read at my funeral, the King James one, because it's the prettiest . . ."

"Mm-*hm*."

"And I want Hymn 702, 'Lord, Thou hast searched me,' to go with it, though I expect some other organist besides myself will have to play it."

Inclusive laughter.

Merry quashed the upsurge of guilt she always felt when remaining silent. She had never been brave when it came to speaking up in a group. Like the day in Dr. Worley's class, when everyone was interrupting everyone else to get in their two cents about that magazine story's provoking last line: "But there was one thing Queenie missed."

"Well, I don't mind going next." It was Lavonne Blake, funeral director and mother of Rachel, who would be entering Lovegood College in the fall.

Lavonne was their loveliest and best-dressed member. You looked at her, cool and tall in her stylish apparel, and imagined her in the plastic apron she wore while embalming a body laid out on a steel table. Lavonne had been a junior at Chapel Hill, in the premed program, when her father died, and she had to quit and come home to run Blake's Funeral Home. "Just like me," Merry had told her, already sensing they were going to be friends. "Though I only made it through one semester of my college life."

Lavonne said, "Verses seventeen and eighteen touch on a question that has bothered me for years. Here, I'll read the passage again. 'How precious also are thy thoughts unto me, O God! How great is the sum of them! If I should count them, they are more in number than the sand: when I awake, I am still with thee.'

"Now here is my question. How do we know it is God thinking those thoughts inside us? How can we be sure it's not something *else* thinking those thoughts? I'd love to hear *your* thoughts on this because I've worn myself ragged studying on it."

A courteous pause, either because no one wished to be first or because each member was mulling over her reply.

Sister Simone murmured something that sounded like scripture.

"Sister Simone?"

"Well, verse thirteen, 'For Thou hast possessed my reins,' tells us who's in charge here. And the person speaking *knows* God is in charge because their relationship has been going on for a long time."

"Mm-hm."

"And the person also understands that God knows he's not perfect. But they have been together since the womb. And if you keep company with someone that long, well, their ways are going to rub off on you."

"Mm-hm."

"So I believe this person has fallen into step with God's way of thinking, not *all* of the time, because he's imperfect, but because he's slipped into the rhythm of God's thoughts."

"Mm-*hmm*."

"It's like recognizing a tune we've heard over and over. Whenever we hear that tune, the words just sing themselves out of us by themselves."

"That is really wise, Sister Simone," Lavonne said. "I would never in a million years have thought of that."

"Wise, I don't know. But the person's got to be *in step* with his maker before he can recognize his maker's thoughts."

An enthusiastic chorus of "Amen!"

Merry was gauging whether it was time to put out the food the members had brought when she realized they were all looking toward her. She was the only one who hadn't spoken a word. She felt her face and neck heating up as they took on their predictable color. ("Boy, are you ever a cinch to read, Merry Grape. Your face is as red as a fire engine.")

"I don't have anything very substantial to add, but I do want to say that our meeting today has only intensified something I have felt ever since you welcomed me to your Bible group five years ago this month. I remember when we were studying Ecclesiastes, and I had never heard that verse that begins 'Two are better than one,' and then it goes on to explain why. If one falls, the other will lift him up, and if an enemy prevails against him, there'll be two to withstand the enemy.

"That verse has meant a great deal to me. Tabitha said today's psalm always reminds her of her moral life, and she went to the trouble of searching out those other translations for us. And then

Lavonne said verses seventeen and eighteen of today's psalm asks something that has bothered her for years: How do we know when it's God's thoughts we are hearing? And Sister Simone got us all a little further when she said what she did about having to be in step and a familiar tune bringing back the words to it.

"Which I guess is my roundabout way of saying that the Ezekiel Bible group has shown me that I may be alone, but I am not by myself."

Chapter One

A little girl opened the door. "Who are you?"

"My name is Mr. Blue."

"What do you want?"

"I've come to see your father."

"My father can't see anyone. He is sick."

"Yes, I know. Here, I have this letter from him. See? That's his signature. And the line just above says . . ."

"I can read. I know what it says."

"Of course you can. I only wanted . . ."

The little girl sighed. "I will have to go and see. I am closing the door now. You stay out there."

He turns his back to the closed door and looks out at the fields.

It is midsummer, and the sun is just setting. A breeze ruffles the leaves. Acres of ripening leaves as far as the eye could see. ("If you are all you say," the father had written, "you had better come quickly.")

The little girl's face. Closed like a door. You stay out there.

What was she, six? Eight? He had little knowledge of children.

Soon, with another sigh, she would invite him in. Because she had to. Time would pass. They would see what he could do. The little girl would learn to respect him. She would have to. Fear him a little, but respect all the necessary things he could do. She would grow in stature and in pride. But the day might come when that imperious face would open, and, perhaps with another sigh, she would stand aside and allow him to enter.

—*Mr. Blue*, a novel by Feron Hood, illustrations by Joachim Maglia. Knole, 1982.

32

The Ezekiel Bible study group, as per their tradition, had cleaned up the hostess's kitchen and set the dishwasher going before they left, and Merry had another hour and a half to get through before driving over to Laurel Grove to see her husband. The best time to visit was after the residents had finished their supper and were gathered in the leisure room to watch television; some others in the earlier stages of forgetfulness preferred to play cards. Television had never taken hold of Mr. Jack; he had been too busy managing Jellicoe Enterprises and, having worked with his family in the fields since he was a child, had never been taught any card games.

This she had learned about living alone. You fared best when you knew what you wanted to do next. Presently she returned to the west porch, equipped with notebook and pen, a pack of cigarettes, and Feron's troubling second novel, *Mr. Blue*.

She had been flattered into writing another historical article for the state magazine. ("I am in awe of 'The Slave Who Discovered Bright Leaf.' It was one of the most substantial and readable pieces this magazine has ever published. Could I tempt you into doing another in-depth treatment of the unfiltered cigarette throughout the history of our country's smoking? Lots of our readers still smoke, you know.") The new editor had actually offered her one thousand dollars and a lifetime subscription to the magazine. Her notebook was already stocked with more material than she could use: little-known facts and lore about a subject she had never given much thought to, even back in the bygone days when Jellicoe Enterprises was being admired and envied all over the state for the desirable "toasted" leaves they grew.

But first, light up a Lucky (her last pack had been Camels, the next would be Pall Malls) and then inhale as best she could and try to note the distinctions of each unfiltered brand still available in the marketplace.

Merry hadn't read Proust but knew the story about his "madeleine moment," when, upon biting into a little sponge cake, he was flooded with involuntary memories. She had never smoked until now, Daddy had forbidden it to the family, though he occasionally lit up a pipe or a Cuban cigar. But now every time she applied her match to the processed leaf-bits ("toasted, not sun-dried!"), she found herself immersed in recollections: Ritchie singing all the verses of "Smoke! Smoke! Smoke! (That Cigarette)"; the smell of roasted corn, the tastes of caramels, nuts, and toast; her disobedient mother disappearing to "sneak a cig" in hidden spots and always keeping a pack of Clove gum on her person.

Question: Hadn't Daddy smelled it despite the Clove gum? Had they fought over it? Had Mama smoked *more* during those depressed months when she slept in a room by herself?

Merry paged through her notebook, gloating over her extravagance of facts and lore. Fact: because the unfiltered cigarette used higher-quality tobacco, the smoker got his fix quicker. Lore: When did Lucky Strikes become "Luckies"? During World War II, soldiers would open a new pack and "flip" one cigarette over. That was to be the last cigarette smoked from the pack. If you survived the war long enough to smoke it, you were Lucky. (She wasn't going to use that one, because how would you know the cigarette was "flipped" if it didn't have a filter tip?)

After she got past the coughing fits, she continued to be repelled by nasty aftertaste in her mouth. How long did it take to become a "nicotine fiend," as the old song called it?

It astonished her that she had never thought about it from the "nicotine fiend's" side. Jellicoe bright leaf had been a source of family pride as well as income. When the antitobacco movement got going in the late sixties, she remembered worrying with Mr. Jack how they could make a living without their star crop. When she came across gruesome articles telling the stories of particular "fiends" who were dying horrible deaths, she read them with a shudder and then would think, "I'm glad Daddy isn't around to read this." Now, with the aftertaste sticking to her tongue, she imagined a person who grew to accept the unpleasantness as part of the "quick fix." Did this mean she was on the way to abandon the unfiltered cigarettes article as she had abandoned Stephen Slade?

Merry put away the notebook and assigned herself to begin *Mr. Blue* again. On the very first page, she knew that even as a child she would never have been so rude to a stranger at the front door. I was just not like that. If anything, I overdid my friendliness to put the other person at his ease.

Then she had a further thought: this unnamed girl who grew up to become Mrs. Blue was some unquiet combination of herself and Feron. Merry could perfectly well picture an eight-year-old Feron demanding of the stranger at the door: Who are you and what do you want?

33

Identified simply by its name on a small slate plaque affixed to the entrance gate, Laurel Grove could have been a private home. You ascended a winding drive flanked by fifty-year-old laurels, ablaze in pinks and whites in spring, a shiny wall of lush green before and after, leading up to the former house whose classical facade had been preserved to grace the semicircular new building with wings on either side.

An artfully arranged cluster of seasonal flowers always greeted you at the entrance of the skylit reception room. "Smell their fragrance," Mr. Jack had instructed Merry, stopping beside the vase. "I have loved them all my life. Damn it, why can't I remember their name?"

Jack had been living at Laurel Grove for two years. Feron's Cousin Thad had recommended it. "It's pricey, but what with the sale of all that acreage you can afford it. Lou and I discovered it when we were looking for the right place for her mother."

"Did she go there?" Merry had asked.

"Unfortunately she passed away while she was still on the waiting list. But she was excited at the prospect of all its amenities."

Sherry, their amiable guide, a nurse, gave them the tour. Jack would have a suite with a visiting room of his own. Everything was even better than they had anticipated: no skimpiness or jarring taste or bad lighting. The common rooms were skylit, with a large TV screen, magazine racks, and card tables. The residents could have TVs in their rooms as well. There was an on-site barber and stylist, a fitness center, and an indoor pool. A masseuse and acupuncturist were on call. Out of sight, at the rear of the semicircular building, were the medical facilities, including a lab and a dental office. But Jack couldn't stop brooding over the lost name of the flowers in the vase.

"Okay, I give up," he finally told Merry. "What were they?"

"They were peonies."

"You see, I have these holes in my brain," Jack confided almost gallantly to Sherry.

"Well, Mr. Rakestraw, everyone does. Some more than others, but you've come to the right place." The nurse carried herself with the easy buoyancy of someone who appreciated herself and knew others did, too. Merry saw Jack taking her in: something unexpectedly nice that had just materialized in a hallway of Laurel Grove. She felt a bittersweet pang as the realization came to her that he was still a desirable man.

Each visit to Laurel Grove Merry approached with a bizarre mixture of first-date excitement and an increasing measure of terror. She never knew who was going to be in Jack's place. People had prepared her for the day when he wouldn't know who she was. And that day had come and gone, and come and gone again. It was like being on a roller-coaster ride next to a partner who kept shapeshifting into someone else. The two of them now met in a place where one minute she was unrecognizable to him, and the next minute he was the one presenting an alien personality to her.

Yet the deeply embedded characteristics of the old Jack hung on: his pride, his restlessness, his solemn courtesy, his mistrust of strangers until they proved their mettle, and his single-hearted devotion to her, long before she had given it a name. The mistrust remained, also the courtesy, but absent like a great gaping hole was his single-hearted devotion to "Miss Meredith."

This evening she was late because she had forgotten that Laurel Grove switched supper to five o'clock during the daylight savings months so the day staff could have time to garden or relax outdoors when they got home. The residents were already deep into their card playing or watching TV. There was a new resident absorbed in some crewel embroidery, a woman to whom time (and money) had been kind. Merry tried not to "compare" residents, but the differences were visible. Why were some humped and others upright? Why did some hands but not others bear liver spots—she had a crop of them herself—and some faces but not others get stamped with those unsightly dark splotches? Mr. Jack had had a splotch above his left eyebrow for years, but when they went for their semiannual visits to the dermatologist to be checked for suspicious new growths, the doctor always offered to remove it, but Jack said as long as it didn't bother Merry, he'd wait till it bothered him.

"Oh, isn't Sherry here today?"

"Sherry leaves at five. You're later than normal, Mrs. Rakestraw. By the way, we haven't met. I'm Doreen."

"How do you do, Doreen. Please call me Merry. How is he?"

"We've been in a bit of a mood today. At least since I came on. He's never happy when Sherry leaves. But she has a life, too."

"Did the laundry room straighten out the mistaken clothes he was wearing last week?"

"I'm afraid I don't know about that. But if it makes you feel any better, they don't really notice the difference. But Sherry did leave instructions about him needing some shoes he can slip into, like loafers."

"My husband has never worn loafers in his life."

"Yes, well, you see, he needs some that don't have to be laced up. He's forgotten how to do it, so somebody else has to do it for him."

Standing with his back to her in front of the window of his private visiting room, he wasn't that much changed from the old Jack. He had come to Laurel Grove fairly soon after his disintegration became apparent to others besides Merry. His hair, no longer flattened by a baseball cap, floated in wisps above his head. The Laurel Grove barber shaved rather than trimmed the back of his neck. He had lost all of his muscle and bulk. Some people gained, others lost, Sherry had said. ("Mr. Rakestraw eats what's on his plate, as long as we remember to serve him small portions. However, so far, there's been no need for supplemental drinks. He's restless when he has to sit down or remain in one place for long, and he's not exactly the sociable type, but he's always polite and considerate with the other residents."

"That's what he always is," Merry had told her, carefully stepping around the past tense.)

"Jack?"

He turned from the window. Outside was a perennial garden, a bit too well kept, bordering on a grassy lawn still bright with late afternoon sun.

Immediately she saw that this was to be one of those days when he hadn't the slightest idea who she was. She watched him reluctantly surrender whatever he had been thinking and dig deeply into his reserves of courtesy. (What thoughts *did* he have these days? She wished she had just a flicker of access to them!) Except for the diminishment in volume, he looked reassuringly like the man she had known since she was eight and had been married to for fourteen years, but she held back from going closer.

"I've just come to see how you are," she said.

"Won't you sit down?" Which he continued to say, whether he recognized her or not. He pointed to the chair she always sat in.

Jack-like, he kept standing. After he got past his mistrust stage, he would come closer and pace back and forth in front of her chair, glancing down on her with friendly curiosity, as though straining to recall who she was.

"I'm just about the same, thank you. All of us here are."

That was one of his Laurel Grove phrases. Then, digging into his reserves again, "And how about yourself? What have *you* been up to?"

"Well, today it was my turn to host the Ezekiel Bible group at our house. We sat on the west porch and discussed a psalm."

"A *psalm*," he repeated blankly.

"Then after they left, I looked over my notes for an article I'm doing for that tobacco magazine. This time they have asked for a history of the unfiltered cigarette in American life."

He gave her an opaque stare, as though she had suddenly switched into a foreign language. But at least he was past the mistrust and had begun to pace back and forth in front of her chair with friendly curiosity.

"So what have *you* been up to?" he asked again.

"Well, as I said, the Bible group came and we studied a psalm, then we had a late lunch, and when they left, it was still too early to come here—or at least I thought it was. I forgot that you have supper an hour earlier in daylight savings time."

"We've had supper. There's a new lady."

"Yes, I saw her. She was doing some crewel embroidery."

The word *crewel* seemed to alarm him. Did he think she meant *cruel*?

"It's embroidery done with wool, and you use a hoop to stretch the fabric. There are a great many stitches." Corinne, who was absent today because of her great-grandson's kindergarten graduation, always brought her crewel work to the Bible group. She had embroidered an elaborate banner for the church.

But now he had turned away from her and gone back to his post at the window. "Why don't they come like they're supposed to?" he asked angrily. "What is holding them up?"

"Who is supposed to be coming?"

"The fucking excavators. Why don't they come and get it over with?"

"They've already come and gone, Jack. I told you, but I expect you forgot. Now we're waiting for the graders and the landscapers. Thad said he would have left the old trees, instead of leveling everything and planting young ones in the sun that will take years to grow."

Turning to face her, he looked startled to see her sitting in the chair; she might have just arrived.

"How faithful you are to come back," he said in a gentler voice.

"Jack, I will always come back."

"So, tell me, what have *you* been up to?"

"Well, you know I told you I was writing this new magazine piece on the history of the unfiltered cigarette . . ."

"Oh-oh, can't buy those anymore."

"Well, you can if you go to the right places. I've been trying each brand. Today was Lucky Strike day."

"You know better than to smoke."

"I don't inhale. I try to, but I do it poorly. But just breathing it in and holding it in my mouth brings back all these old tastes and memories."

"You know he doesn't like it. You'd better let me check your breath before you go back. Get over here."

"You want me to—?" He was motioning impatiently for her to stand up, so she stood up.

But he was already coming to her, with his arms open. Next thing, she was folded into a viselike embrace.

"Oh," he groaned. "Oh, oh . . ."

Pressed against his diminished form, she smelled the Laurel Grove soap on his skin, the Laurel Grove laundry on his shirt. At least it was his own shirt today.

She felt his tears wetting the top of her head.

"Oh, Annie, my God." With a force almost violent he elevated her chin. "Is it really you?" He kissed her mouth, then kissed it more urgently, as though trying to get inside it.

"Oh, Annie, what took you so long?"

34

When Merry left Laurel Grove, she had two and a half more hours of daylight to get through. Summer solstice had been a month ago, but the days were not all that much shorter. Their mother had been the family's solstice marker. If you were interested in knowing how much daylight had been lost or gained since the day before, their mother could always tell you to the minute.

Annie, their mother.

When Merry reached home, she put off going inside. She didn't believe in ghosts, though there had been a period following Ritchie's death when she had longed for him to appear to her, even if he could only come to her in a wraithlike form. But, as with little Paul, she was only permitted to dream about him.

This evening she didn't long for, or expect, any family phantoms. What waited for her inside the Jellicoe house, built by great-great-grandparents and added onto by their descendants, were not spirits of the departed but only the need—the *task*—of reconfiguring all its spaces to assimilate her new knowledge. Reluctant to begin that task, she went again to her chair on the west porch and watched the light fade moment by moment from the sky above what she had come to regard as "Alda's stables."

You have searched me and known me . . . you are acquainted with all my ways.

If she could not believe in full that, from somewhere up there in the changing sky, she was being looked at and known, then how far could mere storytelling take her?

From up there or out there or over there, the story begins, imagine an ever-present Knower whose knowledge is so vast you can only praise it. The Knower, having watched her being knit together in her mother's womb, knows every thought she could think and every place she could go, however dark that place might be.

The darkness and the light are both alike to thee.

How can we know it's the Knower thinking, how do we slip into the rhythm of the Knower's thoughts?

The women in the Ezekiel Bible study group asked these questions every other week. Each offered up her ideas, her research, her speculations, and all of them sought guidance from the group's mind.

So, in her story, a woman in late middle age looks up at a sky she has known all her life and, on this evening as it darkens, asks the Knower for help.

You will have to be more specific than that, the Knower in the story says.

All the things I took for granted, trusted to be as I saw them, what happens when that certainty topples?

Certainties are always toppling. Are you still the person you thought you were?

I think I am, but I'm not sure I admire that person.

Why not?

For being so complacent and stupid. Once when Feron and I were lying on the lawn back at Lovegood and she had finished telling me her horrors, I said, "The worst that's ever happened to me was my dog, Sam, dying."

How were you feeling when you said that? Smug? Proud? Ashamed?

Not smug, not ashamed, and certainly not proud. More like "so far so good." Maybe just a shadow of fear about what could happen in the future.

And how are you feeling now, here on the west porch, while you await the stars?

I'm feeling close to those psalmists of thousands of years ago. All their anguish and rages and petitions. I feel *accompanied* by them. In fact, I am comforted to know they had the same stars.

Everything that is said or sung enriches what can be known.

Enriches even *you*, the Knower?

Of course. We're in this together. Let me ask you a question. Where do you think I am? Up there in the sky, hiding among the stars? Where do I dwell right now when you are sitting on the west porch, waiting for the stars? One just blinked into sight, look to your left, above the red maple you planted for Paul nine years ago. Now I ask you, Meredith Grace, whose name is written in my book, where am I now, and how is it you can hear me so clearly?

A motor switched off on the other side of the tall hedge. It sounded like Thad's car, but Thad never came after dark.

But around the hedge came Thad. It wasn't quite dark because his shoes were still brown against the light pea gravel of the walkway.

"Have I come too late?"

"Not at all. Pull that wicker chair over. I hosted the Bible group today, and everything's still arranged in a circle."

"So you've been busy."

"For me, I suppose. Then I drove over to see Jack at Laurel Grove."

"How's Jack doing?"

"His mood and his location in time is always a bit of a surprise. Today he was railing at the excavators for not coming, and then when we were saying good-bye, he thought—well, he took me for my mother."

She hoped it was dark enough for him not to see her Merry Grape blush.

"You aren't tired?"

"Not really. I have been putting off going inside."

"Why?"

"Today I took in more information than I'm used to, and I've been sitting out here in the—what would you call what it is now? When it's not quite dark but passes for dark until you see someone coming toward you on the path."

"Gloaming is nice." In a sweet unaffected tenor, Thad began singing:

> In the gloaming oh my darling
> When the lights are dim and low
> And the quiet shadows falling
> softly come and softly go . . .

Merry felt his "darling" was addressed to her.

"Oh, please don't stop."

"That's all I can remember," he said.

"Me, too. Sister Simone said such an interesting thing today, about how words can sing themselves out of us if we already know the tune. She was comparing it to slipping into the rhythm of God's thoughts. We were studying Psalm 139, the one that starts 'You have searched me out and known me.' Tabitha, that's our church organist, said she wanted Psalm 139 read at her funeral. I think I want it at mine, too."

"Please don't talk about your funeral, Merry. It cuts me up."

"Sorry."

"To be without you is bad enough. To be without you in the world would be awful."

That was the closest he had ever come to saying what she knew he felt.

"Have you just come straight from work?"

"I have. I was way up in Alamance County. A rich-as-Croesus fellow tried to bribe me. I'm fifty-four years old, and it's the first time anyone ever tried to buy me off."

"But what did he want?"

"A higher appraisal on his property than it was worth."

"Oh, Thad. What did you do?"

"Well, luckily, it was *said*. He didn't foist a roll of bills on me. So I pretended I hadn't heard him, and he got the hint and didn't try it again."

"That's probably what I would do. Though nobody's tried to bribe me yet."

"What's this about too much information in one day?"

"Maybe it's my age, but I'm suddenly waking up to how stupid I've been about so many things right under my nose."

"Like what?"

"Oh, the evil consequences from the plant that has made us so prosperous for nearly two centuries. I had known, of course, the surgeon general made it pretty clear, but it was a kind of *padded* knowledge. Up until this afternoon, I hadn't felt the remorse. I was writing another article for the state magazine on the history of the unfiltered cigarette in America. I had a notebook full of interesting things, and I was smoking all the unfiltered brands so I could describe the taste of each. The editor had said, 'A lot of our readers still smoke,' and I was sitting in this chair when I suddenly crossed the line from thinking, 'oh good, they're going to love my article,' to 'they should stop right this minute.' I'm going to call him tomorrow and explain."

"You're jettisoning it? Yes, that sounds like you."

"Then I started rereading Feron's *Mr. Blue*, to see if I could justify why she had used a story I had told her about my family. I realized for the first time that *I* felt used."

"I'm not much of a fiction reader, but Lou read *Mr. Blue*. She said it confused her, and Lou's not the sort to get confused."

"Then when I went to see Jack, he was in one of his other time zones, and he . . . well, he revealed something about our family that I hadn't known. I stayed outside because I didn't feel ready to face the rooms in the light of this new information."

Thad bowed forward in his chair, clasping his hands. Since she had known him, his hair had gone completely white. She loved the way he didn't go in for snappy comebacks. He was thinking over what she had said.

"Do you feel ready, now?" he asked.

"Not really. But I realize I have to go indoors sometime."

"Would you like for me to go in with you? We can take a tour through all the rooms, and I'll keep quiet unless I'm spoken to. And you can be quiet, too. How does that sound?"

"The tour guide just leads the way and doesn't say anything."

"Something like that."

"You are a mainstay."

"I take that to be a yes for the silent tour."

They went into the house without a word. Kitchen. Dining room. Living room. Ritchie's room. Thad had been in these downstairs rooms, but Merry did wonder what was going through his mind now. She went ahead of him into each room and casually walked around, noting objects, letting the room guide her own thoughts. Thad followed. His naturalness kept the proceeding from seeming absurd.

As she went first up the stairs, she broke the silence. "These upstairs rooms are mostly bedrooms. This room at the top of the stairs was the old master bedroom, where my grandparents slept. At the end of the hall is the new master bedroom with its own bath. They were added when my parents moved into the house. The grandparents' old bedroom became my mother's workroom, where she sewed. She later preferred to retreat to the third floor, to what we called the loft room because it was once a loft. She went to the loft room when she was in her low periods. We were not allowed to go there because she said that's where she went to put herself back together. When Ritchie was little, he thought that meant if he entered he would find her in pieces."

A barely audible laugh from Thad. It was a warm laugh. Thad knew how she felt about Ritchie.

"Across the hall is my girlhood room, now a rarely used guest room."

She stopped to pat the double bed. "There used to be twin beds in here, but they weren't long enough for adults. The day my parents were killed, I was making up the bed Feron was going to sleep in that night, if she had come. I had switched her over to my bed so she wouldn't have to look out at the black barns. You remember them. Ritchie thought they were beautiful."

"They were regal. I was sorry to see them go."

"Soon after we buried my parents, I started sleeping in the new master bedroom, if a forty-year-old room can still be called new, and, well, I've been sleeping in it ever since. Did I say something wrong?"

"No."

"You look distressed. What's wrong?"

"Only that I'm dying to hold you."

"Please don't die, Thad. Life would be awful without you in it."

35

Susan Fox
Dean Emerita
Dinwiddie House
Lovegood College

September 10, 1996

Dear Feron,

Two years have passed since you so thoughtfully sent me your latest book—at least it was your latest book two years ago. As with your other novels, I sat down and read it straight through. I remember warming to it immediately. "Now, here is something fresh," I said to myself. "Something fresh—and true."

And then, let's see, my dear friend Eloise Sprunt died. It was not an easeful death. Far from it. I moved in with her during the last months, helped out under the guidance of the hospice people, and spent the remainder of the week cleaning her beautiful self-designed apartment after the undertakers had loaded her body on their gurney and taken her away to be embalmed. Her children, now in their sixties, wanted an open casket funeral and asked me to deliver the eulogy. It was done at the funeral home because Eloise was not a churchgoer.

Then—what happened next? (I am still recovering memory after a triple bypass, after which I awoke and remembered nothing!) Oh, next came a depression, which was worse in its way than the surgery, because during the depression I could not anticipate a recovery date. What saved me, I think, was that Lovegood was being sued, and I was able to help out while the search committee went looking for a new president.

I just glanced over what I had written, and it reads like a missive from Calamity Jane. However, I'll finish the rest of the bad news, and then I want to return to happier subjects, including *A Singular Courtship*, which I have just this week read again.

Two girls broke into the sports center to go for a midnight swim, and one of them drowned. The parents sued and won big. President Brook offered his resignation, and it was accepted. Now we finally have a new president, Jillian Norden, a powerhouse with a background in banking and public relations. She is only in her midthirties, but comes to us with a formidable reputation for fund-raising and cost cutting. Married to a quiet, agreeable man some years her senior, with a son about her age.

I was forty-five when I came to Lovegood. Now I am eighty-four. After my recovery from the bypass(es) and the depression, I feel almost dangerously vital. So much so that I forget my age and get reminded of it in myriad ways. The other day, I was in the pharmacy picking up a prescription when an angry young person accused me of "breaking in line." I stepped aside to let her go ahead of me, but this seemed to increase her annoyance. As I was leaving the pharmacy, she was complaining to the manager, and when she spotted me, she pointed and said, "That's the one, that's the old woman who tried to shove ahead of me." And, you know, it took half a second for me to realize I was "the old woman."

I have seen Merry Jellicoe (Rakestraw). She drove up with a friend whose daughter is a student at Lovegood, and we had a wonderful visit here at Dinwiddie House.

I don't know if I told you this, but the trustees allow me to live here as an on-campus emblem of old Lovegood values. It is an elegant, rather inconvenient old Victorian house, but after my surgery I moved downstairs, and Mr. Peeler, President Norden's husband, now has his offices upstairs. Mr. Peeler had a small, very profitable investment company that he sold to a bigger one, and he advises friends about their stocks and carries on an extensive e-mail exchange with friends all over the country. His son has equipped the upstairs offices with the latest connections, and he is giving me tutorials on how to use this daunting new addition to our technology. And Mr. Peeler and I have embarked on a team-teaching elective course for juniors and seniors. In 1989 Lovegood became a four-year college, as you no doubt know from the annual report.

You and Merry are among Lovegood's most faithful donors. When Merry was here at Dinwiddie House, she mentioned your Sophie Sewell Hood scholarship and said she wanted to set up a Paul Jellicoe Rakestraw scholarship. That was the little boy who died, which I am sure you know about. You might not know that Mr. Rakestraw has been in an assisted-living home for a few years now. Merry says he doesn't know who she is anymore, but he seems happy to see her most of the time. She has a full-time job in a funeral home, which she loves.

And now for your novel. I fell in love with Isobel, Tom's mother, on the first page. Oh dear, I thought, I hope she stays on through the story, and she did. And Nora, whom Tom brings home unannounced, I immediately saw was an extremely smart but untrusting young woman, socially awkward but aware of her lacks. While she's not saying much, she is always observing others. I didn't see it coming but found it convincing that someone like Nora would look over at Tom during their drive back to school and picture herself marrying him and becoming part of the family.

And the letters, on both sides, were wonderful. Each woman knows herself fairly well and allows the other to know her. As for Tom, I think I got to know as much about his emotional life as Tom does himself. When we are inside his head, it is like suddenly being lifted into lonely, rarefied air. He isn't at all the sort of person who is interested in figuring out others. He has become one with his vocation. I got excited just by learning a fraction about the subjects he is pursuing. Especially about those medieval centuries when some individuals were striving toward the highest feelings human nature could achieve. "A new respect for human possibilities was in the air," as he tells them in his first lecture. And Nora was attracted by this idea before she was attracted to Tom. I caught myself wishing that Miss McCorkle could meet Tom and had to remind myself that Tom was a character in a novel! (Miss McCorkle, now Mrs. Radford, and her husband have moved to a retirement center. They are both still active in their church and politics and travel all over the world. They send one of those Christmas letters that goes to everybody, only theirs is full of news worth reading.)

Dear me, I have just started an eighth sheet of notepaper, writing on both sides. This must come to an end, though I have enjoyed it. Speaking of ends, I was, once again, unprepared for their wedding night. "Passionate abstinence," what a thoroughly medieval concept, but with Nora and Tom it didn't seem far-fetched. I expect you got some outcries from the reviewers in this "let-it-all-hang-out" era of ours. Which, in its turn, will go its way, and who knows what comes after? What goes around comes around.

I eagerly await your next book.

Yours,

Susan Fox

This is deserving of a P.S., after what I wrote above. The president's husband and I are team teaching an elective course for juniors and seniors listed in the Lovegood catalog as Social Skills in Business. Mr. Peeler's son, while searching for a profession, spent half a year in England going to Butler School. We are working from his old syllabus. Starting with how to set the table, which fork is for what, moving on to conversational and wardrobe dos and don'ts and so on. And guess what? The class is oversubscribed! What goes around comes around?

36

December 8, 1996

Dear Feron,

I am counting back and realizing my last letter to you was in 1988. After you wrote in your thoughtful note about little Paul that you might be coming down soon, I finally got up the nerve to write back and tell you I had abandoned my Stephen Slade novel. As it turned out, you didn't come down, and now, somehow, eight years have gone by.

I say "somehow," which I'll get to now. Ritchie used to say, "Do you want the good news or the bad news first?" and I always said the bad first because then there would be something to look forward to.

So, let's see, Jack went into an assisted-living place in 1990 and is still there, or some of him is. Laurel Grove is top of the line, Cousin Thad found it for us (of course!), and we are fortunate to be able to afford it.

I received an announcement of Mr. Sterling's death from the literary agency last year.

The last time you and I met face-to-face was in 1979 at the Neuse River Café. How can that be, when you are with me every day and so frequently in my night life? As you once said of me, you are one of the regulars in my dreams. I do get to hear about you from your cousin Thad. He said that someone left you a beach house, and you are hard at work on a new novel, which you have to finish before you go anywhere. I heard that Blanche Buttner had moved out of your Pullen house and gone back to Benton Grange. I have had a job working in a funeral home since 1993, but no, that has to wait for the good news.

Early in 1994, I finally went back to the dermatologist (after Jack went to Laurel Grove, I got careless about checkups), and he found a melanoma on the back of my leg. It turned out to have metastasized to other places (lungs, liver) and I went through the whole regime—some "site" surgeries, then chemotherapy and radiation, and felt pretty bad for almost a year. My Bible study group was wonderful; I couldn't have got through it without them. Your cousin Thad kept asking when I was going to let you know, and I would say, "I hope never, because I intend to get through this. And if she finds out through *you*, I am not going to be pleased."

Now, here is the good news. I am in remission, back at work at Blake's Funeral Home. My boss is Lavonne Blake, who's in my Bible study group. Her daughter, Rachel, is graduating from Lovegood in May. Lavonne had to drop out of premed and take over the family business when her father died. I felt close to her from the start, because her story is similar to mine. My job is mostly being a glorified receptionist, but I do lots of other things—except what I can't do without a funeral director's license. Do you know one of the things I love most about going to a real job for the first time in my life? Getting dressed! I often think of you when I'm deciding what to wear. "Feron has been doing this for over thirty years," I say to myself. Dressing for work is like putting on a costume belonging to a different part of yourself.

I am typing this at home on a desktop computer which your cousin Thad kindly set up for me and taught me how to use. It's not easy to learn these skills when you're our age. I am slowly getting proficient with e-mail, if you will let me know your e-mail address. Mine is jellicoe@aol.com. Meanwhile, I've learned to write my stories and letters on the computer and print them out. It's amazing what you can do—move things around with cut and paste, delete whole sections without having to copy pages over. Remember how I had to rewrite a whole page, just to change *ordinary* into *optimistic*, as you had advised after reading my story for Miss Petrie? Young people now will never know the messy, smelly experience of Wite-Out-ing whole paragraphs.

I've started writing again. After my remission, I reread a bunch of stories by Chekhov, and then I chose the title of one—"The Teacher of Literature"—and wrote a story about a young woman like Maud Petrie meeting a young woman like Miss Olafson when they were at the same college. Chekhov's teacher of literature is a young man who makes a bad marriage which he longs to escape, but I actually got my Maud character and my Olafson character to where they realize their passion for each other and I shamelessly concluded it by stealing phrases from the ending of "The Lady with the Little Dog": *("Then they spent a long while taking counsel together, talked of how to avoid the necessity for secrecy, for deception . . .* [though] *it was clear to both of them that they still had a long, long road before them, and that the most complicated and difficult part of it was only just beginning.")* I felt comfortable with my theft because my "Teacher of Literature" will never see the light of day, but I gained a great confidence by seeing it through.

Now, to *A Singular Courtship*. I'm not a critic, I never even finished my freshman year as you know, but I think it has taken you to a whole new level. Remember our Algonquin meeting, when you told me a little about your marriage to Will and his mother's "courtship" and how you hadn't been able to find a way to write about your married life. "Nothing really fits what Will and I had together," you said. But in *A Singular Courtship* I think you have pointed the way. Remember how Miss Petrie quoted Chekhov about how a story can be wholly satisfying if the problems are convincingly set out? Well, you did that in *A Singular Courtship*, Feron, and now it feels like you have crossed some barrier and can go anywhere you like.

And your writing is so realistic, though there will always be a touch of the beyond about the way you see things, Feron. Your idea about our "reference auras," for example. Or that time on the lawn at Lovegood when you tapped your fingers in the grass and said the class poet of 1918 would be in her upper fifties and her life might have become "congealed, like Jell-O." I still ask myself from time to time, "Does anyone think I have congealed?" And unbelievably we are now in our upper fifties, like Mary Louisa Summerlin was when we talked of her on the lawn.

Feron, you've got to come back down here some time. Please finish your novel and come again. Since we had to cancel your visit that terrible day following the Christmas of '58, you have yet to see where I live.

Much love,
Merry

Merry read through her e-mail, cut out a few too many mentions of Thad, and added "your cousin" to the others.

Feron would never hear *that* personal story from her.

If my "day of too much information" in the summer of 1992 had not ended with Cousin Thad's inspired "house tour," I might have missed possessing the dearest secret of my life.

She printed the revised pages, folded them into an envelope addressed to Feron's office, and deliberated between the remaining thirty-two-cent stamps on her Commemorative Year sheet. She had been holding back the four "Indian Dances" to feel close to Ritchie, but now, for Feron, she picked the scariest one Ritchie would have loved best, "Raven Dance."

37

1996

Feron had at last confronted Cuervo. "You once said you could tell me what I don't know about myself, but then you never did."

"I said, 'When you're ready to ask,' but you never did."

"Would you still do it, if I asked?"

"You'd better ask soon. I experience tolerable and less tolerable days."

"You ate your flan, and it stayed down, and you aren't wearing your nosepiece right now. Is this a tolerable day?"

"There is more to tell, now that I know you better."

"What is that tune you've been humming all morning?"

"'September Song.' It was high on the charts when I arrived in this country thinking I was Prince of the World. As I was for a while."

"'September Song' was the favorite request my first year at Lovegood! There was this evening radio program called *Our Best to You*, where people called in. We loved that program, only Merry made us turn off the radio after lights out."

"It is embedded in my memory. *Incrustado*. When I am remembering that time in my life, the song starts up on its own. When I woke up, a phrase was playing in my head."

"Oh, which phrase?"

"'One hasn't got time for the waiting game.' I will spare you my off-key singing."

"I can't sing, either." Nonetheless Feron did: "*When the autumn weather / turns the leaves to flame / one hasn't got time for the waiting game.*"

"Yes."

"Yes, what?"

"Yes, those are the right words, and yes, neither of us can carry a tune.

I would begin my assessment of your character as follows: A *tortuga*'s resistance to being known, a shunner of society, quick to see the worst in others but unforgiving when it comes to your own faults. Envious. Competitive. A hungry singularity of mind. Once I would have said a procrastinator, but it is more of a stubborn holding back, an endurance test with yourself to see how long you can *not* do something. And frugal."

"You called me a skinflint."

"Let me revise. Having known you for over twenty years, I would choose a more attractive word from my country: *amarette*. It means 'always saving.'"

"I know I'm tight with money, but 'always saving' sounds much nicer. But I already knew most of these things about myself! Hard on myself, envious, unsocial, wary—though my husband, Will, did say he loved my 'wary grace.' He said I moved like someone antici-pating a lightning strike, but I kept marching on, my face revealing nothing."

"But you haven't awakened to your rarer strengths. I remember telling you in our first conference that you have more strangeness in you than you know. And you have tapped this strangeness to some degree in your fiction. I can guarantee there is more if you will find openings for it. How many years have you lived in this city?"

"I came in the late summer of 1963. Will died in January, and then I spent six months with my uncle and his fiancée."

"Please, you add it up. My brain is running low on energy. As a matter of fact, I am going to need that nosepiece again."

"Oh, no, I've tired you out. Maybe you should rest now."

"I have all the resting time I need ahead of me. I count more than thirty years."

"Ninety-five minus sixty-three is, oh God, thirty-two years. How did that happen?"

"And how many places did you 'apartment-sit'?"

"Offhand I can't say. I would have to make a list."

"I'm not asking you to go into numbers, but you must have saved some money living this monastic life for three decades."

"Hardly monastic. There have been some encounters. Mostly unwise and regretted. A few downright embarrassing."

"I don't wish to hear about them, as I don't wish to share my own encounters. Some of us simply are not adept at maintaining the part that comes after the encounters. Then let's say monastic in your lack of possessions. While I had to teach myself sparsity after I purchased this tiny apartment, the discipline seems natural to you."

"When Will was my professor, he said if you could answer the question 'What is my discipline?' you were on solid ground. But he meant discipline more in terms of vocation. I hadn't found my discipline even after I was married to Will. But during the lonely hours in England when he was over at the university immersed in *his* discipline, I began to worry that I might never find it. It was beginning to get to me."

"Yes, I can see that it would."

"Did you get yours earlier in life?"

"In early life, my main occupation was planning my suicide. I wanted to be under the soil before they realized I was a monster. Then one day I was playing around with a story about a family who *does* know it has a monster in its midst. I made the father rich and powerful enough to do anything he wants. He builds a walled garden and populates it with other freaks like Nito. But I was telling you how I had to teach myself sparsity, where to you the discipline came naturally."

"My not acquiring things began when I moved to New York. While I was living in other people's places, I couldn't load myself down with possessions, and the 'while' turned into three decades. When I did finally commit myself to a sublet, I found I had lost the getting urge. Except for clothes, but for those I always waited till I went back to Uncle Rowan's, and his fiancée would take me to her stores and they'd put it on her bill. So my sparsity is tainted with mooching."

"Now you have a sublet. When does it end?"

"Oh my goodness, next year already. But if worse comes to worst, I can always retreat to Pullen and live in my own house."

"Is that something you want?"

"No, I like it here. In New York, you can be invisible, if it suits you. I feel timeless and free, like an untethered artist floating above the buildings in the night sky."

"In that case, I will leave my tiny 'beach house' to you. But I haven't finished my assessment. Do you want to hear the rest?"

"There's more?"

"Just a little. You are a faithful friend. Now, don't wince. Learn to accept a compliment. And you are unemotional . . ."

"That's a compliment?"

"Sometimes it is, sometimes it isn't. In Latin America, they might call you *vacana*, a cool person. Free from what the psychoanalysts call *affect*. You don't show much emotion. Why is that, I wonder?"

"I don't know. It's like when you said I could be funny. I never thought of myself as funny. Though Merry said I was. The other, the *vacana*, hasn't always worked in my favor. At my mother's inquest, which I told you about, I didn't cry. My stepfather cried buckets. Everyone thought my behavior was unnatural and suspicious."

"When your husband died, did you cry?"

"Not at first. I was more angry with him, his carelessness. I felt abandoned. I felt scared. I didn't cry until I was living with Blanche Buttner. And it was a strange sort of crying. More like suppressed sobs. I remember crying a lot when we lived with my grandparents, but they were temper tantrums to get my way. After my stepfather took us over, I don't remember crying. Though I must have. I was only four at the time. People of four cry, right?"

"I was not a crier as a boy. The less I was noticed, the less my monstrousness would be suspected."

"I will have to think about it. I really don't know why I'm this way."

"Perhaps you will discover why in some yet-to-be-written tale."

"I wouldn't know where to start. 'The woman who couldn't cry'? Like the Grimms' story about the boy who wanted to learn fear?"

"It will come in its time. If it has a time."

"In *Nito's Garden*, it's only the rich, powerful father. The mother is never mentioned."

"*De acuerdo.*"

"What about your mother in real life?"

"She was useless to me in real life, so I omitted a mother figure in my book."

Walking around Cuervo's beach house, Feron continued murmuring to him. He had been gone a year. The last time she had seen him in the hospital—or rather the last time he would allow her to see him—they went over his burial arrangements. Paid in full, including gravestone. Plot bought ten years previously.

Green-Wood Cemetery in Brooklyn. Take the R train to the Twenty-fifth Street stop and wear walking shoes. "I'll be in good company: nineteenth-century lesbian artists, piano virtuosos, Civil War soldiers, Henry Ward Beecher, and now even Lenny Bernstein!" Feron took the R train a single time. When she returned to the beach house, he was waiting just inside the door. He was not under the soil at Green-Wood.

The afterlife Cuervo had many comments to make, so many in fact that she had stopped trying to distinguish between which ones she'd actually heard him say and which were new ones. She asked him questions and was rewarded with oblique answers, some of them useful.

"When you arrived in New York feeling you were the Prince of the World, were you planning to write a second novel *then*?"

"I hadn't decided *not to* yet."

It was not unlike consulting a Ouija board or having a fruitful session with your active imagination.

Blanche had returned to her home after Orrin had been carried out of Buttner House on the undertaker's gurney. The dreadful Daphne stayed on awhile, then vanished one day. Taking a number of valuable items with her.

"I had way too many things," Blanche wrote. "Some of the things she nicked I never liked anyway. If you want anything, now is the time to say, because I am embarking on a long-overdue dismantling of Buttner House. There is no way I can ever adequately thank you for those years in your Pullen house. I know this is only a fantasy but I do feel I was given a taste of being Rowan's wife, even though he was only there in spirit."

*   *   *

The novel Feron had begun in Cuervo's beach house on his little Olivetti was stalled because of—what? Dislike? Disgust? Discomfort? *The Woman Who Lied*, it was called, or was going to be called. With *Beast and Beauty* and *Mr. Blue*, she had begun with models of fairy tales. *A Singular Courtship* had evolved out of her needing to record the underlying—Cuervo might use the word *strange*—realities of her short marriage. "It was more like an impressionistic elegy" she had described it to Merry at their Algonquin meeting. What more had she told Merry at the time? Oh, God, the lie about the kind old editor who praised the draft but said it needed more "bed scenes"? Beginning *The Woman Who Lied*, Feron had once again felt the urgent need of a model, some other piece of literature to lean on, and she had chosen, perhaps stupidly, a combination of *Notes from Underground* and *The Fall*. Both were confessions, Dostoevsky's narrator enraged and disgusted, and Camus's lawyer ironic and suave.

She had got her lying woman onto the bus, as in her failed story for Miss Petrie, and had kept the momentum going through the woman's narration of falsehoods through her childhood and teen years. ("My lies were safety barriers I put between myself and what others wanted to make of me.") An excellent reason for lying, Feron had thought, typing away: to save yourself from what others wanted to make of you!

Then Feron had started second-guessing her original plan. How could you have a whole novel take place on a bus ride? Well, but Camus had kept his nameless narrator and listener inside a bar for the whole 147 pages. Should she keep her narrator nameless? If she gave her a name, what would be the most fitting one? Vera was a little *too* ironic. Maybe something ugly: Bertha? No, that was the name of Mr. Rochester's crazy wife.

Feron's mother's name had been Leona. Like the hotel woman who went to jail.

But *The Woman Who Lied* stopped dead when the woman, still unnamed, confessed to taking Ergotrate to get rid of a fetus. After two prescriptions of Ergotrate had failed to do the job, she had rushed into a (short-lived) marriage.

More than once in a mood of drunken spite, Feron's mother had told her daughter her own Ergotrate story. ("But you hung in there!")

The woman on the bus told her listener, "Alas for *my life*, she hung in there like a tick."

At which point, Feron put the cover on Cuervo's Olivetti, which fit better than her old Royal on his desk, and went out for a walk. When she returned to the beach house, she spoke aloud to Cuervo's spirit.

"What should I do with this thing? Please help me."

"It has a propulsion, it may be leading you toward something you don't yet know. But perhaps you could use a short sabbatical."

Out of fear that he would stop speaking, Feron kept herself from reminding him he had suggested this in their first conference.

"It will come in its time. If it has a time."

That's what you said about "The Woman Who Couldn't Cry" before you died.

Cuervo's tiny apartment looked much as he had left it. The only art on the wall facing the windows was his great-uncle Eugenio's framed pastel of Cervantes dreaming the character of Don Quixote.

"Would you like me to set you a task?" Cuervo's voice inquired.

38

Your task is to outwalk the sponsor.

"Refrain from all writing and thinking about writing. You are a walker, so walk. When something interests you, pause, take it in, and walk on. Pause and absorb but do not form words about it or try to shape it into something else. No trying to 'capture' it, like tourists with their cameras, who frantically click and click and return home with nothing but little squares. No planning, no plotting. One cannot stop the *recuerdos*—recollections are inevitable, but refrain from all planning and plotting and fabulating. Resist anything calculated to impress the eyes of others. Walk and look and walk on. *Anda . . . mira . . . anda.*

"Outwalk the sponsor!"

It sounded like genuine posthumous Cuervo returning to elaborate on one of his memorable figures of speech. Ah, yes, the good old sponsor. ("All the influences outside yourself—or between you and your work.")

She intended to accept his task, but first some letters on the little Olivetti. Having kept faith with her Blanche correspondence, she could certainly honor the longest letter she ever received from her oldest friend. Even as she was reading Merry's letter, responses were tumbling out of her. But when it came to rolling in the sheet of paper and typing the opening words, she regressed into a childlike stupor. How do you start a letter when your oldest friend has just written to tell you that she had cancer but didn't tell you?

She would tackle the other letter first, which had been forwarded from her publisher after languishing for four months in someone's nonurgent pile.

This from "Josefa Maglia," twin sister of the artist who had illustrated *Mr. Blue*. Joachim Maglia, whom Feron had never met, had died, the sister said. Feron assumed AIDS, since Josefa Maglia's film, which had won best Independent Short Documentary at the Atlanta Film Festival, was titled *Brother Death: An AIDS Elegy*.

> Joachim and I shared a loft, so I watched the art for your book come into being. First he would apply a monochrome layer of wash, usually in sepia, though with *Mr. Blue* he started experimenting with an almost transparent overlay of indigo. We would go over a passage he was thinking of illustrating and talk about the possibilities. He would try different approaches. You might be interested to know that the first frontispiece for *Mr. Blue* was a man in work clothes carrying a suitcase and a hat standing as seen from below by the little girl who has just opened the door. His face is in shadow because the sunny fields are behind him. The giant jaw, seen from so far below, dominates, with grim line of mouth, nostrils, and eyes slanted downward. "Too threatening," said my brother, and he started over so the man with the suitcase and hat has his back to us and is looking down on the little girl blocking his way. She was a success because he caught the juxtaposition between the little-girl body and the closed imperious face.

> My purpose in writing you is to make a bid for a two-year film option on *Mr. Blue*. Ever since Joachim died, I keep seeing scenes from your story. I have read multiple versions

of the Bluebeard story, and watched the best film treatments (*Gaslight*, *Spellbound*, *Suspicion*, *Shadow of a Doubt*), and then tried to turn it around, as my brother turned around your frontispiece, to see if I could come up with why a woman, a wife, a woman of property, would make a certain room off-limits for the man. More perplexing is why he honors her injunction? Even more mystifying, what does the sparsely furnished old loft room tell him, and us, after her death?

Why, really, does someone of either sex keep a private place no one else may enter? Or does that place already exist because each and every one of us spends the majority of our time at the mercy of our interior life?

Joachim threw away many attempts before he got that room the way he liked. We walked up and down lower Broadway looking for The Chair. Joachim said, "Nobody's going to try to sell a chair with stuffing coming out of it, but I can do stuffing." And the table and the folded blanket and the window and those lines still showing where the loft had been plastered over.

I believe that filming and editing a story can convey dimensions of time and the way the mind works that are not so accessible to the writer or the painter. *Brother Death* was black and white and silent in the dying sections, and was in color with minimal dialogue when he was making his paintings. Whether I would take that route with *Mr. Blue*, I can't say until I begin. But if you are willing to take a chance on me, we could meet and talk. That is, if the book isn't optioned to someone else.

Hoping,
Josefa Maglia

* * *

Walking without planning and plotting was no easy task. What had she thought about during all those months and years, when she was swinging along the pavements to and from work? She remembered her shoes, every damn pair of them, it seemed, but nothing of the mental travels that accompanied them on their daily rounds. Had young women really traipsed back and forth to work in three-inch heels? Blanche had schooled Feron in footwear before she left for Lovegood College. Better to go half a size bigger than what you *thought* you were, if it feels roomier. Besides, longer is more elegant. Through all of college and for the (few) Institute of Medieval Studies gatherings at Durham University in England, when she was known as Mrs. Avery or "Will Avery's wife," the 8AA black pumps with three-inch heels were her set of social feet. On excursions with Will to ruined monasteries and holy places, she had a pair of lace-up walking shoes that lasted until fifteen years later, when one morning they began to pinch because her feet had grown. She remembered the exact morning: before the lunch with Merry at the Neuse River Café. Feron had worn pants and a sweater and a jacket and the suddenly-too-tight walking shoes, and Merry had dressed in beautiful clothes and announced that she had married Mr. Jack. Why, you could write a whole essay revealing a person's life through their choice of shoes.

STOP!

Pause and absorb but do not form words about it or try to shape it into something else.

Stop "capturing" the shoes: the three inch, then the two inch, then the eighties when young women sprinted to work in gym shoes and carried their social feet in a bag.

"Scores," Cuervo had said.

"Scores! You mean as in 'threescore and ten'? That kind of scores?"

"Let's see, when did you enroll in my class?"

"Seventy-two?"

"Yes, in seventy-two I had scores of friends. Counting colleagues, students, social acquaintances, and publishing people, not all of them close, but some of them were. A decade later they started dying mysteriously. One day a friend asked me to go with him to see his friend in the hospital. He said, 'He's got something strange and they've isolated him and we will have to wear masks and gowns.' From then on, the mystery disease started picking them off. I was lucky to be among the living when they discovered a pill that inhibits the damage. Inhibits. Not cures. My ugly sores have disappeared but my lungs are too compromised. I have made it to my threescore mark but won't complete the extra ten."

If you really got into the walking task, you noticed more things than you ever supposed could exist in the same period of time within eight to ten blocks of Cuervo's beach house. One could write a guidebook, *How to Absorb New York without Trying to Shape It into Something Else*.

Get lost, sponsor!

How deeply ingrained was this habit of plotting and planning how to attract the sponsor? How far back did it go? Not to the walks in Pullen and Benton Grange. In those walks she had been trying to think of ways to improve herself in order to remain welcome to the people in her new life. At Lovegood there was little walking, except to seedy Cobb's Corner with Merry. At the university, her walking steps around the quad drummed to the beat of how to pass the courses, how to impress, how to graduate. Or had they begun after her bathroom reading of Merry's "Lingering on the Lawn," when envy and competition had reared their heads? From then on, perhaps she had carried plottings of how to turn her despoiled childhood into something artistic that would snag the attention of others—as Joyce had struggled for ten years to find the right form to hold his young years.

She walked up and down Bleecker Street and thought about Will. The rainy trip back to school when he broke a long silence:

"You and my mother have become friends. I was wondering how you thought of me."

It was deep winter, cold with icy rain, so he kept his eyes on the road ahead of them. Driving back to campus from his mother's house. For the eighth, or was it the tenth, time?

"You mean, as a friend, or what?"

"I think I'm asking more about the 'or what?' "

Was this it? Was this on the way to being it? Whichever it was, her answer had to be clear and true but not frightening or tell-all true.

"Well, I think you are the first man I have ever admired."

"Admired." He tested the word, still staring hard at the road ahead of them.

"Wait, I haven't finished. I like spending time with you. I am a little envious of your work. I hope that someday I become as engrossed by something as you are, something I'd rather do than anything else. And as I already said, I really admire you."

"You do like spending time with me?"

"I have no other person who has come as close. The nearest was my old roommate, Merry, at Lovegood College. But you're the first man I feel at home with, though I don't know you as well as I do your mother."

The windshield wipers swiped back and forth against the icy rain.

"I am thirty-seven years old. Did you know that?"

"I'd more or less figured it out from talking to your mother."

"You are how old?"

"I was twenty-two last June."

"So you're twenty-two now and I'm still thirty-seven until February. For four months every year I will be fifteen years older, and for the other eight I'll be sixteen years older. Will that be too much difference?"

"I think it will be just about right."

"Why, really, does someone of either sex keep a private place no one else may enter?" Josefa Maglia had written. "Or does that place already exist because each and every one of us spends the majority of our time at the mercy of our interior life?"

Sometimes during a walk around the Village, Feron began experiencing moments of transitioning out of herself and evaporating into an excursive mind with no personal needs to hold it back. Sort of similar to Joyce's wish to refine himself out of existence in his writing. Or did this count as a sponsor thought?

No, it didn't. It didn't want anything. It was merely a *recuerdo* of having been struck by that Joyce passage in her university dorm room.

Taking off from Josefa Maglia's speculation about being at the mercy of our inner lives, Feron walked one day into a comprehension of what Will had probably been doing on the windy, misty day he stumbled and fell off the eroded edge of the cliff at Saltburn-by-the-Sea.

She remembered Aurelia Avery's description of young Will's ferocious walking. (". . . in fact he seemed not to be aware of where he walked, but he set a fiendish pace . . .") The doctor had told Will's parents that brains worked better when one walked.

January 2, 1997

Dear Josefa Maglia,

Sorry about the long delay. Your letter had been sitting at my publishing house for four months.

Your project sounds promising. Let's meet and talk about the two-year option. I feel I should tell you I have never been satisfied with *Mr. Blue*. Your questions about private places and interior lives were intriguing. The film medium may indeed convey dimensions of time and the way the mind works that I failed to capture.

Let's get together and explore this further. Here's my street address. I don't have e-mail yet.

Sincerely,

Feron Hood

39

January 10, 1997

Dear Merry,

Just think: three years from now we will be in the new millennium. I am learning e-mail. I have a young friend, a filmmaker, who is doing her best to drag me into the twenty-first century. I'm already familiar with the internet from my job at MacFarlane's, from which I have been "bought out."

I don't really know where to start. How does a friend begin a letter to a friend who had cancer and didn't tell her? I am surprised Cousin Thad held out. But the last thing he would want in the world would be to go against your wishes.

Maybe, like you, I'll begin with the dreary stuff. My great friend and mentor Alexy Cuervo died in 1995. The "beach house" Thad mentioned that Cuervo left me is a small fifth-floor apartment in Greenwich Village. Cuervo called it his beach house because if you stick your head out the window and look left, you can see the Hudson River.

Let's see. My "retirement" from MacFarlane & Company. (By the way, use my home address on this envelope from now on.) The young woman in Human Resources, as Personnel is now called, looked into my folder and exclaimed: "I wasn't even born in 1963!" (The year I started at MacFarlane.)

"I expect *you've* seen a lot of changes at MacFarlane in your time," she said.

"Mostly just the computer screen that ruined the tranquility of my office," I said. "But human nature at MacFarlane has remained pretty much the same."

Her desk name plate said *Trudi M. Schube*. Trudi M. Schube said, "I heard you wrote some novels under another name than Avery. I stopped in to Barnes and Noble hoping to buy one so you could sign it for me today, but they didn't have any books by Feron Hood."

At the end, when she stood up and came around the desk to shake my hand for graciously accepting "the package," she said, "I am planning to write a novel when I can find the time."

"Oh? What will it be about?"

"It will be about a modern woman in the city, sort of contemporary."

I said, "Well, don't wait too long. Time has a way of slipping by. Before you know it, you'll be receiving *your* buyout package."

I am really sorry to hear about Jack, but as you say it's fortunate he can be in a place like Laurel Grove.

And I'm sorry about Mr. Sterling, your literary agent. I will never forget opening that *Atlantic* and seeing a story by "M. G. Petrie." I'm glad you are writing again. It's a way of life, isn't it? I just killed off the novel I told Thad I couldn't go anywhere until I finished. Yes, Blanche is back at Benton Grange, getting rid of all the furniture that the dreadful daughter-in-law didn't make off with.

I love your idea of picking out a Chekhov story title and writing a story with the same title. Maybe I'll try that myself. After my young friend Josie acquaints me with the laptop she says I am going to buy, maybe I'll break it in by writing a Chekhov story.

Thank you for the good things you said about *A Singular Courtship*. I, too, thought I had crossed some barrier and freed up a little more of myself, but then the old panicked ambition kicked in, and I started thinking, *A Singular Courtship* was published in 1994, better get going on another book. And up popped *The Woman Who Lied*.

Are there certain poisonous topics lying in wait to bring a too-determined writer down?

I had a good letter last year from Dean Fox.

Your job sounds fascinating. Tell me more.

Love,
Feron

———————

Blake Funeral Home
January 20, 1997

Dear Feron,

It has been so hectic around here. In this business, you can go days without a service or a burial, and then suddenly there are pileups. But I want to clear up something about my not telling you. In your young life you were tested so much.

I guess I didn't want to add to the weight. I didn't want you to feel you had to drop everything and fly to my bedside. But if, God forbid, it should happen again, I promise I will let you know.

Love,
Merry

January 30, 1997

Dear Merry,

Thank you for your promise. Think of it this way. If you didn't tell me and I found out too late, it would be the worst test of my life and I could never forgive myself.

Will had a student in his Medieval England class who asked him, "Shouldn't a person's improvement count for part of the grade?" During our marriage, we often quoted Mr. Tribby, who dropped the course after Will said no. When Will and I were being hard on ourselves for one reason or another, one of us would ask, "But shouldn't a person's improvement count for part of the grade?"

Which is my way of telling you that during our thirty-nine years of friendship, I believe I have improved. Don't worry about sparing me.

I am off to buy that damn laptop with my young film-maker and mentor.

Love,
Feron

February 14, 1997

Dear Merry,
My e-mail address is fhood@aol.com.

And now I will compose my very first e-mail on Valentine's Day. Here is a short-short story: My young mentor, Josie, told me I had to go out more. ("If people don't see you, they forget about you.") So I dressed up—a nice pantsuit and makeup, and went with her to a party. Artists, filmmakers, a few writers. I was introduced to a woman about my age, who said, "Feron Hood, the *writer*?" "Yes, that's me," I replied modestly. "Oh," she said. "I thought you had died."

Love,
Feron

February 14, 1997
Oh, Feron, how awful. But happy Valentine's Day back. And I am so glad you're on e-mail now. You know what I love? The *instantaneousness* of it! With a letter, you wait until you accumulate enough to fill it up, but with e-mail it's okay to send off a sentence or two. Whatever is on your mind that day, that hour.

May 1, 1997
Oh, Feron, we have planted trees between us and the new development, but we can still see over the tops of them. Speaking of trees, the developers have cut down all the mature trees in our shelterbelts. Trees form a shelterbelt, which

changes the energy in the air and the moisture of the soil in the fields. I am glad Jack will never see the new landscape.

May 21, 1997

Dear Merry,

I'm so glad I have you to complain to. My editor asked if I was "working on anything," and I told him I'd had some promising false starts. I said, "Why haven't I achieved more? In twenty-one years I've only published three books." He said that writers were like fingerprints, no two alike, and you didn't compare fingerprints. "Balzac wrote eighty-five novels in his last twenty years, averaging two or three a year. Flaubert's wildly successful debut was never repeated." "But I haven't done either one of those things," I said. "There you go, comparing again," he said. "Be grateful for what you have."

On August 31, 1997, early morning, Merry wrote:

Princess Di is dead. It's all over the news. I feel I have lost a lovely friend I was always eager to keep track of.

On December 14, Merry wrote:

Jack died this morning, at 6 A.M. A Laurel Grove nurse he liked was with him. The bewildering part, Feron, is they had kept the body in his bed so I could say good-bye, but I was already seeing the old Jack in my mind as I was packing away his things to take home.

40

1998

Feron's fifty-seventh year was turning out to be a year of reckoning. (Though, counting forward from her June birthday, it was her fifty-eighth year.)

She slipped on an icy sidewalk and broke her foot. Trapped on the fifth floor of a building with an elevator that broke down at least twice a month, it occurred to her that it might not be practical to spend her aging years in New York. What held her here? She had been bought out of her day job, though fortunately MacFarlane's health benefits would last until she was sixty-five. Which was only eight years away.

For the first time, she was dependent on others. Josie now served her as Feron had served Cuervo. Josie admired her—maybe a little too much—and would have moved in if there had been space. The two men on the fourth floor, who had known Cuervo, checked in to see that she had food and books. One of them, an organist at a nearby Episcopal church, baked, and the other was a librarian in the branch library.

Even her editor, by turns emboldening and deprecatory, showed up with an orchid from his greenhouse. "This will live, if you take proper care of it. So: with your foot in a cast, have you started anything new?"

Feron told him what she had been reading. A novel about a contemporary hostess built on Mrs. Dalloway's story, and the suicide of an AIDS-stricken man built on the suicide of Septimus Warren Smith. 'Standing on the shoulders of giants,' as my husband Will would have put it. But it made me want to reread *Mrs. Dalloway*, so I did."

"Any giant tempting *you*?"

"Oh, I don't know. There was the English writer Ian McEwan's *Amsterdam*, which got me contemplating the power of envy and spite."

"*Amsterdam* was a scathing little treat, wasn't it? Are you sardonic enough? I don't know."

"I've also been toying with the idea of a young widow, but I don't feel like basing her on myself, so I would have to invent whole new circumstances."

"If you could find new circumstances, young widow has a built-in allure."

"Except I've promised Josie Maglia a draft of the screenplay for *Mr. Blue* in a month."

"How is that going?"

"It's not. The more I'm with these people, the less they want to say."

"*Mr. Blue* was your bête noire novel. Or should I say bête bleu? Though it didn't do too badly, and Joachim's paintings make it a collector's item. Perhaps Josie will end up doing another semi-silent film. She was certainly rewarded for *Brother Death*. Maybe your screenplay won't be required."

Blanche wrote that she had sent a "small truckload of nice furniture over to your house—courtesy of Thad. He says he'll store it in the guest house/study, which so far is bare. There's the walnut pedestal writing table, where you spent many hours writing during your six-month stay with me, and the sturdy chair that went with the desk. How Daphne overlooked the chair, which is a Chippendale, I don't know."

The librarian on the floor below asked if she had read all of Jane Austen.

"All but one. I couldn't stand that goody-goody heroine in *Mansfield Park*."

She tried again with the copy he brought her and found herself in a wholly different moral place than the one inhabited by the scornful younger Feron. Fanny Price's transplant from low to high on the privilege scale was painfully similar to her own. She cringed when Sir Thomas said of the poor niece he is about to bring into his family:

"We shall probably see much to wish altered in her, and must prepare ourselves for gross ignorance, some meanness of opinions, and very distressing vulgarity of manner; but these are not incurable faults."

But Fanny was nine when she came to live at Mansfield Park, and Feron was eighteen when she walked up the wooden stairs and into her uncle's office and identified herself.

She exempted her eighteen-year-old self from gross ignorance and meanness of opinions, but when it came to distressing vulgarity of manner, she could hear Blanche Buttner as clear as yesterday: "But Rowan expects it."

Did moral life grow more attractive as desires narrowed?

She had tired of her "color game." Black, fake white, misty green, verdigris, and so on. It was time to find other means for measuring her improvement, to quote Mr. Tribby.

If you could "age out" of concern for what would get you further and concentrate instead on what you really wanted to become, what would life be like? A clarified, simplified landscape? No longer always to be focused on means to an end, but just staying alert for the worthy seeker of your consideration. And being glad you are able to provide it.

Like Uncle Rowan, at ease behind his desk in his upstairs office, ready for her when she walked in the door.

Like herself, perhaps one day, at ease with herself after having stopped trying to turn everything into the next book. Alert, yes, but not trying to imagine beforehand whose footsteps are on the stairs.

41

1999

B lanche Buttner had died. Easter fell on April fourth that year, and Blanche had been found collapsed over the side of her bed on Good Friday.

Blanche would have been pleased. Or maybe she *was* pleased in her afterlife. Good Friday was her favorite day in the church calendar. Starting with Maundy Thursday after the altar was stripped bare and remaining bare until the dawn of Easter Sunday. ("Everything is going, going, gone, and then we have to submit to the darkness and desolation in between. For me, the desolation has always been my high point. To fully grasp the magnitude of what you've lost requires the experience of having to do without it.")

Blanche's housekeeper found her in a kneeling position on a pillow on the floor beside her bed. Her body was still warm.

Cousin Thad phoned Feron on Friday evening. Since she had acquired the device, Feron had become an answering-machine lurker. She never picked up until she knew who was calling. Even then, she usually waited until the caller had dispensed a portion of the message.

"Okay, Cousin Feron, if you're there, pick up. This is Thad, and you know I never call unless I have something necessary to tell you."

Those closest to her were aware of this. Their total number did not begin to add up to one of Cuervo's "scores." But, as friends do, they accepted her ways.

"What's up, Thad?"

"Oh, good. Feron, this is about Blanche Buttner, whom I know you were close to."

"You said 'were.'"

"Yes, this morning. Her housekeeper said she passed away while she was praying. What a way to go. Listen, knowing how travel arrangements rattle you, I've booked you on a flight from Newark for Monday the fifth, arriving in Raleigh at 2:45 P.M. The funeral is at ten on Tuesday."

"Where do I stay overnight? I suppose the house in Pullen."

"Well, here's the good news after the bad news. Merry will meet you at the airport, and you'll stay at her house. Then she'll go with you to the funeral Tuesday, and after that she'll drive you back to the airport for the afternoon flight to New York. I've booked the return, too."

"Thank you for that."

"One more thing. Blanche's priest called me and asked if you'd like to do the second reading at the funeral mass. It's—wait, I've got it here: Romans eight, verses eighteen to the end. I have to call him back either way."

"Either way, what?"

"Whether you agree to read it or not. It was in Blanche's funeral suggestions that you read that passage."

"Well, then, of course I will read it."

Romans 8:18–end, Feron scribbled on a notepad.

* * *

Like everything physical, the airport had altered over time.

The first Raleigh-Durham Airport Feron had known had been like a good-sized warehouse set in the middle of farmland. As the plane was descending, you could look out the window and see whoever was waiting for you standing out on the tarmac. In those years the airport was hardly more advanced than Swain Eckert's flying school with its metal-roofed hangar and offices.

She had departed with Will from this airport as a bride and returned with Uncle Rowan as a widow. Then came the years when Uncle Rowan, or sometimes Uncle Rowan and Blanche, awaited her inside a glass enclosure separated from the tarmac. After Uncle Rowan's death, Blanche had waited for Feron at a "gate," inside an expanding terminal, always under construction.

Rolling her handsome carry-on bag (a present from Blanche) up the carpeted exit ramp, Feron prepared for the physical reality of the friend who would be awaiting her at her gate.

As there was no immediate sighting of Merry when Feron emerged through the door, she revised her expectations and began searching the faces of older women craning their necks to spot whomever they'd come to meet. But anyone remotely resembling any of the earlier Merrys she had known was simply not there.

Was the plane early? No, right on time. What, then? How long should you stay put and wait for the expected one to arrive? Blanche Buttner would be the ideal person to advise on this quandary. ("I'd give her at least ten minutes before you do anything at all. And stay close to the gate you came out of, because that will be where she's expecting to see you.")

There were no pay phones in sight, as most savvy people now traveled with their own little flip-top cell phones. Josie Maglia had been urging her to get one. Having talked Feron into writing the screenplay for *Mr. Blue*, Josie, who was young enough to be Feron's daughter, dispensed frequent advice about what the up-to-date Feron was going to need when the new century kicked in.

A figure was racing toward her. "Feron! Oh, Feron! Thank God!" She had never seen Merry running and was surprised at the boyish straight-ahead-ness of her gait, even in a skirt, unlike the customary female sidekicking. Must be the result of having had a brother to run with.

"I got completely lost, I thought I heard concourse B but it wasn't B, it was D. I think I'm losing my hearing. And I got here early so you'd be sure and see me first thing when you came through the door! This airport has turned into a monster. The last time I was here, there wasn't any such thing as a concourse. Oh, God, Feron, I'm sorry."

She was out of breath. Smaller, thinner, enviably well-dressed, beautiful, even with a large band-aid crossing the bridge of her nose.

"But I'm here and you're here," said Feron, embracing her and experiencing the Merry-ness of her. So this was what a human friend felt like: a body thrumming with exertion, warm, damp skin, a remembered smell, a forty-one-year connection zapping between them. "We are both here *together* in this monster airport. Let's sit down for a minute and catch our breaths."

"I'm waiting till we get out of this confusing parking garage and onto a familiar road before saying anything meaningful, Feron, but I'm sorry that Blanche Buttner's death had to be the occasion of our reunion."

"That sounds meaningful enough to me."

"I am so glad to have you next to me in the car," Merry said, as she whipped the svelte silver hatchback through the airport traffic.

"Do you still have the red truck?"

"No, I sold it to a woman who keeps horses in a stable we built and never used. Jack had always wanted to have horses, but . . . many things haven't continued the way we'd planned. The tobacco acreage is now a gated community with a man-made lake and a golf course. I'm sorry you never got to see our tobacco fields, Feron. Right about now we would be transplanting from the seedbeds into the ground. This time of year will always make me feel nostalgic. Did you have any warning about Blanche?"

"It was there if I had known to look for it. In recent letters there had been a certain tone of letting go. She sent the pieces of furniture she wanted me to have to Pullen, and spoke a lot about her romance with Uncle Rowan, sort of summing it up. You know they dated for years before their long engagement that never turned into a marriage? And she was two years older, she told me, and managed to keep it secret from him to the very end."

"You used to talk about them a lot when we were at Lovegood."

"I did? What did I say?"

"Well, I was thinking about it as I drove to the airport. You thought she was formidable, but you admired her taste. And you could be so funny about their long engagement."

"Funny, how?"

"Oh, you would speculate about their sex life. Sometimes you'd do their voices. Or their thoughts. Like, 'Not yet, Rowan, I don't feel right about it just yet.' And he would say, 'Honey, is it because you think I'll respect you less?' Or you'd have him think, 'Why is she putting me through this? At our age? When is *yet* going to be?' Or you'd have her thinking, 'Wives are supposed to go and live in their husband's house, but what if the wife's house is nicer?'"

"Merry, I do not remember one single word of this."

"That's what friends are for. And family. Even during Ritchie's brief life, we often remembered entirely different versions of the same event. And Jack and I were always comparing our different versions of the past until he lost his memory."

"It must have been anguishing, losing him little by little like that."

"The doctor explained to us that it would be selective at first. It was different in each person, he said. He told me we would have to wait until his particular pattern of deterioration presented itself. Isn't that an awful way to put it? Jack's 'particular pattern of deterioration.'"

"I love these old county roads. Uncle Rowan used to drive me around on roads like these and tell stories about how it used to be."

"I love them for the same reason," said Merry. "Plus, on this route I won't have to drive you by Windbourne Oaks until we're forced to pass it on the highway tomorrow."

"Windbourne Oaks?"

"What used to be Jellicoe's tobacco fields. Why on earth any developer would cut down mature hardwood trees planted purpose-fully over the land for two centuries and put in saplings somewhere else seems moronic to me. Jack said it was because the developers needed to arrange trees where *they* wanted them to be around the new houses going up. This was back when I could still take him out for drives from Laurel Grove. Then he was still enough himself to name the species of every old tree that was gone. He said there had been many other trees besides oaks on our old land, and the commu-nity might equally have been called Windbourne Maples or Windbourne Cottonwoods. Then one day he turned on me like an enemy and demanded why I would bring him to see a thing like this."

"I'm really sorry I never saw your tobacco fields, Merry."

"So am I. It just didn't work out, did it?"

"Do you have a Bible at home?"

"Sure. Why?"

"Blanche left instructions for me to do one of the readings at the funeral. I want to rehearse a little at your house so I won't let her down."

"Do you know which passage you're supposed to read?"

"Romans Eight—here, I have it in my purse. Verses eighteen to the end."

"She's a Catholic, right?"

"Devout."

"Listen, Feron, I apologize for wearing this ugly bandage on my nose, but the hole underneath is even uglier."

"You had more of those things taken off?"

"He thinks he got it all, but if not he says he'll have to cut out more. 'We'll have to dig to China' is the way he put it. This was just the basal cell kind, but after my bout with melanoma he's not taking any chances."

Why were they stopping in front of the African Methodist Episcopal Church?

"I won't be a minute," Merry said. "I need to pick up something."

How lightly Merry ran up the walkway to the white clapboard church. Glimpsed from behind, her movements were those of a girl in her twenties. EASTER SERMON: WE'RE DOING ALL WE CAN DOWN HERE IN GOD'S LOVING ARMS was posted on the billboard on the lawn. And below, in smaller letters: Sunday Easter Service 11 A.M., with Communion.

Merry slid back into the car, handing over a single sheet of paper to Feron.

"What's this?"

"Romans eight, verses eighteen to thirty-nine. From the New American Bible, which is the one the Catholics use. So you can rehearse properly. I photocopied it out of Pastor Ford's Complete

Parallel Bible. Sometimes we use it in our Bible study group; you'd be surprised how different some passages can be in their various translations. And these are just the English translations."

Feron skimmed the photocopied verses. "I think I can manage this. I wonder why Blanche chose this particular passage for me to read."

"You two got along, didn't you? I mean other than you thought she was formidable."

"Oh, yes. But she was an acquired taste. And I certainly was one for her. She taught me many things I would be worse off without."

"Like what?"

"Oh, everything from how to buy shoes to how to be gracious. I knew no one like her in my previous world. I never completely got over being a little intimidated, but, funny enough, after I was in New York and especially after she went to live in Uncle Rowan's house, we became comfortable together. And she liked my last book; that may have helped some, too."

"You know, Feron, our dorm mistress once told me in confidence that Cynthia Chasteen was supposed to be my roommate. But when you enrolled at the last minute, they decided we might make a better match. Miss Darden said the dean compared it to horses who were comfortable together in the field."

"Horses!" Feron laughed. "But she was right about our being comfortable together. Oh, shit!"

"What's wrong?"

"I didn't bring a hat for Blanche's funeral. Hell, I don't own a hat to bring."

"Don't worry. We'll find something that will work. Oh, Feron, those were such unreal days, after I had to leave Lovegood. Everything was completely changed for us. I ran the farm along with Jack, then there was Ritchie to feed and help with homework, and after he went to bed the evenings went on and on. But you know who saved me? Miss Petrie. She always closed her letters with 'Keep writing!' So I filled up one of the Lovegood composition books I had bought in the campus bookshop. And then I filled up another, and when those were all filled, I went out and bought some more. But not the Lovegood ones, with the Doric columns on the cover."

"What did you write?"

"Oh, first just little vignettes. The weather and the crop worries. Lots of nature descriptions, too many, I'm afraid. I love doing clouds. And little stories of things that happened to Ritchie, his ups and downs at school. I started copying them over and sending them to Miss Petrie. She was having a difficult time. Miss Olafson had been offered a better job, but it meant they had to leave Lovegood, and Miss Petrie wouldn't have a job. She chose to go with Miss Olafson, and I guess in the new place I was her only student. Feron, we corresponded for six years! And then Ritchie was killed, and I started writing this story about the curing barn, which got more detailed the more the narrator lets herself remember. And Miss Petrie helped me make it better, then she told me to submit it to the *Atlantic* First contest. By then she was very sick and never knew they'd accepted it."

"That is such a *pure* story, Merry. In comparison, my trajectory seems so erratic. Other than term papers, I didn't write at Chapel Hill. I was hanging on by my fingernails to keep from flunking courses. Oh, I was still thinking about writing and envying the great ones, subtracting their birth dates from their publication dates. And then I was occupied with Will and how to get him without scaring him off. It was only after we got to England and he was off at Durham University all day that I started regretting I didn't have a discipline like Will. The first thing I wrote was for Will. I typed up his notes for a chapbook on Aelred of Rievaulx, this English medieval abbot who must have been quite an unusual person."

"I'm so uneducated, Feron. What is a chapbook?"

"I didn't know either till Will told me. It's a booklet, usually under forty pages, that sticks to one subject. Scholars and poets tend to make them. Abbot Aelred was Will's star. He represented all that a person could be if he kept reaching toward the highest feelings human nature was capable of. He was a leader and negotiator, he preached, he trained novices, he traveled the continent, he made the abbey prosper, everybody loved him, he was known for his sympathy and gentleness. Luckily, he wrote well, so he was able to record some of his progress. He wrote a treatise on friendship, which is still in print."

"Oh, I want to read it!"

"I'll look for a copy in Barnes and Noble. It's probably in a Penguin edition. Well, after I came to the end of the notes, I decided to try writing a story about Aelred the abbot. He suffered from various ailments, kidney stones, arthritis, shingles, and had to lie down a lot, so the monks would gather around his bed just to discuss things and be near him. First I planned to do it like a little diary by a twelfth-century monk. I was going to surprise Will. But then I got ambitious and tried to do the different monks' points of view, what they thought of Aelred. And that meant stopping to sort out what sort of personalities they had. I was actually making notes on them when Will's professor came to our flat and said he'd been notified by the constables at Saltburn that a man carrying Will's identification had fallen off the cliff. It turns out that someone or some animal or even farm machinery falls regularly off that eroding cliff, but I didn't know about that until later. But you know the thing that still upsets me about that night when we had to go up to Saltburn and identify the body? One of the constables asked me if Will and I had been having troubles in our marriage. You know the first thing that flashed through my mind? This is my punishment for lying about Swain hitting my mother and then leaving the house. Now I'm having it done back to me, someone assuming that Will jumped because our marriage was in trouble. And then when I was staying at Blanche's, a widow of twenty-three, I started scribbling down everything I could remember about Will before it faded. Things he said verbatim. Even the way he smelled."

"Did you save your notes on the monks?"

"Ah, no. I threw them away. I can't believe all the things I wish I hadn't thrown away."

"Did I tell you how I abandoned my Stephen Slade book? Sometimes I mix up what I told you with what I thought of telling you."

"God, yes. 'I wish my master was still alive and I was his slave.' The news item in the tobacco museum. What a killer. I owe you an apology for all the time you wasted on my presumptuous idea."

"Oh no, Feron. Without your task, you see, I would never have gotten up the courage to attend a service at Ezekiel Church. As it was, I changed outfits until there was a pile on the bed. I was afraid I wouldn't be welcome. Well, when I pulled up in the church parking lot, I saw I was the only truck, but at least I was dressed well. And even before I reached the front door, they were coming out to welcome me. Most of them knew who I was, one of them had a father who had worked for Daddy during the harvest. What was I saying? Oh! I would never have thought to go there if I hadn't realized that for Stephen's sake I needed to be among living African Americans.

"And that was because you set me that project, Feron. Otherwise I would never have gone. I would have missed so much. Our Bible study group, new friends. My first job! They gathered around me and saw me through my pregnancy. Paul was baptized at Ezekiel Church, and he was buried from there. And they were there for me through Jack's decline. I wish you could meet them. Well, you'll meet Rachel Blake, the daughter of my boss. She's bringing over our supper later. Rachel will be graduating from Lovegood in May. Now, look, I'm going to turn off the main road. We're going on a slight detour so you won't have to see Windbourne Oaks. Oh, Feron, I can't believe you are finally coming to my house."

"Well, I was a long time coming."

What a disgustingly lame response, Feron thought. I should have had a tutor like my late father Woody, who taught his sister, Aunt Mabel, how to gush.

42

Feron was here in this house. Getting settled in Ritchie's room. And they had found her a hat for the funeral tomorrow.

Without comment Feron had entered the room where she was to sleep. "What did you do with the flag?" she asked after looking around.

"What flag?"

"The flag that was draped over the footlocker."

"Oh, that was just in my 'Curing Barn' story. In real life I left it folded, the way his comrades presented it to me. It's inside with his other treasures. I keep his air force blanket draped on top."

Merry had opened the locker and there, beside the folded flag, was Ritchie's black straw trilby that he had worn in his starring role as Stage Manager. Feron tried it on in front of the mirror, Merry adjusting the angle until it looked captivating. She could see from Feron's studied nonchalance that she thought so, too.

"I should probably not wear the purple feather, though."

"You can wear it. Purple is for death, too."

"Well, you're the funeral home expert, so I will."

They had agreed to "rest up" until six, when Rachel Blake was to bring over their hot barbecue supper from the Three Little Pigs. Merry was surprised at how glad she was to lie down. Her headache had returned, and she had chugged down more pain pills. In her room, formerly hers and Jack's, before that, Mother and Daddy's, she thought of Thad. ("Will you tell Feron?" "Tell her what?" "About us." "No, Thad. We have to remain our own secret.")

She heard no sounds below. Feron must have felt like lying down, too. It was hard to believe they were getting close to the sixty mark. She remembered how congealed they'd thought the class poet of 1918 must have been in her midfifties.

She dreamed that Feron flew in the window as a supersized gray bird and embraced her with the large wings. Merry could feel the softness of the feathers and the support of the spiny shafts. "Horses!" the Feron-bird exclaimed. "Well, we must thank the fates for dropping us into the same field."

Murmurs rose from the west porch beneath the windows. Feron seemed to be holding forth to someone. In the bathroom, Merry splashed and brushed herself into shape. She could tell from the outdoor light that it was way past six. A tiny spot of blood had oozed through the gauze pad in the band-aid. She slapped another band-aid on top to cover it up and went downstairs.

Through the kitchen window she took in the two seated figures. Her long legs pretzeled around each other, Feron was reading aloud in stops and starts to Rachel Blake.

". . . nor height, nor depth, nor any other creature will be able to separate us from the love of God."

"That's good," said Rachel. "Even and unemotional. The words will carry the feeling."

I couldn't have laid it out any better myself, Merry thought. Feron's Coke bottle and glass across from Rachel's glass and backup pitcher of iced tea. Someone had set the oven at 150 degrees to keep the barbecue and the hush puppies warm, and she knew without checking that the meal's cold accompaniments were in the refrigerator.

She felt a great release and an equal amount of sadness. If the moment could have spoken aloud, it would have said, "See, Merry? You don't have to keep carrying the world on your shoulders all by yourself."

It was as if her spirit were registering this scene from some future place. A woman watching the people in her life doing what they needed to do without her.

"I had planned to lie down and refuel or reconnoiter or something," Feron said, "but the air outside was too reproachful. I thought, tomorrow I will be breathing in jet fuel and recycled air. So I walked the complete circle of the paddock. First the horses pretended I wasn't there, then one by one they got curious, and by the time I completed my circle, all three were lining up to smell my hand. Oh God, Merry, what a beautiful place this is."

The barbecue had been eaten, they were on their second bottle of wine, and the stars winked at them through the closed window. It was still too early to eat out at night.

"I wish you could have seen it in its grandeur. All around you, nothing but fields. Now on the east side we have planted trees between us and them—a mix of white pines and poplar and pin oak, but they're still too young to blot out what isn't there anymore."

"If I had made that Christmas visit, in 1958, how would it have looked?"

"All plowed under by then. But a horizon of loamy soil holding up the sky. I don't know if I saw the grandeur back then. I saw it as a lot of acres and a lot of responsibility."

"Then I took a side path into the woods and found the Jellicoe family cemetery. But Merry, I was a little shocked to see you've already put in the stone for yourself."

"That's what happens when you work in a funeral home. You learn to think of funeral directives like you would your grocery list."

"Don't tell me you've made your grocery list."

"During the melanoma scare, I did—right down to the hymns and the readings. All the members of my Bible study group have made their funeral directives. Rachel Blake will play Lovegood's processional hymn. You know she was offered a music scholarship to Converse for her last two years, but she chose to stay at Lovegood and graduate with her friends."

"She was a real help with my reading tomorrow. Keep it even and unemotional, let the words carry the feeling. Honestly, when you meet people like Rachel, you can't be too much of an old woebegoner about the future. Their spirits seem less . . . knotted. I've got one in my life, Josie Maglia, a young filmmaker who's taken a two-year option on *Mr. Blue*. She's been after me to write the screenplay, but during my refreshing walk around your land I realized writing a screenplay for *Mr. Blue* was the last thing I wanted to do."

"Why?"

"I need to let it go. My motive was skewed from the start. I was out to repeat my success with *Beast and Beauty*. But *Beast and Beauty* had a firm foundation. Its key idea was that Beauty can love Beast as long as she doesn't go outside with him, and I built the story around that."

"It was exactly right."

"But with *Mr. Blue*, I wanted to set myself an impressive challenge. I know, I said, I'll turn the Bluebeard story upside down. I'll create a female Bluebeard. She'll be the one in control. She has the property and the power. She has all the keys. She can make the rules and punish. I started her off as a bossy eight-year-old opening the door to a stranger who has come to work for her dying father. Right away, the little girl asserts her power by making him wait and closing the door in his face. And for a while, the chapters sped along. She grows into a young woman and keeps setting herself new ways to keep him in his place. And he works skillfully and hard, determined to make her acknowledge his worth. Finally she marries him because belonging to her ancestral land is more important to her than anything else, so why not share the burden with him? But she keeps one place for herself that he must never enter. And he obeys! She becomes so sure he will not betray her that she no longer locks the door. Though Joachim Maglia made that wonderful painting of a big gothic lock. Well, so far so good. *Beast and Beauty* was 150 pages. I was already on page 118. My editor liked what he had read and commissioned Joachim to illustrate it. Joachim was Josie's twin brother. She shot a film that documented his work as an artist while he was dying. The work part was shot in color and the disease part in black and white. Very minimal dialogue. She called it *Brother Death: An AIDS Elegy*. It won several awards at film festivals.

"My editor said he was waiting with bated breath to see how I was going to resolve my audacious feat, as he called it. Well, it was like he put an evil spell on it. How indeed was I going to turn her into a female Bluebeard? She has no secret. She hasn't murdered anybody. She's tested his loyalty, and he has passed the test. So she gets pregnant and dies in childbirth, the good old-fashioned way. Females who assert themselves too much have to die. Naturally she has insisted on a home birth, to keep everything inside her fiefdom, as Miss McCorkle would call it. I was whining to Cuervo about my failure, and he said why don't you write it over again. But who would publish it, I said. And he gave me this maxim that sometimes artists have to choose between the work and the sponsor."

"The sponsor?"

"The sponsor, he said, was anything *outside* the work that underwrites or influences it. You have to break free and walk away from the sponsor. A sponsor can be anything from publisher to editor to critic to reader. Cuervo believed that a book's need to exist should be enough. Maybe that's why he never wrote a second book. Anyway, that's my sad story of my misbegotten *Mr. Blue*."

"I think I know what her secret was."

"You do?"

"She's fallen in love with him. But she thinks she would lose her power if she let him know."

"I never even considered that! That forbidden room, by the way, is from that story you told me at Lovegood about your mother's secret room, where she put herself together again."

"I sort of guessed that," Merry said and chose not to elaborate. "But there's a conclusion to my story, too. More of a nonconclusion. The day after our parents were killed, Ritchie came to my room and said we had to go up to the secret room right away. He was convinced that she was in there. So I played along, but guess what?"

"What?"

"It was completely stripped. The chair, the table, Mr. Jack had cleared it out. He said he was only trying to make things easier for us, but Ritchie screamed and called him horrible names. Eventually he cried himself to sleep, but I don't think he ever forgave Jack. Did you see little Paul's stone in the cemetery?"

"How could I miss it? His name followed by those dates wrenches your heart. I wanted to leave something beside his grave, so I looked around and found an unusual pinkish stone. It was shaped sort of like an arrowhead."

"It *was* an arrowhead! You must have found one of Ritchie's sacrificed collection. When he was ten, he developed this passion for the Coree Indians, who settled near the Neuse River, where we had lunch. He did a school project on them—by the eighteenth century they were extinct. Then he branched out and got interested in all the eastern North Carolina tribes, and he reached deep enough to get really incensed by how they were treated. 'I mean, it was their land, they were here first . . .' and one day in a fit of grief he buried his entire arrow collection in the family cemetery. Where did you find your pink stone?"

"It was over in the old section, by a Jellicoe who had served in the navy in the War of 1812. I thought how fortunate you were to know where you came from so far back. Uncle Rowan provided me with some forebears in the Pullen cemetery, but nothing like your spread."

Feron was here in this house. Only now it was the next morning and Merry smelled the coffee she had been planning to bring to Feron in bed.

Merry had said goodnight and gone up to her room, counting on having time to steep in all that had passed between them, but then she had given in and chucked down one of the doctor's pain pills in case her scooped-out nose were to give her trouble at night. That, added to the wine, had knocked her out.

She went to the window. Down below was Feron with a coffee mug, sitting on the edge of the porch. Over her pajamas she wore Ritchie's blue air force blanket wrapped around her like a shawl.

Merry slipped a sweater over her nightgown, changed the band-aid, and hurried downstairs.

"Oh Feron, I was planning to bring you coffee in bed."

"I've been up for a while. I had this dream, I'm not sure what it was. Whether I was asleep or I dreamed I was asleep. I realized I was being watched by someone in the room. I thought to myself, if I open my eyes I'll wake up. So I opened my eyes, and there was this figure sitting on Ritchie's footlocker. I could tell it was a man, but it was so blurry I hardly saw him. He was trying to speak to me, but it faded in and out like voices do when you're scanning radio stations. The only thing I could make out was 'five black barns,' and he kept calling me by some name that sounded like 'Errol.' Then light started filling the room, and he dissolved. All that was left on top of the footlocker was the black trilby I'm going to wear to Blanche's funeral today."

43

"We know that all creation is groaning in labor pains even until now; and not only that, but we ourselves, who have the first fruits of the Spirit, we also groan within ourselves as we wait for adoption . . ."

Reading Blanche's assigned passages from the lectern of St. Athanasius Church, Feron was feeling less and less like her usual self. Whether this was an agreeable or an ominous occurrence she couldn't tell, because she had never felt this way before. Whichever it was, it would have to wait, because her main purpose was to get through this reading without failure in any of its many forms.

Since the dawn appearance of the man on Ritchie's footlocker, she had felt both light-headed and spacious. Her mind could hold more things at once, but a precarious floatiness was part of the experience.

For instance, having read aloud the verses ending with "adoption," she grasped clearly that she *had* undergone adoption when Uncle Rowan took her in and she had gone to live under Blanche's roof. Henceforth, she would never be the same. She could never go back to being "the old Feron" again. As she moved through her reading, sticking close to Rachel's advice to "let the words carry the feeling," she saw—not a visual manifestation, like the blurred man on the footlocker, but vivid portraits of Rowan and Blanche on her inward eye.

That wasn't all. She looked out at the congregation. "A sea of faces" still held up well for a cliché. She saw Merry, leaning Cousin Thad's way. Not touching, just . . . and she saw rangy Thad folding himself into a closer curve to guard the space of "the sublime little lady in the black hat."

Of course. Anyone could see it. If they observe as I am observing now.

Had she stumbled into a higher level of perception—or was she on the verge of a stroke?

"Now hope that sees for itself is not hope. For who hopes for what one sees? But if we hope for what we do not see, we wait with endurance."

Please get me through the rest of this funeral and then the ride to the Benton Grange cemetery, and the burial, and there's not going to be enough time for the reception. And after that, the drive to the airport with Merry for the return flight to Newark and then the taxi through the tunnel and, if the elevator is still out of order, the five flights of stairs to the beach house on Christopher Street. Once you're safely there, and lying down, you may inquire further into this.

The funeral had started late, past eleven, and it was ten past one before they left the church. It was almost quarter to two by the time everybody got into their cars to follow the hearse to Benton Grange cemetery, where Blanche would join her parents and grandparents. If Blanche had married Uncle Rowan, would she be going to the Pullen cemetery to join the Hoods? Or not?

Merry was saying the Roman rites had been impressive, something entirely different from Ezekiel's services. "At Ezekiel, it's more like we're all lifting one another up, rather than the priest dispensing everything from above. I don't mean to sound critical. Your reading was beautiful, Feron. You looked elegant as you stood up there. I was so proud of you. The next time it's my turn to choose the reading for our Bible study group I'm going to suggest Romans eight."

Blanche's coffin was lowered into its hole by a cranking device turned solemnly by someone on the funeral staff. Going down with her was a sumptuous spray of white lilies and roses "from all of us in the Hood family," sent by Cousin Thad in disobedience to Blanche's "in lieu of flowers" stipulation in her obituary.

Uncle Rowan's coffin had gone down the old-fashioned way, six red-faced, straining pallbearers inching it down with straps.

After the crank had been unscrewed and the rest of the lowering equipment discreetly carried away, the priest uttered the words of committal and produced a stream of loose black soil from his lacy sleeve.

Everyone waited. Thad nudged Feron. "They're waiting for you to go first. Grab a handful of dirt from that pile and throw it down on the coffin."

Afterward, a handsome lady approached Feron.

"Marguerite Steed! How wonderful you look."

"Thank you, Feron. Daddy died late last year. He almost made it to a hundred."

"Blanche told me in a letter. You must miss him."

"I do, but he's still very much around. I have lost forty-five pounds. This summer I plan to travel. I have invitations from doll collectors all over the world. My first stop is Tel Aviv to see an exhibit of Israeli folklore dolls. I'm staying with relatives of Edith Samuel. I once wrote her a fan letter, and she responded. Her dolls are mostly in museums now. Of course she died back in the sixties."

"Do you know, Marguerite, I wanted to send you a doll once. Actually a pair of dolls: a rat in formal dress riding a horse in a

Madison Avenue shop window. It was called 'Rat Race,' and priced at twenty-five hundred dollars."

"What a kind thought. If I'd had the money when Edith Samuel was still making dolls, I would have spent all of my savings on one of her forlorn little émigré dolls. Feron, your Aunt Blanche was a great-hearted soul. She left her world much better than she found it."

44

Standing between Feron and Cousin Thad, Merry was remembering funerals in her life. Mother and Daddy, Ritchie, little Paul. Oh, and Feron's Uncle Rowan. And Sister Simone's twenty-four-year-old grandson who fell off a roof of a house he was shingling. And, of course, Jack.

Desire had been between them, well, not from the beginning, but after the deed was done and Jack had plunged into self-castigation. He would never forgive himself. But then the months passed, and while working together outdoors, she saw him glance at her and she felt something. Although they stayed apart for two years, she thought of him as hers. Then Ritchie went off on a camping trip, and they fell into bed. Then his remorse again and her shame, which kept them apart until Ritchie left for the air force. His death drove them into their separate corners of self-reproach. Until they abandoned all pretense and got together as often as they wanted. And after the 1979 harvest was in and they were congratulating themselves, she said, "Mr. Jack, would you ever consider marrying?" "Marrying? Who?" He had looked completely bewildered. "Well, me," she said. "Merry Grace."

*   *   *

Cousin Thad was telling Feron he had an ideal tenant for her house if she would agree to a three-year contract. "I can vouch for this person. Your property couldn't be in safer hands. Of course, we'd put in a cancellation clause for if you change your mind. It's my son, Simon. He's been promoted by his Raleigh bank, and he's planning on getting married. Think about it, and we'll talk numbers when we get to the reception."

"Thad, I'm not going to the reception. I get antsy if I have to worry about missing my flight."

"Oh, no! But your flight's not till almost five!"

"And now it's almost three. And it's more than an hour's drive from here. Your son can rent the house and bring his bride there if he wants. We can work out the numbers over the phone when I get back to New York."

"If you'll pick up!"

"I did when you called about Blanche."

Cousin Thad's disappointment had showed too much when Feron said they were skipping the reception. If Merry worried about anything, it was Thad's openly loving her with his looks and gestures when others were around. In church today she kept having to slip out of his inadvertent nearness.

She and Jack had made all they could of their marriage. Until the night of Paul's death, she had never felt anguish. Until the night of "too much information" seven years ago, after Jack thought she was her mother, she had not wished anything had been different. Their marriage was all it could be.

It was the undreamed-of love that came after that had thrown her for a loop. It didn't surprise her that some kind of suffering should accompany this love. It seemed right that there should be a price. The new love came weighted with the knowledge of all she could lose. Being so high meant farther to fall. "What if I lose it?" always goes with the undreamed-of gift.

"Life would be awful without you in it" each had told the other on the night it began.

"Poor old Thad," Feron commented from the passenger seat. "He was counting on seeing you at the reception. It was all over his face. It must be nice to have a courtly lover. I was sorry to drag you away, but it would have been cutting it too close."

"I don't mind. I hate having to rush, myself." The flippant courtly lover remark meant that Feron was no wiser.

"Uncle Rowan always insisted on waiting with me at my gate. I told him it wasn't necessary, but he said he wanted to. So we would both sit there nervously, making polite conversation. There was no talking him out of it."

Merry had been planning to wait with at the gate with Feron, but Feron was sending her a pretty transparent message.

"Oh, I should return Ritchie's hat. Shall I just sail it into the backseat?"

"You looked great in it, Feron. Listen, I have to tell you something. That day you were supposed to come visit us in 1958? Ritchie was helping me make up my bed for you so you could have a view of the apple orchards and not our five black barns. I was afraid they would depress you, but Ritchie thought they were beautiful and was looking forward to telling you why we painted them black. To hold in the heat and give the leaves that famous Jellicoe crackle. And you said this morning he kept calling you something that sounded like 'Errol.' Well, he said, that day you didn't come, your name sounded like 'Feral,' and he teased that he was going to call you that."

"You think—?"

"I do. You have a sense of the beyond that I just don't, Feron. All these years I've been going into his room longing to see him again, and all you had to do was open your eyes and there he was sitting on his footlocker."

"If you want to know the truth, I did feel spooked. It was on an entirely different plane than what I have with Cuervo. I talk to Cuervo and ask him questions. But I knew Cuervo so well that I can think his afterlife-thoughts in safety. There's not that head-on collision with something I know comes from outside the range of what I can control. I'm wondering if that apparition had anything to do with the strange way I was feeling while up at the lectern."

"How did you feel?"

"It was peculiar. I had this floaty feeling. I couldn't tell if it was going to turn into something good or bad—you know, like they say people about to have an epileptic fit are extra lucid. Or I thought maybe a stroke was coming."

"Oh, Feron. I didn't see anything. And I was watching you."

"And I was watching you, too. It seemed I knew everything about you. Even things you never told me."

"Are you still . . . having it now?"

"No, it stopped when I was talking to the priest after the service. He was telling me Romans eight was Blanche's favorite reading, and she had wanted me to have it. And how well she thought of me. And he was explaining that the church was so full of flowers because they were left over from Easter. Blanche had wanted flower money to be spent on worthy causes. Somehow that conversation with the priest brought me back to earth. Frankly, I'm not sure I'm ready for that degree of perception. Have you ever felt you were getting more enlightenment than you could handle?"

Yes!

"I think I understand what you mean," Merry answered.

They were close now. You could see the jets lining up and lifting off, less than a minute apart.

"We covered so many subjects last night, Feron, but I forgot to tell you why I thought *A Singular Courtship* was so good. It was as if in the simplest way you had opened a door and invited us to share the complex way you saw the world. I felt intimate with your characters, even with Tom. He was so often up there in the ether, but I felt I understood him as well as anyone else did, and I understood why someone like Nora would love him. Was your Will anything like that?"

"Oh, yes. Oh, yes."

Merry did go so far as to insist on getting out of the car at Feron's terminal and hugging her.

"Oh, Feron, I'm always afraid I'm never going to see you again."

"You know that can't happen. We are embedded in each other's reference auras forever."

Yet she was already wriggling out of Merry's embrace.

"And besides . . ."

Off-key and with a complicit twinkle at Merry, she broke into the school refrain:

> *That soul, though all hell should endeavor to shake,*
> *I'll never, no never, no never forsake.*

Repeating the refrain, Feron turned away and wheeled her carry-on bag through the automatic doors.

45

Cousin Thad had booked window seats for Feron on both flights. Now she waited to see what unwelcome possibility would drop into the empty aisle seat beside her. She had changed out of her funeral clothes in the terminal restroom. Now she put on her "not at home" mask and made a point of staring intently out her tiny window.

Someone was pausing, lifting belongings into the overhead bin. She didn't feel looked at, but she side-glimpsed the figure of a man folding himself into his narrow seat and clicking his seatbelt.

After the aircraft had reached cruising altitude, she felt it was safe to courteously acknowledge him and at the same time convey that she wanted her privacy and hoped he did, too.

He was not looking her way.

The attendant asked if she would like a beverage.

"Oh, a coke with ice and a slice of lemon if you have it."

"Thank you, I'll pass," said her seatmate in a civilized voice. Still not acknowledging Feron's presence.

After which he lapsed into some deep inner space like someone taking advantage of the empty seat beside him.

Back in the early seventies, before Cuervo entered her life, Feron had read a new Doris Lessing novel about an aging woman who suddenly realizes men no longer see her. She experiments by walking past a construction site as her gray-haired dowdy self, and the workers don't see her. She goes away, tucks her hair up into an exotic scarf, changes into a tight skirt that shows off the sway of her hips, and walks past the site again. This time the men see her.

At the time, Feron had been close to despair. She hadn't published anything, her marriage novel had lost its momentum, and she was already thirty-five, only ten years younger than the Doris Lessing woman.

Today she was more than ten years older than the Doris Lessing woman. Was this the beginning of her transition into a woman unseen?

On these return flights to Newark, Will always came back to her. On their first full day as a married couple, Will was in the window seat, and she saw his back more than his face. Though they had awakened in bed together in his mother's guest room, he was now far away from her.

(What was it Merry had said? "Up there in the ether.")

He will always be like this, she had thought as they had ascended into the clouds, but at least now he's mine. She had known this about him, expected it, was made safe by it. Will Avery would never invade her boundaries, and she must never invade his.

If he had lived, he would be seventy-four. What condition would he be in? Deteriorating like Jack, or would he still be the Will she had known? Would they stay married? She believed they would. Unless she had done something pretty bad, Will would not have left her, just retreated deeper into the ether. She was sure that she was the only person Will would have wanted to marry. And not without his mother's sagacious courtship on his behalf.

He liked her wary grace, as he called it. For different reasons they both had been wary people. She because she had known invasion and did not want her boundaries breached again. He because he had bound himself, faithful as a monk, to a mysterious period in history where certain elements of the population were reaching toward the highest feelings nature could achieve, and, having pledged himself, he remained with them when they fell short. ("There was something in that period that made them eager to try," he had told them the first day of class.)

Lying side by side, faces up. Breathing in complete concordance. Or sometimes lying on their sides facing each other, but not moving or touching. Who would understand the prolonged rapture without having experienced it? They continued to practice it after they had discovered it through necessity at his mother's house. They did the other, too. The first few times were failures. No concordance, not in sync, embarrassing, and messy. "We both get an F-minus, if there's such a grade," Will said. "But don't we get points for effort?" she asked, parodying Mr. Tribby, who had transferred out of Will's class the first day. But Will felt comfortable with her clumsiness because they shared it. At last they fell into a rampant coupling that satisfied them both. But it wasn't prolonged, and when it was over, they felt they had missed something.

Nobody told the truth about sex. She still couldn't imagine the bed life of Merry and Jack. Though she had never laid eyes on Jack, Feron had somehow incorporated Cousin Thad's description of him as "a man who never sat down." Yet they had made a child together. As for Merry and Thad, if Feron had guessed right, she couldn't picture that, either. However, from the lectern, she had seen two people trying not to show that they were lovers.

In Durham, she and Will lived in a "medieval tower" flat in the cathedral close. On rampant nights she was the one who got out of bed and descended the curved stone staircase to remove the

Dutch Cap, as Blanche called it, wash it in soap and water, and replace it in its case. Another thing about rampant nights, one had to plan ahead and put in the Dutch Cap before climbing the stairs to bed. And also feed the gas heater with a shilling so the room wouldn't be freezing when she got out of the warm bed afterward. Funny, that you got to be "spontaneous" only on the nights of disciplined restraint.

From the beginning, dating back to when Will had more or less proposed on the drive back to campus by asking if their age difference was too much, Feron knew that he was always making an effort to appear relaxed around her. Her goal had been to get him to the place where he no longer felt the necessity to make an effort.

Paradoxical that the only man in her life she had wanted to marry had been gifted to her by the man she hated above all others for raiding her girlhood. For on that fateful Sunday she had fled to the campus coffee shop because she couldn't stand being alone in her dorm room with her powerless rage at Swain's lying self-acquittal during his visit the day before.

During their short marriage, Feron had practiced watchfulness. Will was a rare bird, unacquainted with being in another person's company night and day. She had watched him without seeming to watch during their flight from Raleigh to Newark (then, in those days, helicoptering across to Idlewild Airport for their transatlantic flight). For much of that journey he had been reading Aelred's treatise on friendship in Latin, which he said was an inadequate translation and he intended to give it a deserving one. Or he had been staring at the seatback in front of him—just as Feron's current seatmate was doing now.

Then he would snap to, as though remembering he was married, and look at her and touch her. "Are you okay?" And they would talk about the wedding the day before and how his mother hadn't seemed quite herself (she wasn't) and about what it would be like to live in England. Neither had set foot abroad. Or about Aelred, the abbot of Rievaulx, whose life offered Will the closest clue he had to those higher feelings that medieval people had been reaching toward.

Soon they would be walking among the grassy ruins of that abbey, Will telling stories about the great abbot who made Rievaulx into a place of spiritual welcome and prosperity. Before it was over, Feron felt she knew and appreciated Aelred as well as Will knew and appreciated Miss McCorkle.

"Why did you never marry again?" No one she could think of had actually asked her this, but if they had, she might have replied, "For one thing, nobody else asked me. For another, I guess I wasn't exactly putting myself forward."

Even as a young widow, she had not offered herself in the marketplace—"presented her body to the public" as the aging woman in the Doris Lessing novel had put it. She'd had an affair with only one person, a management consultant at MacFarlane whom she had helped write a better report. A soft-spoken French Canadian, who seemed to intuit what she was all about. A man of nuances, he was based in Montreal, and on weekends they met halfway in Albany. She knew he was married from the start. They had blended in mind and body. Then he was transferred to South America and after a fervid weekend in Albany they parted at the train station with a fond embrace. (Similar to hers and Merry's farewell embrace today.)

She was not proud of "the encounters" that followed. Increasingly she recoiled from the intimacy. Getting close led to disappointment and demands and, in the worst cases, disgust. Repeat performances became fewer and farther between, until she understood the next step, if she were to take it, would be one-nighters with strangers.

"Some of us are simply not adept at maintaining the part that comes after the encounters," Cuervo had said.

The plane taxied to its gate, and the passengers strained against their seatbelts until they heard the permission bell. The seatbelt next to hers clicked, and the man beside her came back from whatever faraway place he had been.

He was speaking to her. "Is there anything I can lift down for you from the overhead bin?"

"Oh, thank you, yes. It's the dark green bag with leather trimmings."

The passengers were slowly pushing toward the exit door. He had set her bag upright and pulled out its handle so she was ready to precede him down the aisle.

He was looking at her at last. A man somewhere between sixty and seventy with an interesting face and benign demeanor. He said, "I want to thank you for the most restorative airplane ride I have ever had."

She was too surprised to have a ready answer. Perhaps it was better that she didn't.

The beach house elevator was still out of service, so Feron began the five-story climb, bumping her carry-on behind her, step by step. Halfway up, she permitted herself to sit down on the landing and catch her breath. Was this what it was going to be like, not being young anymore? She closed her eyes and leaned against her bag, rubbing her cheek against its sturdy canvas material. For a moment she thought she was going to faint. Or that the lectern thing was returning. At last she reached the top and entered her apartment.

Leaving the bag just inside the door with its handle up, as the man on the plane had presented it to her, she made it to Cuervo's bed and lay on her side, breathing in and out. Her face tingled and she felt light-headed. If she should die, who would find her? How long would it take them? The pesticide man? Josie? Someone, Cousin Thad, would have to come and get her body and bury it. Merry would weep forthrightly. ("I said to her, 'I'm always afraid I'm never going to see you again,' and I was right.")

What would she leave behind?

Not much *stuff*, Thad would thank her for that. ("Over thirty years in New York, and it all fit into one load, bless her heart.")

Two modern fairy tales that had made her visible on the literary scene and a novel that almost won a prize about three peculiar people in the sixties.

To whom had she made a difference? Cuervo? Uncle Rowan? Blanche? Merry? Will? Will's mother (although Feron had let her down, pleading her own desolation so that Uncle Rowan would make the phone calls)?

Maybe the lover from Montreal? Maybe Dale Flowers? The man on the plane?

The interesting part of this exercise was the relief, the pleasure, the "restorative" qualities that came with visualizing her completion. Done. Over. The End. Dust to Dust.

At least she hadn't killed anyone. Or taken what wasn't hers. Oh, wait. What about Swain's money in the shoebox?

My admirable points were my industriousness and my fierce discipline, founded though they were on envy and competitiveness and the belief that no matter what I did, I would never be good enough.

Once she had asked Will as they walked among the ruins of Rievaulx Abbey, "Did you ever consider becoming a monk?"

"Funny you should ask that. I did. I did think about it. But then I asked myself why. I'm not religious, and I would have to give up my freedom and pledge obedience to an abbot I might not even like. Besides, it would take away too much time from my work."

Feron slept. The sound of raindrops awakened her. She went to the window, lifted the sash, and unfastened the screen so she could stick her head out and acknowledge the river that had made Cuervo call his apartment "the beach house." He told her that some of his friends—rather, late friends—had called the Hudson River "the dump."

Now there was a color for you. "Hudson River Blue" on top, a million pounds of GE's toxic waste below. Toxic waste would comprise which colors? Dirty gray, slime green, a writhing, wormy white, some deadly pink?

She sat down at Cuervo's desk and gazed at Great-Uncle Eugenio's pastel drawing of Cervantes dreaming Don Quixote. The writer, in voluminous shirtsleeves, topped with a seventeenth-century black silk vest, was in left profile, his balding forehead lightly leaning against his left hand. He was looking down, or across, or at some invisible place, as the silent man on the plane had done. Cervantes's mouth was pursed in an intense, abstracted way.

Behind the power of Cervantes as he dreamed his character, Feron felt the power of Great-Uncle Eugenio's respect as his art evoked his subject.

You had to be careful with the posthumous Cuervo. Feron would continue to ration her questions to him, fearful of using them up. Cuervo didn't speak unless she asked a question. She would not dream of "sharing" this morning's encounter with Ritchie. She knew Cuervo's spirit spoke through her, whereas Ritchie's manifestation came from somewhere else.

"Maestro, what do you advise me to do next?"

"You are already in the desk chair. Forget the new laptop for now. Pull a sheet of typing paper from the drawer and roll it into the little

Olivetti. Type a single-spaced page of what's on your mind. You abandoned the woman who lied, now evoke a woman who tells the truth."

"It has to be single-spaced?"

"Single-spaced."

"Just one page and stop?"

"Just one page and stop. Not a word more."

Feron's Single-Spaced Page

My late husband was pursuing a medieval abbot who wrote a book on friendship. He had been my teacher first. When I met with him to discuss what topic to choose for my term paper, he invited me to look at the books he had placed on a certain shelf and see if anything caught my attention. I paused at Peter Abelard's *History of My Calamities*, but I knew my teacher had become weary of term papers about Heloïse and Abelard's ruined sex life. Next I paused at a bound green thesis with my teacher's name on the spine: *Cicero and Aelred of Rievaulx on Friendship*. I was excited more by *Calamities*, but at this time in my life my paramount desire was to please my teachers so I would not flunk out of school.

"What about friendship?" I asked.

"What about it?"

"I see you wrote about it, for one thing, but it's also a subject that fascinates me."

I was a suck-up, but I was a crafty suck-up.

"Why?" he wanted to know. He asked me to sit down.

"Well, I've only had one friend in my life so far. My roommate at Lovegood College. I'd like to know why it was we clicked the way we did, and why we were always at rest in each other's company. We were completely different people from different backgrounds. For an English assignment she wrote a story about our friendship. I was the dark one, haunted by a troubled past, and she was the light 'ordinary' one who hadn't had any troubles. I made her change 'ordinary' to 'optimistic.' She was the first person to arouse my competitiveness, but she also made me aware of my lack of goodness. She remains my standard for what a friend should be, though I might not ever see her again."

"Why not?"

In those days my teacher was a pair of black-rimmed glasses reflecting me and a disembodied intelligence who had power over whether I succeeded or failed.

"She had to leave school after first semester because her parents died and she had to take over her family's tobacco farm. She lives in North Carolina, but our lives are going in opposite directions."

My teacher said, "Take the Cicero next to my thesis because it's a good translation. And you may borrow my thesis if you'll take care of it. I've translated much of Aelred's treatise because there's no dependable translation. And you know not to make this about yourself, don't you?"

"I certainly won't make it about myself."

"Although some of what you said about your friend you will recognize in Aelred's treatise on friendship."

46

jellicoe@aol.com
to Feron Hood
April 6, 1999, 6:30 P.M.

Dear Feron,

You are still in the air. This time yesterday you were here. Today's daylight is close to yesterday's daylight, so if I wanted to play unwise games with myself, I would imagine you suddenly appearing down at the paddock, making friends with the horses, or sitting on the west porch with Rachel Blake rehearsing Romans 8. I say "unwise," because I've done this before, picking a scene and then trying to bring Ritchie back into it. The imaginer always runs smack into the barrier between what is and what isn't and goes to pieces. I never tried it with little Paul, though I once dreamed of Ritchie carrying him in his arms. You are still very much alive. Why shouldn't we end up tottering together into the middle of the next millennium? One thing I know for sure, we will never run out of things to say.

Merry left her desk to answer the phone. It was the dermatologist.

"We got it all on the nose, but there's something else. I want to send you back to Duke for a scan—what time is good for you?"

"Has the melanoma come back?"

"It's a new site. Let's just pray this one's contained."

Merry returned to her keyboard, deleted most of her message, added a few lines, and pressed "send."

> Dear Feron,
> You are still in the air. This time yesterday you were here. Your visit was lovely. Please come again. I don't think we will ever run out of things to say to each other.
>
> > Love,
> > Merry

The treetops were tossing and the sky had gone gray. Across the field, Alda was clapping her hands to call in the horses. Merry went out and stood on the west porch and let the wind whip at her skirt. She had not changed out of her funeral dress. Miss Petrie had taught them a literary term for when the weather in a story serves as a comment on what a character is feeling, but she couldn't remember what it was.

When compiling a list of all the ways she could lose Thad, she had overlooked the possibility that she might be the one to exit first. After he had seen her through the last cancer, the next awful "what if?" that popped up was, "What if Thad, who is six years older, goes first?"

47

Shaken by their interview with Jocelyn Williams, Lavonne Blake and Merry Jellicoe sat down in Merry's little office at the funeral home to pull themselves together.

Merry said, "I'm glad this state allows two people to be buried in the same casket."

"Yes, as long as they can fit. Daddy buried a husband and wife once, but I remember him saying, 'If that man had one more inch on him, we couldn't have squeezed him in.' In our case one of them was less than a day old. She will fit nicely in her mother's arms."

"The resilience of the human spirit—doesn't it amaze you, Lavonne? Mrs. Williams went out of here with a spring in her step because she had a living purpose. To choose their clothes."

"It couldn't have been easy for her," Lavonne said, "taking those photos."

"Jack and I did that. It was only moments after Paul stopped breathing. His skin was still pink and warm."

"Oh, Merry, I'm sorry, I didn't even think . . ."

"No, it's fine. We were glad we had the photo . . . well, eventually we were. And it's a good thing when you can draw on your own experience to understand somebody else's pain. What was especially strong of her was to get to the neonatal unit and take the picture while the baby was still alive. Then she had to go back to the delivery room and take a picture of her dead daughter."

"They weren't very successful pictures, but there's enough to go on. We'll have a professional photographer do shots of mother and infant at the viewing."

"If we could get those shots even an hour before the viewing, I could scan them into the program."

"What a good idea!"

"Before you go below, Lavonne, I'd like to run a couple of things past you."

"You look serious."

"It is serious, but it's also okay in the scheme of things, I promise. The melanoma has come back. Or rather this one's a new one. This time it's taken up residence in my brain."

"Merry, you said this was going to be okay!"

"I meant in the larger scheme of things it will be, either way. You of all people should understand that. The drill is pretty much like last time. Only, because of where it is, I'm going to be fitted for a radiation mask. I'm trying to think positive. There's a chance you'll be stuck with me for years more, until I'm an ancient crone."

"May it please the Lord we stay friends though our crone years. Meanwhile, just like last time, you can count on me."

"I know I can. Right up to the end and after the end, if it comes to that. No wait, I meant it when I said it will be okay *either way*. What I'm thankful for is, well, my mother and father never got a chance to plan, my brother, Ritchie, never got a chance to plan, either. The funeral I took Feron to last week was for a lady who'd had time to plan everything. A complete Catholic funeral mass, with directions for which people she wanted for the readings and for the pallbearers. There were to be no eulogies and no sermon. Just the funeral mass. She gave away furniture, left money for the church to build a new food hall. She had no heirs, so she left her house with some of the best furniture in trust to the town of Benton Grange, to use for community events. As you know, my funeral directions are already in your files and my will is at the bank, and stone is already prepared, except for the closing date."

"Oh, Merry, you make it sound like you're planning a big party."

"Well I am, in a way. I'm thankful I have a chance to plan. There's one more thing, Lavonne. This has to stay strictly between us. Not even Rachel can know."

"Strictly between us. But what about Feron? Aren't you going to tell her?"

"Yes, she made me promise I would, but I'm going to wait until I think it's time."

"And when will that be?"

"I'll wait until I know more . . . till I see how it goes."

48

Feron was calculating. The three-year rental contract with Thad's son, Simon, would end in 2002, the year she turned sixty. Then she would either sell Uncle Rowan's house or go and live in it. But she would keep and sublet the beach house to give herself the option of fleeing back to it should poky little Pullen make her crazy. If the stairs of the beach house became too much for her, she would sell—the men on the fourth floor said the value had skyrocketed since Cuervo bought it in the seventies. She would buy some small apartment and continue to take her daily walk up and down Fifth, like the lady with the gray gloves. Only she wouldn't have to stop anyone and ask for bus fare home. Feron still had a hard time picturing herself as old, except when she had to depend on others.

fhood@aol.com
to Merry Jellicoe
May 13, 1999

Dear Merry,
I felt close to you today. I went over to Josie's loft to watch
a Spanish tourism documentary I was dreading, but it showed

tobacco farmers in Extremadura bringing in the harvest and
gave me an insight into your life's work and the work of your
forebears. Having you in the middle of things made the documentary tender and meaningful. I saw how Ritchie would
have straddled those rafters, and you when you were young
checking through the fresh-cut leaves for "lugs." Spain is a
huge producer of tobacco, and the season in Extremadura is
the same as yours because the two of you are within three
degrees latitude of each other, and their harvest begins in
mid-August. Josie has this bee in her bonnet about filming
parts of the harvest and then finding some ancient farmhouse
for the setting of *Mr. Blue*. She wants me to go with her, even
though I'm not writing the screenplay anymore. No one is
at the moment. I will have to get a new passport.

I tried your exercise of taking off from a Chekhov title
to break in my new laptop, but "A Woman's Kingdom"
was a train wreck. I based my tale on a lady in Pullen who
is a world-class doll collector. Ask Thad to tell you about
her. First I tried it from her point of view, and it was
tedious. Then I tried it from the point of view of the
"visitor" (me) whom she invites upstairs to see her "more
personal" dolls, and it was tediously bizarre.

Haven't heard from you recently. But now I can picture
you in your beautiful surroundings. You were right when you
said we will never run out of things to say. Recently I have
been trying to imagine old age in Pullen. I think together
we might face it with aplomb, but it would be impossible
without you.

Love,
Feron

49

August 1999

Feron had locked her door and was halfway down the first set of stairs to drop off her key with her friends on the fourth floor before taking the elevator the rest of the way. She heard the phone ring three times followed by the automated male voice: "Please leave a message after the tone."

"Feron, please pick up. This is Thad. I'm afraid Merry—"

She left her suitcase on the landing and raced back upstairs. She must have stored this scene into her reveries of the future. It seemed she had experienced it multiple times and could predict all her thoughts and responses.

He was still talking when she picked up.

"*What?*"

"Feron, you're there."

"I would have been on the elevator and out of reach in another five minutes."

"Did you hear any of what I said?"

"I was trying not to because I knew you were going to have to say it again. What's happened with Merry?"

"They were doing whole brain radiation at Duke, and she had a seizure on the operating table."

"Is she alive?"

"She's home again. She's able to speak, but her right side . . ."

"Damn it, she promised to tell me!"

"I'm calling because she has asked me to tell you now."

"Five more minutes and I wouldn't have heard the phone! I was on my way to the airport to fly to Spain."

"Which airport?"

"Kennedy."

"Well, I've booked you an afternoon flight from Newark. It's the same flight as you took last time for Blanche."

"Are you saying she's about to die?"

"It's more like"—he broke off to collect himself—"that she's all right with whatever's going to happen next. But that's kind of hard on the rest of us."

Josie, waiting with a taxi below, had been remarkably practical. If she was let down, she didn't show it.

"What will you do about your ticket?"

"I'll just have to forfeit it."

"No, when I check in, I'll explain for you. You'll probably get a refund. Eventually."

"Well, at least I had a bag already packed."

"A forty-one-year-old friendship is a lot older than me."

Thad was waiting at the gate, which brought back Merry, last spring, racing toward her, running like a boy. ("Oh, God, Feron, I'm sorry!")

Thad held her. He smelled of some agreeable masculine scent. What a dear, good man. Her first cousin.

"When did this happen, Thad?"

"End of June."

"June! It's the middle of August!"

"Everything got kind of turned around. More hospital. More scans. Some rehab. She was on the up and up, could put weight on her right leg but couldn't use the right hand yet, then they took another scan, found more tumors in other places, and that's when she . . . well, I won't say gave up hope, but started looking at a new ending. Back in May you wrote that you were going to Spain and she wanted to be sure you got to do everything you needed to do over there before she gave me the okay to ask you to come down here."

"I would have come sooner if I'd known."

"I know you would have."

During the drive, Thad brought her up-to-date. "She has an incredible support circle. The women from her church have organized themselves to take care of everything. And she has what they call a palliative care doctor, who phones every day and adjusts her meds as required. A calibrated combo of stimulants and painkiller and, I believe, steroids. To decrease fatigue and make her sharper. She has her plans all in place for while you're here. How long will you be staying?"

"As long as I'm wanted."

"Better tell her that. Be prepared for her sleeping a lot. She's lucid pretty much most of the time, but she sometimes has to search for words. And she'll suddenly leave you and drift off to a place you can't go. Oh, and she wears this bandage in bed to protect the back of her head from touching the pillow. A wonderful old lady from her church fashioned it into a sort of turban. Before I forget, my son, Simon, is so pleased with your house. He says if you ever want to sell—"

"I don't think so."

"That's what I told him."

"Have they set a date?"

"They've broken it off."

"Oh, no!"

"It's okay. It's always been a sort of irresolute business. She wanted to be married, and he felt he was in too far to get out."

"That's not good."

"No. Lou and I never wavered. Nothing could have stopped us. I snatched her out of junior college to follow me into the navy, and now forty years later she's becoming an arborist up at State. She has a nice little apartment there."

"What exactly does an arborist do?"

"Takes care of trees. When we returned home, she had her parents' house moved to a big field in the country, and we planted all these young trees, which started dying, but she was hell-bent on saving them. Now they are big, beautiful shade trees, and she's gone off to study how to save other people's trees for lots of money. I had my main career first, and she's having hers now. A person can lead sequential lives. In a long marriage, you can watch your partner in the act of morphing into someone new."

"Ah, I wouldn't know. I wonder if Will and I would have become sequential people."

"Feron, I've been wanting to ask you something if it's not too painful."

"Ask away."

"When you lost Will, how did you manage to carry on? You really loved him, Merry says."

"It happened so fast. One minute I was in our apartment waiting for him to come back from one of his walks, and the next minute I learned that he had fallen off a cliff. I suppose I owe my carrying on to Uncle Rowan. He came over to England and took care of things, and then I stayed with Blanche for six months. It took a while to get my bearings. In a way, I'm still getting them. It takes . . . Thad?"

Hunched over the steering wheel, Thad was sobbing.

"Why don't you pull off the road for a minute?"

"Good idea. I'm sorry, Feron. It's just that . . . how will I manage to go on without her in this world?"

Okay, so now I know for sure, thought Feron. He wants me to know for sure.

She took her first cousin in her arms, allowed him to cry himself out in the car, and then they continued on.

"The day nurse is at the end of her shift," Thad informed her. "The night nurse comes on at seven. As soon as I take you to her, I'm going to head home. I still sleep at home nights."

Merry lay, apparently asleep, in a raised hospital bed in Ritchie's room. The carefully wrapped turban reminded Feron of the scarf Merry had worn low on her forehead to their lunch at the Neuse River Café. The nurse on duty left Feron sitting beside her friend. Her anxiety over how she might find Merry faded. Merry was smaller and bone-thin, her face pale but not gray or anything. She wore ironed pajamas, which Feron bet anything had once belonged to Ritchie. She was simply grateful to sit quietly beside her sleeping friend, matching her breaths to Merry's.

At last the eyes opened. "I was dreaming you were here," Merry whispered.

"I *am* here. Can I touch you?"

"My right side is not . . ." Merry reached her left hand across to grasp Feron's. "How long can you . . . ?"

"I can stay as long as you want."

"But your harvest?"

"What? Oh, the one in Spain? I can see it in the film later. Maybe we'll watch it together."

"Maybe . . ." The eyes closed again.

This time Feron was given the upstairs bedroom, formerly Merry and Jack's. Outside the late sun was still strong. From this window you could see it beating down on the silvery rooftops of the new development. Oak-something. Feron hated it when her memory played hard to get, which was happening more often these days. The recently planted trees were still too young to hide the roofs and upper stories. Feron squinted and tried to replace the houses with the grand old tobacco fields she had never seen.

("All around you, nothing but fields . . ."

"If I had made that Christmas visit, in 1958, how would it have looked?"

"All plowed under by then. But a horizon of loamy soil holding up the sky. I don't know if I saw the grandeur back then. I saw it as a lot of acres and a lot of responsibility.")

In mid-August, the golden leaves in those former fields would now be ripe and ready for harvest as far as the eye could see, like the picture on the cover of the state magazine with Merry's Stephen Slade piece inside.

Josie still had several hours before her flight to Spain. One day in the future, Feron would sit in a darkened room and be shown waving Spanish leaves being harvested, and a man and a woman in an ancient farmhouse working out a mode of existence.

She realized she was counting on Josie to redeem her misbe-gotten *Mr. Blue*, or at least shine some fresh light on it. Will said medieval artists strove to copy or embellish an old subject. ("Making something original was not at all what they were aiming for.")

"She's fallen in love with him," Merry had said of Mrs. Blue. "But she thinks she would lose her power if she let him know."

50

"Merry, do you remember 'September Song'?"

"I loved that song."

They sat together on the west porch. So far, the calibrated drug combo seemed to be doing its job; Merry had dressed in slacks and a shirt too loose for her and a silk scarf in place of the bedtime turban. She wore Ritchie's blue air force blanket wrapped around her shoulders. She was always cold, she said. It was going to be a fine day. A gentle mist rose from the paddock. The horses hadn't been let out yet.

"Cuervo said it was on top of the charts when he arrived in New York in 1958."

"When we were at Lovegood."

"He was just a little older than us, with a book already published in two languages!"

"That song was . . ."

Feron waited for Merry to find her words. Wasn't waiting what she had come for?

". . . it was sad," said Merry. "But a *good* sad."

"I know what you mean. How we love our '*good* sad' stories and songs. But even if it was playing on *Our Best to You*, you always made us turn off the radio after lights out."

"Mmm . . ."

Which could have meant "yes, I remember," or equally could have been a polite acknowledgment that people still bound to life, healthy people like Feron, persisted in bringing up personal anecdotes from the past.

Often Merry gazed into immeasurable space. As though distancing herself from her surroundings, even from Feron. It must have been that sort of distancing that had made Thad say Merry was all right with whatever happened next. ("But that's kind of hard on the rest of us.")

But then Merry would make a sudden remark about what was going on inside her. Like the day Feron noticed how she was trying to move her right hand, not having much luck.

"Can I get you something?"

"No, thank you. I'm writing my book but it's hard."

"What book?"

"The one about us."

"How much have you done?"

"A good bit."

"Can you talk about it?"

"I do it in short takes, like my notebook vignettes for Miss Petrie."

"Which one are you on now?"

"I move around, so it's hard to keep track."

Feron got to know Merry's support circle. There was the elegant Lavonne Blake, the undertaker. And her daughter Rachel, who had coached Feron in her Romans 8 reading for Blanche's funeral. ("Even and unemotional. The words will carry the feeling.") And Sister Simone, who must be pushing ninety, the one who had made the bandage-turban for Merry. Sister Simone wore colored turbans herself and large hoop earrings, and would sing Merry to sleep if asked. Dedra the surgical nurse was the one Feron asked about medical matters.

"What exactly is a seizure? Is it like a stroke?"

"A seizure is caused by a surge of electrical activity in the brain. A disruption of blood circulation in the brain causes a stroke."

"Which is worse?"

"They're both serious. And a stroke can be followed by a seizure. With Merry, they said it was a stroke and then the seizure."

"So it was the stroke that caused the right side to . . . ?"

"More than likely. A seizure could have done it, too. There's so much we don't know for sure. That's the main thing I've taken away from twenty-three years of nursing: there's so much we don't know for sure."

Corinne had great-grandchildren, embroidered church banners, and baked pineapple upside-down cakes, which she left cooling on the table for anyone who wanted a slice.

Tabitha, the church organist, also cooked: mac and cheese, which everyone liked, and rice pudding, which was about the only thing Merry would eat.

As a whole, the group treated Feron like an honored guest, summoned by their beloved Merry. Feron felt sure that Lavonne considered herself Merry's best friend, but then Feron knew how she tended to insert competition into almost everything.

Merry had been gazing at her. "You have changed, Feron."

"Oh, how?"

Merry waited for the words she wanted. "You are more . . . *near*."

"I've never heard anything as beautiful as that bird song. What is it?"

"I think it's a Carolina wren. Jack would know for sure."

* * *

Merry's compromised right hand was moving steadily across her lap.

"Are you writing your book?" Feron was dying to hear more about that book.

"Listen, Feron . . ."

"Yes?"

"If you should ever write about a mother losing an infant child, I want you to describe . . ."

"Describe . . . ?"

"Every soul is unique. So, be sure and . . ."

Feron waited.

"Each child is his own gift. Am I making sense?"

"I *think* so."

"No, I'm not. What I want to tell you is when Paul was just born, when he came out of my body, we looked into each other's eyes. I knew him for his individual self. It is there from birth . . . the personality like no other before or after . . . not just a baby! You understand?"

"I do."

"Try to get that in. It's important. In case I don't finish . . ."

Merry's compromised hand was hard at work, but it was a different tempo.

"Are you writing your book?"

"I'm going over my list. To see if I've left anyone off. Rachel Blake gets a . . . what's the polite word for money?"

"Legacy?"

"Thank you. Ezekiel gets a church hall. Your aunt Blanche gave me the idea. What can I give you? Please don't say 'nothing' like your cousin Thad."

"I'd like to have one of your notebooks, if you've kept them."

"Take all of them. They're in a box in the closet of . . . where you sleep."

"I will treasure them."

"Something else I wanted to say, but I forgot. It makes me really happy you want my notebooks."

51

The calibrated drug combo had lost its magic. Merry didn't dress and limp out to the porch anymore. Merry slept. Dedra the surgical nurse told Feron nature was taking its course.

Upstairs in the old Jellicoe farmhouse, Feron heard worsening moans and violent vomiting in the night. Heard the nurse, a new one, ask shouldn't they send her back to the hospital, and a scolding voice that sounded like Lavonne's reciting a list of no-no's: no 911, no ambulance; call the palliative doctor. Feron heard the phrase ". . . passes away . . ." and was about to go down when she heard Merry's welcome moan. She was still there.

Next day there was a feeding tube and what they called "the pain pump," which the patient could press when she'd had enough.

If she took a walk, Feron stayed within sight and hearing in case they had to summon her back.

Rachel gave Feron a copy of the list of people Merry wanted at her funeral. With their contact information. Scanning the list, she saw Dean Fox's name. "I will help you call them," Feron told Rachel.

The night sky outside Feron's window was unusually crowded with stars. How could there be so many *more* than usual? Feron narrowed her eyes, trying to make sense of these extra stars. They seemed to merge right down into the landscape below. She had acquired patience so she looked and looked until she got it. They were the lighted upstairs windows in the Windbourne houses on the other side of the trees.

Feron was sitting beside Merry's bed. Someone was always there. Merry wasn't asleep, but her eyes were closed.

A new kind of uncounted time had come to the house. It seemed to stretch itself out and out and out. As she had grown accustomed to doing, Feron tried to match her breaths to Merry's.

The eyes opened. Just like the night Feron arrived. "You're here," Merry whispered.

"I'm here," said Feron.

"This is not delirium."

"It's not delirium."

"I know you're really here."

"I'm really here," Feron said, enclosing her friend's weakened right hand in both hers. It came to her that this was the way Merry had enclosed *her* hand in Lovegood's chapel during those "never, no never forsake" lines of the processional hymn when Merry had probably assumed Feron was thinking of her lost mother, when actually Feron had been grieving and yearning for something she couldn't name.

A long, easy silence stretched between them.

"I remember now . . ." whispered Merry, "what I forgot to tell you. I love you."

"And I love you."

January 7, 2001

Susan Fox, Dean Emerita
Dinwiddie House

Dear Feron,
What to say!

I will do everything in my power to honor your largesse in memory of Merry. But first I'd better bring you up-to-date on Lovegood news.

Having survived the turnover of millennia without Armageddon or crashing of computer systems and fizzle of the electric grid and the collapse of civilization, we have now completed the first year of the new century with its bitter election and hanging chads and a contested decision that I fear may reverberate through the decades to come.

I am still alive and compos mentis, as is my friend Mr. Peeler, whom you met when he escorted me to Merry's funeral in September of '99. Mr. Peeler's wife, our ambitious president, continues outdoing herself with changes and improvements. Lovegood is in the throes of becoming a coed university with an evening division and a new name. The best legal team and the best PR firm are on board for the big turnover scheduled for this coming June. As of September 1, 2001, Lovegood College will open its doors as Horace Lovegood University.

There were some frenzied murmurings that we should change our motto as well. Was *Esse Quam Videri* sufficiently "goal-oriented"? We went through a few dicey months while the board considered a new motto worthy of our ambitious new endeavor. A consensus came up with "To Aspire and Achieve" to replace "To Be Rather Than to Seem," but the

Latin version was awkward ("Aspirare et Merere"). At last the foolishness abated after several of our big donors, one a former state senator and one a current one, reminded us that *Esse Quam Videri* was, and always had been, the state's motto.

Winifred Darden often said that the secret of Lovegood's extraordinary endowment fund could be expressed by the acronym GET: Gratitude, Enclosure, and Tradition. I wonder what she would have said about our name change. Probably something like, "Let's be thankful they kept 'Lovegood' in the title, and we've still got our Doric columns and our grateful girls."

Which brings me back to your proposed endowment for a lecture series. Mr. Peeler and his son ran the numbers and concluded that with your initial installment alone we could schedule the first Meredith Jellicoe Rakestraw lecture for May of 2002.

However, I am keeping your proposal and generous check in a drawer until I hear back from you. You might not be as excited about funding a lecture series for Horace Lovegood University.

I'm glad that your filmmaker is finally satisfied with her early rushes of what is now *Mrs. Blue*. Mr. Peeler and I looked at Extremadura on the internet. What a lovely unspoiled place. I never knew the Spaniards were big tobacco growers.

You asked if we had a copy of the Lovegood pageant for a scene in your novel in progress, which led me to explore Winifred Darden's bountiful preservations. I also found the words to the Daughters and Granddaughters hymn, and some other treasures I thought might interest you. I scanned them all myself. The enclosed CD, as you'll see, is Mahalia Jackson singing "My God Is Real," the song Sister Simone

sang at Merry's funeral. Though I can't send the unforgettable spirit of that day, this should bring back a touch of it.
As we were driving back to Lovegood, Mr. Peeler said I
must have been a keen judge of girls to have had the fore-
sight to put Merry and you in the same room. I said Winifred
and I had talked it out together, and it was part experience
and part fate and perhaps an infusion of that undefined
substance we sometimes call grace.

I can't wait for you to finish what you call your "friendship novel." I will try my utmost to remain a lucid reader
until it's in my hands.

(Your filmmaker may be taking a risk with a silent film,
but I cheer her on. We could all do with some silence, just
sitting back in a dark theater and watching humans living
and working and discovering their affinities without any
words. How interesting, as you say, that an attempt at a feminist Bluebeard tale should contain a love story beneath it.
I like the new title.)

Let me know how you feel about endowing Horace
Lovegood University. If you still want to go ahead, we can
get things in motion fairly quickly.

With warm regards,

Susan Fox
Dean Emerita
Lovegood College

ACKNOWLEDGMENTS

I thank Professor Bes Stark Spangler for educating me about tobacco, particularly from the point of view of a child who was brought up in the tobacco world when tobacco was still "king," and has lived into an age in which everyone knows that it kills smokers.

I thank Evie Preston, who for ten years has given me feedback as I talk out in safety what I haven't written yet.

I thank Rob Neufeld, who edited volumes I and II of *The Making of a Writer*, and is completing *The Art of Becoming: Gail Godwin's Contributions to Literature*.

I thank Robb Forman Dew, who has been the trusted acute reader of my manuscripts in progress for thirty-seven years.

I thank Moses Cardona, my agent, who reads with his heart and always tells me the truth.

I thank Nancy Miller, who has edited eight of my books, fiction and nonfiction. This time we not only conversed, but we felt free enough to do a little dance that led us to scenes that otherwise would not appear in this novel.